Jacqueline Webb spent two years as a student nurse at Guy's Hospital in London, and worked at a school in France, before training as a teacher at Bath University. She now lives on the Wirral with her partner, Shane, and their two children. This is her first novel.

THE SCARLET QUEEN

Kate Whitaker is the spoilt daughter of a Victorian Egyptologist; she enjoys playing tricks on her father's assistants on his desert digs. She anticipates amusing herself with her new prey, Adam Ellis. But Adam is made of sterner stuff and soon puts her in her place. Seven years later the pair meet again in London. Adam, now an archaeologist himself, accompanies Kate back to Egypt where her father is searching for an ancient fabled statue known as the Scarlet Queen. And when Kate discovers that she has a rival for Adam's love, her troubles are just beginning . . .

JACQUELINE WEBB

THE SCARLET QUEEN

Complete and Unabridged

ULVERSCROFT
Leicester

First published in Great Britain in 2005 by
Robert Hale Limited
London

First Large Print Edition
published 2006
by arrangement with
Robert Hale Limited
London

The moral right of the author has been asserted

British Library CIP Data

Webb, Jacqueline
The scarlet queen.—Large print ed.—
Ulverscroft large print series: adventure & suspense
1. Excavations (Archaeology)—Egypt—Fiction
2. Romantic suspense novels 3. Large type books
I. Title
823.9′2 [F]

ISBN 1–84617–521–6

Published by
F. A. Thorpe (Publishing)
Anstey, Leicestershire
Set by Words & Graphics Ltd.
Anstey, Leicestershire
Printed and bound in Great Britain by
T. J. International Ltd., Padstow, Cornwall

This book is printed on acid-free paper

1

London 1900

I was fourteen when I first met Adam Ellis and he was twenty-two. Within minutes of our meeting he had told me I was an impudent chit who deserved a good whipping and I had told him he was an idiot who probably couldn't date a gravestone without help.

He was right, actually. I *was* impudent, but in my own defence I defy anyone who has spent two whole hours in the company of Mrs Mercer not to be in a bad mood by the end of it. Normally Mrs Mercer would not have dreamt of accompanying one of her former pupils to the station in order to be returned to the bosom of her family. That chore would have gone to one of her menials and we would all have been happy. But Mrs Mercer had decided to see me well and truly off the premises herself, the premises in this case being London, and England too, I've no doubt. Certainly she wanted to make sure I was never going to return to Mrs Mercer's Academy for Young Ladies of Gentle Birth, which is why she was with me.

We had been waiting for some twenty minutes by our hansom cab that dull spring morning in 1900, me in my ugly school hat and smock and Mrs Mercer in her black bombazine, when Adam walked up to us. I was too callow at fourteen to notice how good-looking he was. All I saw was the long drooping moustache which made me want to giggle. He later told me it was intended to make him look older; we were in love at the time, but even then I don't think he appreciated me telling him he had looked like a starving walrus. Sometimes men have no sense of humour.

'Mrs Mercer?'

Mrs Mercer had looked at him as though he were one of the tiniest pupils in the first form.

'Yes?'

'I'm Adam Ellis. And this must be Katharine.'

'Mr Ellis! Of course, you're going to Cairo with Lady Faulkner. To be Professor Whitaker's assistant.'

'Just for three months, ma'am. To finish my thesis.'

'Of course. And Lady Faulkner . . . ?' Mrs Mercer peered behind him. Neither of them was taking any notice of me.

' . . . will be along very soon. She asked me

to make myself acquainted with you in case she was late.'

Mrs Mercer's smile switched off. This was not what she wanted to hear. She glared at me for several seconds as though the tardiness of my new guardian was somehow my fault, then seemed to come to a decision.

'No matter. Professor Whitaker mentioned you in his letter regarding the arrangements for Katharine's return. Well, here are all her health certificates and travel documents. Good day to you, sir.' She handed him a bundle of papers and turned back towards the cab.

Adam looked horrified. 'Do you wish . . . I mean, will it be all right . . . ?'

Normally, Mrs Mercer would never have left an unaccompanied young girl alone with a strange male. But as I have already said, these were not normal circumstances. I have no doubt that the idea of my possibly being sold into white slavery sustained her all the way home. She turned and dealt Adam an icy smile.

'I'm sure Katharine will be quite safe with you, Mr Ellis. If Professor Whitaker is happy for his daughter to be travelling thousands of miles with a young gentleman in her party, then I'm sure it's not for me to criticize, even if she is one of the most impudent, troublesome gels it has ever been my misfortune to meet. Goodbye, Katharine,' she said, turning to me at last. 'Perhaps your manners will improve once you're back with your father.'

I had just finished sticking my tongue out at her behind her back.

'Goodbye, Mrs Mercer.'

She glared at me a little longer before shaking her head at my deplorable manners and departing, leaving Adam and me alone. We studied each other for a few seconds, sizing one another up.

'That was very rude of you,' he said eventually.

I shrugged. I could see he was mentally agreeing with Mrs Mercer.

'Well, where's your luggage, then?'

I pointed to the two chests over by the ticket-office. Adam instructed a guard to bring them to the boat-train at platform twelve, then beckoned me to follow him.

I had already had a bad morning; now it was being compounded by one of Papa's new assistants treating me like a badly trained puppy. I trailed in his wake with all the ill-grace I could muster. When we arrived at the platform, there was still no sign of my new chaperon.

'Where's Lady Faulkner?' I asked.

'She'll be here soon. Don't touch that,' he snapped as I bent down to examine the scroll he had left on top of his valise.

'It's all right,' I sneered. 'I won't ruin it. It's only a fake anyway.'

The look on his face cheered me up no end.

'It most certainly is not, young lady. And keep away from things you don't understand.'

'I understand when someone's been bamboozled,' I said. 'Look at the illuminations on that lettering. Far too bright. Only a complete amateur would fall for that.'

Before he could stop himself, Adam had bent over to examine the scroll more closely. That was when he called me an impudent chit. But not before I saw the look in his eyes. I was right and he knew it.

I always enjoyed baiting Papa's new assistants. As the only English child on archaeological digs in Egypt, it could sometimes get lonely when Papa was busy. But with the assistants around I always had a source of amusement. Sometimes they tried to ignore me, sometimes they took refuge in treating me like an infant; one had even patted me on the head once. I spent the whole week placing glue on his chairs and workbenches and even his saddle. He never touched me again. But I had never before had the opportunity to torment one even before he left England. For the first time since being forced to leave Papa and spend the whole miserable winter in Mrs Mercer's wretched boarding-school I was actually beginning to feel happy again.

'You are . . . ' he began, but luckily just at that moment, a lavender-scented apparition in a blue coat and skirt appeared and held out her arms to him.

'Adam, darling! I'm so sorry we're late. Rose couldn't find my parasol and I can't possibly go to Egypt without a parasol. Never mind. We're here now.'

This was the first time I had ever met Alice Faulkner. She was tall, fair and beautiful. She kissed the assistant lightly on both cheeks before turning her attention to me.

'And this must be Katharine. My dear, how lovely to meet you at last. I'm Lady Faulkner and I'm very pleased your dear papa asked me to bring you home. We'll have so much time to get acquainted. Darling, is this the right train?'

Sir Henry Faulker, head of the board of directors of the Cavendish Museum, was a wealthy man and besotted with his young wife, so we had a whole carriage to ourselves on the first part of our long journey to Cairo. Rose and the other servants were busy sorting out the luggage, so we were left alone as the train eventually pulled out of Victoria. Alice leaned across from the seat opposite me and patted my arm.

'I had a telegram this morning from Cairo,' she said, smiling kindly at me. 'Your papa says he is looking forward to seeing you again.'

I was relieved to hear this. Now that I was going back home, I had become a little anxious about Papa's reaction to my return. Of course Mrs Mercer and her hired minions hadn't helped. One of the teachers had told me she hoped I would be soundly thrashed for all the trouble I had caused.

'Thank you, ma'am,' I said meekly. I could feel Adam's eyes on me. They were narrowed.

'How many times did you run away from school?'

'Three.'

'Good God.'

He turned away from me in disgust and began reading a newspaper. Alice took my hand in hers.

'Some people just don't take to school, Katharine.'

'I would have thought school was exactly the right place for her,' said Adam disagreeably, talking as though I wasn't there.

Alice glanced at each of us. 'Well, you

7

know, darling, Katharine is very clever and scholarly and sometimes such young people can find restrictive environments a hindrance to their studies.'

'I was very scholarly at her age too, but I managed all right at school.'

Alice frowned. 'Did you darling? I thought you hated it.'

'Certainly not. I was very happy at school. And make her stop doing that,' he said as I stuck my tongue out at him, a mocking smile on my face. By the time Alice turned to me, I was a picture of innocence.

Alice sighed, then, with one last glance at Adam, she began talking to me about how excited she was to be visiting Cairo for the first time. She was kind and charming and vivacious; the exact opposite, in fact, of Adam, who sat with his nose buried in his newspaper while we talked.

The journey passed very pleasantly as far as I was concerned.

★　★　★

That night, as the ship set sail, I sat behind the door to the stateroom where Adam and Alice were talking and eavesdropped on their conversation. I have never really thought about it before, but I actually *was* a most

8

obnoxious child. I had absolutely no shame in doing that sort of thing then. It is only with the passing of years that I have learnt to become more civilized.

They were dressed for dinner and were taking sherry before going down to the dining room. I had already been given my dinner in my room and I had told Rose, who had grudgingly accepted charge of me, that I was going for a short walk around the promenade before bedtime. I lied easily as a child too.

'Darling, you weren't very friendly to Katharine this afternoon,' Alice said, as Adam passed her a sherry glass.

'Friendly! It was all I could do not to box the little brat's ears. Do you know she called me an idiot, just before you arrived?'

'Did she, darling? That was very rude of her. Why?'

'I really don't know. Because she's a spoilt, ill-mannered little urchin, I expect.' But the tips of his ears had become reddened and Alice must have spotted it too, because she smiled.

'Adam, I know James has spoilt her dreadfully, but she is very clever. Even Henry admits that and he finds her as difficult as you obviously do. Why else do you think he insisted on travelling ahead of us?'

'Good God, Alice. Do you mean to tell me that you actually put off the chance of travelling with your husband two weeks ago in order to chaperon that little madam back to Cairo?'

Alice put down her sherry glass on the table beside her.

'Well, I could hardly leave her here. James wrote imploring me to help. The poor little thing was obviously feeling wretched and Mrs Mercer was threatening to put her out on the streets if someone didn't come and fetch her. What else could I do?'

I'm ashamed to say I felt quite smug at this, and had no guilt whatsoever at the thought that a total stranger was forced to inconvenience herself on my behalf. On the contrary, I suddenly saw myself as a timid little waif abandoned by all my protectors and left to the mercy of an evil crone when luckily my fairy godmother had come swooping down on her glittery ephemeral wings to protect me. Alice, I should point out, was wearing a delicate silver evening dress with lacework as fragile as cobwebs along her décolletage, which helped quite considerably with this pathetic image.

'Poor little thing? She needs a good spanking! How on earth does a chit of fourteen run away from school three times?'

'With great determination, I should imagine. So tell me, darling . . . ' here she took his arm in hers and I went off her a bit, ' . . . what did she do to annoy you so much?'

He finished his sherry. 'She said the Franciscan scroll I bought last week was a fake.'

Through the slits of the louvre-door where I was sitting watching, I could see she was biting her lip to stop herself from laughing.

'And was she right?'

'Yes, dammit!' he exploded, then saw the look her eyes and threw back his head and laughed as well.

They both sat down on the couch again, Alice taking his hand in hers.

'Please try to be a bit nicer to her, darling. For your own sake as much as anything. James adores her, you know.'

I nodded at this. Papa did adore me. That was why I had found it so hard to be packed off to cold, grey, miserable England without him.

'I've no doubt. He certainly doesn't seem to care how the little wretch behaves towards his assistants. You've no idea of the stories that circulate in the common room back at Cambridge about her.'

I pricked my ears up a bit at this. It was the first time I'd heard about my reputation among the Cambridge history students who regularly competed for the honour of being Papa's assistant on his digs. It was said that a student who could boast a season with Professor Whitaker could have any job for the asking. It was good to know that I too was famous in my own special way.

'Oh Adam, surely you don't begrudge the child a little fun — '

'Fun! Davitt-Brown says he caught her making tiny rips in his mosquito nets. He'd been wondering for days why he was bitten more often than anyone else. And Tillyard says she kept telling the servants to starch his underwear.'

Alice giggled and I liked her again.

'That's not funny, Alice. Of course he tried to stop them, but she can speak Arabic and he couldn't. And Tavistock says she put glue on his saddle. He was stuck on the horse for six hours before he managed to break free. And of course Whitaker always takes her side. I'm telling you, if it wasn't so important, I wouldn't have touched this sabbatical with a bargepole.'

I would have liked to hear more, especially about all the things I'd done in the past. I'd forgotten how successful the starch trick was. But just then I heard a noise coming from the servants' rooms and I leapt up.

Rose came through the door, her arms full of Alice's beautiful dresses. She glared at me disapprovingly.

'Little girls what listen through doors never hear any good of themselves.'

I shrugged. I was well pleased with everything I had heard so far, but adults were always saying things like that.

'Rose,' I said, following her through to Alice's bedroom and throwing myself on to the bed. 'Have Lady Faulkner and that man known each other a long time?'

Rose placed the clothes on the bed and began searching for hangers in the wardrobe.

''Er ladyship and Mr Adam are cousins. They've known each other since they was little nippers, miss, and keep yer boots off the covers please. Some of us 'ave work to do round 'ere.'

I rolled over on to my stomach and began stroking the embroidered peacocks on the bedspread, my black-stockinged legs waving gently in the air.

'Did she get this job for him then?'

'I'm sure I don't know, miss.'

I continued to stroke the fabulous birds on the cover. Sir Henry and my father were not just colleagues, they were great friends and I knew Papa would be happy to take any student he personally recommended. The

13

winter wedding between Sir Henry and Alice Talbot had been the talk of London, penetrating even the gloom of Mrs Mercer's school. Even I, preoccupied with my own miseries and schemes to run away, knew that he had showered extravagant gifts and jewels on her. At the time it had merely been another reason for me to feel wretched.

'I bet she did,' I said. 'I bet he's really stupid and this is the only way he'd ever get such a good job.'

'Mr Adam 'as a double first from Cambridge,' Rose said, pausing in her work and glaring at me. I was quite certain she didn't know what that meant except that it was good, but it was clear she liked him. ''E doesn't need no favours from 'er ladyship to get a job. And now I think it's time you was in bed, miss. Come on. It's quite late enough now.'

She bundled me off to my room, and didn't leave until I was safely tucked in, making it clear she would be keeping an eye on my door so I couldn't escape. Actually I was very tired by then and only made the minimum amount of fuss. Even so, I lay awake for some time afterwards, listening to the sound of the engines and lulled by the gentle sway of the ship. I had a lot to think about.

★ ⋏ ★

The next morning I found Adam on his own in the private breakfast room. It was quite early and Alice was not up yet. Adam had finished his breakfast and was in his shirt-sleeves, the table piled high with books and papers and reference materials. I grinned, knowing that he was already bogged down with the work Papa would have sent for him. Papa liked to test his new assistants' abilities right from the moment they began their journey.

'Hello,' I said brightly. I was feeling very pleased with myself. I was back on board ship, travelling home and here was a new assistant to tease. 'What are you doing?'

'Working,' he snapped. 'And I'm busy. If you want breakfast, you'll have to go the dining room.'

'No, that's all right, I've already had mine.'

This was true. I always get up early on sea journeys. There's something about the brisk salt air and sound of the waves crashing against the ship that sets my senses tingling. I'm a very good sailor. Besides, I'd had a special reason for getting up early that morning. I was dressed in my best summer whites to get me into the feel of the searing heat of Egypt and wash away completely all memories of my miserable winter. To that end, I had spent a very satisfying ten minutes

15

throwing my school hat and tie over the bow of the ship and watching them first float away and then sink for ever into the dark waters of the Atlantic. Actually I would have thrown my smock and black woollen stockings and boots over too, but Rose had caught me and insisted I give them to her, scandalized by the waste. She had threatened to tell Alice of my behaviour and when I had told her to go ahead, she had surprised me by giving me a sharp smack on the bottom. Outraged, I had then threatened to tell Alice about *her*, but she had just marched off, with a short laugh and told *me* to go ahead. Clearly Rose and I had unfinished business.

'I know. Let me help you,' I said chirpily, sitting down next to him and glancing at his work. It was a passage from Cicero, a real stinker. There was no way he would have known about it until we had left port. Papa always made sure the assistants never got to see the work he set them until they were on board and had nothing but their own wits to rely on. He'd caught out quite a few that way.

'No,' he said even more snappily. 'Now go away and find some other brat to play with.'

I grinned. I could see one mistake already.

'Oh please let me help you,' I wheedled. 'I'm very good at Latin, you know.'

'No doubt. But I'd prefer to do this alone.'

He bent his head again and began scratching his pen along the paper. I edged my foot gently under a table-strut so that it tilted ever so slightly.

'Well, if you're sure, Adam. May I call you Adam?'

'No. You may not.'

'Oh please. I won't insist you call me Miss Whitaker.'

'I had no intention of doing so. In fact, I have no intention of talking to you at all if I can possibly avoid it. Oh blast!' Not realizing the table was now on a slant, he'd pulled the ink-pot over and it ran across his translation, obliterating hours of work.

I stood up, well content.

'Well, I'll leave you to it then, Adam.' And I began to stroll out, whistling happily.

'Wait!'

I turned back.

'All right then, *Miss Whitaker*. Let's see what you can do,' he said as he pushed a chair out from under the table with the tip of his boot.

I stared at him, confused. This wasn't how it was supposed to go at all. Usually the assistants would have died rather than admit they needed help. Especially from a girl. I scowled.

'No, you're probably right, *Mr Ellis*. You

17

should do it yourself. Papa likes to know his students' limitations.'

'But wouldn't you like to know too?'

I stayed where I was. Somehow, this man had pulled the rug out from under me. He no longer sounded harassed and irritable, but cool and superior. I knew that if I left now he would have won the first round. That could not be allowed to happen. I walked back to the table and picked up the passage and the part of his work that wasn't completely ruined.

'You made a mistake here. This isn't the imperative, it's the ablative. Look.'

I pointed to a sentence, but instead of studying it with me, he merely handed over the pen.

'Very well. Correct it then.'

I hesitated. Things were now going badly wrong. Instead of making him feel foolish, I had somehow got myself in the position of doing his work for him. I scribbled a few words down and tossed it back to him.

'Hmm. Not bad, but you've forgotten to take into account the dative.'

I flushed. It was a stupid mistake, the sort of thing a beginner does. 'Well, I haven't got a double first from Cambridge.'

'True. And I'm not a spoilt little brat who eavesdrops on her elders' conversations and throws perfectly serviceable clothes into the sea on a whim.'

I stood up abruptly. 'I hate you.'

'So I gather. But before you run off and start plotting what foul tricks you're going to play on me, perhaps you ought to know I have three younger brothers.'

'I don't care.'

'Maybe not.' He stood up and caught up with me before I could reach the door. Catching hold of my arm, he pulled me back. 'But the point is, I'm very good at dealing with annoying little children. I've had plenty of practice.'

I felt my cheeks go even redder.

'If you ever dare to touch me — '

'My dear Kate, you won't believe the ways I can keep you under control.' He let go of my arm and strolled back to the table. 'But if you want to find out the hard way, then be my guest.'

I took a deep breath. 'If you think — '

'Of course, we could always call a truce,' he said casually, then added: 'And you could do me a favour.'

'Oh really? And why, pray, would I want to do you a favour?'

'Because it would mean you could show off. And you do like to do that, don't you, Kate?'

'Don't call me that. And just because I know more than you about Latin and fifteenth-century scrolls doesn't mean I show off.'

He shrugged and looked down at the Cicero, apparently losing interest.

'OK.'

'And I don't need to do you any favours. Papa always takes my side, remember?'

'Well, we'll see, won't we?'

'You won't last two weeks.'

'Fine.'

It was no good. I was hooked.

'What favour?' I asked at last, going back to the table.

He looked at me, a sly smile on his face and I knew I'd well and truly lost the first round.

'Teach me Arabic,' he said.

Now, in spite of my dislike for him, I was intrigued. None of Papa's assistants had ever bothered to learn more than a few words of Arabic before. Most thought of Egyptians as savages and no self-respecting Englishman would bother with the language of heathens.

'Why?' I asked, intrigued.

'So I can stop the servants starching my underwear.'

In spite of the situation, I couldn't help grinning.

'All right. I might. But you'd have to do something for me in return.'

He thought about that for a minute.

'Fair enough. What is it?'

'Let me come with you when you go into the tombs. Papa never lets me go alone and he's finding it hard to get into the really exciting tunnels nowadays. I hardly ever get to see anything. I know he'd let me go if I was with an assistant, but they never take me.'

'Really? What a surprise,' he said drily, but I could tell he was thinking about it. Then he nodded. 'Very well. But you'd have to follow my orders.'

'OK.'

'No, I mean it. The first time you ignore me, that's it. Your expeditions are over.'

'Yes Adam,' I said meekly; just then the door opened and Alice walked in.

'Good morning. Isn't it a beautiful day? Katharine, my dear, have you had breakfast?'

'We both have, haven't we, Kate? We were discussing Cicero.'

Adam sounded far too pleased with himself and I wasn't happy at him calling me by my pet name. Usually I only let special friends call me that. But Alice just smiled.

'Wonderful. Well, Rose is organizing my breakfast. Let's take a quick turn about the promenade while she's busy.'

I noticed that Adam was quick to pull his jacket on and take her arm, but as Alice held out a hand for me, Adam shook his head.

'Kate won't be able to come with us. She accidently knocked the ink over my work and agreed to do it over again for me to make up. Didn't you, Kate?'

We locked eyes, Adam's mischievous, mine seething. How did he know? Suddenly I could see him winning round two without even trying. But I desperately wanted to go on a tunnel expedition and I knew he was my only hope.

'Yes, Adam,' I ground out.

'Oh, how kind, darling. And when it was just an accident. Surely she can come for a little walk first?'

'Sadly no. I need this done as quickly as possible, because I can't proceed to the next assignment without it.'

'Oh dear. Oh well, we'll leave you to it then, darling. You are clever, aren't you?'

I began to stack up all the books and papers to take to my room, my blood boiling because I knew I'd be stuck inside for the rest of the morning now, while Mr Double First got to spend even more time with his dear cousin. As I started to pick them up, Adam helpfully came over to assist me.

'If you make even one mistake in that

translation and I have to do it all over again myself, I guarantee you the biggest thrashing of your life,' he whispered in my ear.

'And if you go back on your word and don't take me with you when you go out on tunnel searches, I'll make you wish starched underwear was the worst thing you had to look forward to,' I hissed back.

We glared at each other for a second. Then Adam smiled. 'Have a pleasant morning, Kate.'

And he and Lady Faulkner strolled out together to enjoy the fine sea air.

★   ★   ★

My dislike for Adam grew apace on the voyage, but for a while we managed to ignore each other. He was busy with Papa's work and I always found plenty of projects to keep me occupied during the long sea voyage, especially after I met William. William was thirteen, the son of an army captain who had decided to take his family to India, and we had quickly discovered in each other an identical streak of mischief. One day, bored with dropping rotten fruit and vegetables on the heads of passengers on the promenades and ringing for servants in the first-class lounge then running away, we decided to sabotage Rose's laundry. I still hadn't forgotten that smack.

We waited until she had spent the better part of the afternoon washing and starching and ironing. Eventually she decided that everything was as clean as it could possibly be and she went for a cup of tea. William and I sneaked into the laundry area and loosened every peg on the line. When we had finished, we retreated to a position far enough away to avoid suspicion, but near enough to savour the fruits of our dark labours.

We did not have long to wait. Soon a strong gust of wind blew in, sending petticoats and tea-gowns flying way up in the air and along the deck. Then they floated gently down, settling on the first-class promenade where stout matrons and red-faced, bewhiskered military types were taking afternoon tea. Muslin blouses and serge skirts crumpled up in heaps across the tables, knocking over milk-jugs and teapots, and lacy drawers and stockings were strewn over the heads of various gentlemen, causing several ladies to shriek at such indelicacy.

William and I, two decks up, fell about laughing. We were in seventh heaven until we both felt a strong hand grip the collars of our suits and drag us up into a standing position. I turned, scowling, to see who had dared to touch me in this way and found myself staring at Adam.

'You two seem to be having fun.'

'So what if we are?' I snapped. 'It's no business of yours. And let go of me.'

He ignored this and hauled us both nearer to the edge of the deck where we could see Rose running frantically about as she retrieved garments and apologized fervently, her face red with exertion and embarrassment, furious that all her hard work had been for nothing. I grinned maliciously. It was just a pity that Rose would never know who was responsible.

'I hope you're proud of yourselves,' Adam said, letting go of our collars at last. I was so busy enjoying my revenge on Rose I nearly said yes, but remembered at the last minute not to give the game away.

'I don't know what you're talking about,' I said, pulling my pinafore straight and adjusting my straw boater. He burst out laughing.

'Of course you do. You and your little playmate have got guilt written all over you. Well he has, anyway,' he added scornfully, pointing to William who did, annoyingly, look guilty. 'You look as though butter wouldn't melt in your mouth, but since we both know what a lying, scheming little brat you are, that's neither here nor there.'

'I'm afraid you're mistaken, Mr Ellis,' I said haughtily. 'William and I had nothing to do with that débâcle down there, but of course, you must believe what you wish. Come, William. We'll be late for tea.'

Poor William was looking even more worried now, but I still think we would have got away with it if only Adam hadn't shrugged and said:

'What a good idea. You go ahead and have your tea. I'm going to find Alice and make sure she knows who it was who sent her entire wardrobe flying across the promenade.'

I turned back. Adam was leaning against the railings, his arms folded casually, a nasty look in his eyes.

'Care to make a bet on who she'll believe?' he added nonchalantly.

That did it. Suddenly William's nerve broke. 'Katie, if my parents find out, I'll be sent back to England on the next boat,' he wailed. 'Father was against me coming in the first place, but Mama convinced him that the trip would be good for me — '

'We didn't do anything,' I hissed, trying to ignore Adam's laughter.

'Yes, we did, Katie. And Father will know that. No one's going to believe us.'

I glared at him, but knew he was right.

26

William obviously didn't have the experience or the talent that I had for lying. The game was up. I turned back to Adam and took a deep breath.

'All right. Please don't tell on us,' I said as gracelessly as possible.

'Do you really think that's going to do it?' he asked with interest.

I glared at him. 'Well, what do you want us to do then?'

'Hmm, let's see. Rose is obviously going to have to do that work all over again. I think the least you two can do is offer to help her.'

'Help her!' I yelped. 'Do laundry!'

'Good Lord, no,' he said and for a second I felt relief that we were going to be spared the ignominy of manual labour. 'Rose would never let you loose on Alice's clothes. They'd be ruined. No, I'm sure once we explain the situation to her, she'll be able to find some more suitable work for you to do.'

I narrowed my eyes. 'You're going to tell Rose what we did and let her make us do servant's work? She'll be unbearable. We'll be polishing boots and cleaning silver for the rest of the voyage.'

He nodded cheerfully. 'I expect so. But if that's beneath you and you prefer to take your chances with Alice, please do so. I'm sure William will understand. Probably not straightaway, and he'll have to travel back to England alone — '

'I hate you!' I shrieked. Of course I was going to have to give in. I couldn't abandon William, especially when the plan was mine to begin with. Adam seemed superbly unconcerned.

'Fine. Hate me as much as you want. But never try to get the better of me, especially when my best shirts are involved.'

I felt my face flush with anger, but he merely turned and walked through the doors, beckoning us to follow him to the servants' quarters where he proceeded to explain everything to a red-faced, irate Rose.

★   ★   ★

So that was how William and I ended up spending three hours every morning under the watchful, not to say wrathful, eye of Rose, performing endless unpleasant and often dirty jobs. She clearly enjoyed having us in her power and had a particularly sneering way of saying 'miss' or 'young sir' before barking orders at us. Adam was unbearable too. He made it his business to check up on us every morning and he always looked smug.

William turned out to be something of a disappointment after that. For reasons I never understood he became almost pathetically grateful to Adam for not telling on us, no matter how much I tried to get him to understand we were victims of blackmail. Indeed, he actually became friends with Adam and I often used to find them together, Adam teaching him to play cards; bridge, which was socially acceptable, but also poker and faro which I'm sure were not. I felt that Adam had stolen my partner in crime and that was just one more reason to hate him.

The only solace in the entire journey for me was that by the end of the voyage I had discovered that he was infatuated with his beautiful older cousin. Looking back, even that crumb of comfort was to rebound on me spectacularly one day.

★   ★   ★

I was relieved when at last I woke one morning to see the teeming port of Alexandria, the fishing boats already at work. As we drew nearer I could feel the entire ship becoming fraught with excitement, the heat of the African sun warming our faces and sending those not yet familiar with its ferocity scurrying into the shade of their cabins. The more experienced passengers knew to keep out of its glare but, when in open spaces, to take advantage of any breezes.

By the time we had docked and were ready to disembark I was almost dizzy with anticipation. Alexandria was huge and noisy, the water-sellers, melon-sellers and other pedlars thronged around the ramps, while nearby the carriage ranks were full with Europeans come to meet their relations and business partners. As we made our way down the gangplank, I spotted Papa and rushed to him, throwing my arms around his neck and crying with relief, not caring if he was angry with me for running away so many times. I need not have worried. As he squeezed me in his bearlike embrace, he whispered in my ear that sending me away was the worst mistake he'd ever made in his life and he would never do it again. I embraced him, forgetting all about the miseries of the past winter. I was home.

But as I held tightly on to him, I saw Adam watching Alice. She was one of the last to walk down the gangplank, graceful and elegant as always, despite the searing heat. But when she saw Sir Henry her face lit up with joy: she picked up her skirts and raced down the ramp, throwing herself into her husband's arms.

Adam looked away from the Faulkners' lingering kiss, but not before I had seen the absolute crushing despair in his eyes. I remember smiling, pleased that he didn't get everything his own way, and had resolved there and then to do everything in my power to avenge myself on him for all the indignities he had heaped on me during the voyage. Mr Adam Ellis, I decided, would rue the day he had ever set eyes on me.

2

London — May 1907

I gripped tightly on to my second-best straw hat as the wind whipped around my face and the seagulls screamed above me. Ahead, I could see the white cliffs of Dover. The horn from the ship boomed a greeting as we sailed into the harbour. Along with the other excited passengers I waved at the crowds waiting for us to dock, before running back down to the cabin and rousting Papa from his books.

'Papa! You must come. We're here at last!'

Papa looked up from his books; he had a thick woollen blanket around his shoulders.

'In Dover?'

'Yes. Didn't you hear the horn? Everybody's up on deck.'

I began searching for his coat and hat. With a sigh he stood up and let me help him put them on.

'Yes, yes, I'm coming. Is everything packed? Where did I put the transcripts of the — '

'Everything is packed, Papa. I made sure last night. Quickly now — the porters will be here soon. Here's your hat . . . '

I bustled him out through the tiny cabin door. He grumbled every step of the way, because Papa was never really keen on England and he would not have come at all if it hadn't been for the latest texts he had found on Khaemwaset, a little known pharaoh of the third intermediate period. But he needed the Cavendish to authorize more funding for a dig and one could not keep expecting the museum to come to us. Besides I was now twenty-two and somewhat old for a débutante. Even Papa accepted that if I was ever to be presented at Court, it was now or never.

'This wretched country — always freezing — how did we ever stir ourselves away from the hearths, that's what I want to know?' Papa muttered as we reached the top deck.

'Be grateful it's not winter-time, Papa,' I said, buttoning up his thick serge coat against the chill wind.

'My dear, how on earth can you be sure it isn't?' he said caustically and even I had to smile.

'Because everyone keeps telling me how mild it is. Oh look, Papa, there's the sun now,' I said cheerfully as the sun did its best to melt its way through the dismal grey clouds above us. In Egypt the heat of summer was like a furnace; here I doubted I would ever take my coat and gloves off at all.

'Can you see Henry or Alice?' Papa asked, squinting though his spectacles at the crowds lining the harbour.

I shook my head.

'No, it's far too early for — oh, wait a minute. Yes — yes there they are,' I said pointing to a large black hansom cab. Beside it stood a tall man in a top hat and black morning coat. Holding his arm was a woman wearing a sapphire-blue coat with a deep fur collar and a large round toque of pale-blue tulle. I began to wave, not really expecting them to see me, but to my surprise the woman waved a parasol enthusiastically in reply.

'Good. Stout fellow, Henry,' said Papa, sounding approving for the first time since we had left Cairo. 'We'll soon be off this wretched boat and in London.'

★   ★   ★

Since it was several years ago that Papa and I had last travelled home, we had forgotten how time-consuming disembarkation could be. It seemed hours before we were at last off the ship and waiting in the noisy, busy passenger lounge surrounded by our valises

34

and trunks. I still felt cold despite my thickest serge coat and was just wondering if it was the done thing to search among my possessions here in the lounge for a muff to supplement my gloves when I saw Sir Henry striding along the corridor with Alice beside him.

'Lady Faulkner, Sir Henry, how lovely to see you,' I said, walking up to them and holding out a hand. 'I hope we haven't inconvenienced you too much.'

They both stopped, Sir Henry staring blankly at my outstretched hand.

'I'm sorry, young lady, but I think you've made a mistake,' he began to my confusion. But Lady Faulkner's eyes twinkled.

'Henry, darling, it's Kate! How are you, my dear?' she asked, folding me in a brief, lavender-scented embrace before setting me back to look at me.

'Kate? Little Katie Whitaker? The last time I saw you, you were a chit of a thing in a pinafore and pigtails,' Sir Henry said gruffly, as though slightly peeved with me for proving him wrong.

'Darling, I've been telling you for months about Kate's season. Did you think we'd be presenting a schoolgirl at court? Where is your father, Kate? We're dying to see him.'

'He went to find a porter. He's convinced if

he doesn't engage one himself they'll break his specimen jars and put our trunks on the wrong train.'

'Hmph! Well, my dear, it's delightful to see you. You've changed quite a bit since the last time.' Sir Henry shot me a piercing look as he said this.

'I hope so, Sir Henry,' I said solemnly. 'I promise I won't put frogs in your bath-water this time.'

'Hah! It was you! I told you, Alice,' he said triumphantly as Lady Faulkner put her arm through mine. 'Didn't I tell you? I said it was that little minx who — '

'Yes dear, but that was a long time ago. Oh look, there's James. Come along, we don't want to miss the train and we've so much to do. Really my dear, I can't wait to show you all the latest fashions.'

* * *

We arrived at the Faulkners' fashionable London house that evening, exhausted by the journey and with our senses somewhat assaulted by the difference between life in England and life in Egypt. For myself, I could not help but be depressed by the general dinginess of the countryside as we had travelled up on the train. All I could smell was smoke, great gouts of it, billowing out of blackened chimneys, and the only scenery seemed to consist of row upon row of tiny, cramped houses with sad little yards of grey or perhaps the pale green of a solitary bush. The people too, seemed subdued and colourless, clothed in sturdy but dull fabrics of browns and blacks, boots tightly laced against the damp. Ever since Papa had first mentioned the possibility of this trip I had been almost delirious with excitement, but now, after only a few hours in England, I began to remember why I had been so desperate to leave Mrs Mercer's. As we stepped out of the carriage into the quiet residential street of the Faulkner house, I forced myself to quell my misgivings.

'Here we are, James, Kate. You remember Rose of course,' said Lady Faulkner as a familiar figure in a neat grey dress and white-frilled apron stepped out of the house and bobbed a curtsy.

'Of course,' I said, smiling coldly. The look I got in return told me that Rose hadn't forgotten me either.

A grand figure in a black tail-coat and starched white shirt stepped forward.

'Sir, madam,' he said majestically. Sir Henry nodded.

'Jenkins, see to the luggage, would you?

Come along, James, I've got some rather good whisky in my study, if I can tempt you before dinner.'

We all trooped into the house, leaving the domestic staff to see to the menial task of disposing our belongings. At home in Luxor we could only afford Sayeed as a general servant and Sharira twice a week for laundry so I am afraid I stared like an *ingénue* at the swarm of domestic staff who appeared at the command of the stately Jenkins and swept up our trunks. Jenkins was the butler and not some peer of the realm as I had first thought.

Papa quickly disappeared with Sir Henry into his study, but Alice whispered in my ear that she had arranged for a bath to be drawn for me as soon as I arrived, which is why less than an hour later I found myself luxuriating in a steaming tub full of rose-scented lather, soothing away the aches that the long, tiresome train journey had produced.

For a while I did nothing but wallow in the blissfully hot water, feeling truly warm for the first time for days. I was just considering the idea of getting out when I heard the door to my room open. I slipped out of the bath and pulling the huge, soft towel around me, tiptoed back to my room.

'Hello? Is that you, Lady Faulkner?'

'No miss, it's me.'

'Me' was a girl staring at me, her eyes wide in her plump, freckled face. She wore the same grey-and-white uniform as Rose and the other female servants. She looked about sixteen.

'Hello,' I said. 'Can I help you?'

'No, miss.'

'Oh.'

We stood in silence for a few moments.

'Why are you here then?' I asked. Her face cleared.

'Oh. I was sent up 'ere, miss. By Rose. To 'elp you dress.'

'Oh.' I wondered for a few moments why Rose would think I needed help in dressing. Even she couldn't have that low an opinion of me. Then I realized that no lady would be expected to dress herself in polite London society. I pulled the towel slightly tighter around me.

'That's nice,' I said. 'What's your name?'

'Ruby, miss.' She bobbed a curtsy and her cap wobbled a bit. I noticed her mousy brown hair was starting to come undone too. Ruby, it appeared, was as new to this as me.

'So what do you think I ought to wear this evening, Ruby?' I asked cheerfully. To be truthful I was rather glad to have a second opinion because I didn't have much in the way of evening-gowns and as I had soaked in the bath I had rather been wondering which of my two dresses would be the more suitable. However, from the look of fear that suddenly replaced Ruby's former expression of confusion, it was clear that she didn't have any more idea than I did.

'I dunno, miss,' she said. 'Rose never said nuffin' about me telling you what to wear. She said you'd tell me. She said I just 'ad to come up 'ere and do what you said.'

I raised an eyebrow suspiciously. 'Ruby, did Lady Faulkner tell Rose she was to come up here and help me?'

'I dunno, miss, honest.' Ruby all but wailed this and I knew straight away I was right. She looked about ready to cry now, her plump face going red. Her hair was beginning to fall down about her face now, her apron was tied rather inexpertly round her waist, which suggested she wasn't very good at getting herself dressed, let alone me. Rose might never have heard of the expression 'revenge is a dish best served cold', but it was clear she understood the principle very well.

'Well, it doesn't matter,' I said heartily. 'Now you're here, let's just do the best we can, shall we? If you could unlock my trunk and give me my robe, I can take this towel off and we can make a start.'

Given an instruction, Ruby seemed to feel

better and she dragged my trunk across the floor towards the window, finding my rather tatty dressing gown easily. Between the evening summer twilight and the glow from the exciting, modern electric light, we managed to locate my meagre evening wardrobe and soon we were both standing staring at a rose-pink, panne-velvet gown that was only slightly too small for me and a sea-green satin with long, close-fitting sleeves and lace frills along the bust which had somehow got ripped during the voyage.

'It's just Sir Henry and Lady Faulkner and myself and my father for dinner this evening, isn't it, Ruby?' I asked rather desperately as we contemplated this sad choice.

'Oh yes miss, there's no one else,' Ruby assured me. 'That greens's very pretty, miss. It'll suit your eyes.'

'Do you think so? Even with my spectacles on?'

She frowned. 'I don't think ladies wear spectacles in the dining room,' she said.

'Oh,' I said, wondering if I shouldn't wear my spectacles in the dining room then. It wasn't a matter I'd ever had to consider before. In the Valley of the Kings I either wore them or I missed vital evidence. We looked some more at the two dresses.

'Very well, then,' I said at last. 'The green it

41

is. But what about the lace? It's all come away.'

'Oh that's easy to repair, miss. Don't you worry about that.'

'Thank you very much, Ruby,' I said. Then something occurred to me. 'Ruby, have you ever served in the dining room before?'

'Oh no, miss. I'm only the 'tweenie. An' Cook says I'm all fingers and thumbs and can't be trusted with valuable things. But I've peeked in the room when nobody's looking,' she added.

'Of course.' I flinched. Rose really did know how to avenge herself.

Whilst Ruby busied herself with my few possessions, I sat down on a basketwork chair and looked around the room. I had never been in one so grand as this one. There was a brass double bedstead with a feather mattress and an ornately carved dressing table, draped with muslin and decorated with rich red ribbons. Next to it stood a matching wash-stand with a jug and bowl painted with fragile-looking roses. The large window was draped with chintz curtains. I had never felt so elegant or pampered before.

By the time the dinner gong struck at eight o'clock, Ruby and I were staring critically at my reflection in the dressing-table mirror and feeling quietly satisfied with ourselves. I didn't look too shabby and Ruby had managed to put my hair up with rather more success than she did her own.

'Thank you very much, Ruby,' I said as I walked to the door. 'You've been very helpful.'

She flushed with pleasure as she bobbed another little curtsy and I got the impression that compliments didn't usually flow in Ruby's direction.

'Thank you, miss.'

'May I ask Lady Faulkner to let you help me again?' I asked and was rewarded by an even deeper flush of pleasure.

'Thank you very much, miss.'

I walked down the stairs and found Papa and our hosts in the drawing-room. Lady Faulkner was wearing a yellow evening gown of chiffon and watered silk and looked a blaze of colour next to the more severe black and white of the gentlemen's attire. I wondered briefly who had been sent to attend to Papa, but before I could enquire Lady Faulkner rose and came over to me.

'Kate, there you are. You look lovely,' she said, her eyes sweeping over my dress doubtfully. 'I'm very cross with Rose. I specifically told her to help you this evening.'

'Not at all, Lady Faulkner. Please don't scold her. In fact, I was very pleased with

43

Ruby. I hope you'll allow her to help me dress again.'

'Oh? Really, dear?' Now she looked confused and I knew she was picturing Ruby in her mind. 'Well, if you say so. I'm so looking forward to taking you shopping tomorrow. I hope you'll let me advise you.'

'I'm counting on it, Lady Faulkner,' I said and was rewarded by another woman beaming with pleasure at me. I couldn't help wondering what it was like to be so interested in clothes and jewellery and other feminine accoutrements. The last time I had been that pleased was when I had found a second dynasty jar intact.

Dinner was every bit as sumptuous as I had expected, with the table in the dining room laid with a snow-white cloth and silverware that sparkled in the candlelight. We moved from soup to fish to the entrée, aided at every step by silent, attentive servants who replenished our glasses and removed plates with the solemnity of priests observing a pagan religious rite.

Sir Henry and Papa talked almost non-stop about Khaemwaset and his court. About six months ago Papa had discovered some documents on this Pharaoh and he had become intrigued with the scripts which seemed to give patchy directions to his burial chamber. Abandoning the more lucrative sites in the Valley of the Kings and at Giza and Saqqara, he had begun to spend all his time searching for Khaemwaset's tomb in the area known as the Tomb of the Nobles, not far from the Valley on the verdant, fertile flood plains of the Nile. We had had some initial success, but our leads had soon petered out leaving us with little more than a few broken pots and some maddeningly enigmatic yet tantalizing scripts. But Papa, somewhat obsessed by this time, refused to give up until our money ran out and we were forced to return to Luxor. As far as Papa was concerned, this was the main reason for our journey to England and he intended to plead his case for more funding to his utmost. At last, however, as we were served gooseberry fool, Sir Henry seemed to remember that I existed too.

'James tells me you're thinking of going to look over Girton,' he said, looking over the table at me as if I were a new species of animal.

'Oh really, darling?' Lady Faulkner sounded surprised too, but without the same contempt as her husband.

'Yes,' I said. 'I know the University won't give me a degree, but even so, it would be wonderful to have access to the library there.

Papa has told me so much about Cambridge.'

'Sounds like a lot of nonsense to me.' Sir Henry held up his glass and a footman stepped forward to fill it.

'Now darling, you don't really think that,' Lady Faulkner reproved him gently. 'Kate's so clever and I think it's a wonderful idea.'

'Well said, Alice.' Papa beamed at her over the gleaming crystal of his own glass. 'Henry's just an old-stick-in-the-mud. My Katie's the equal of any man when it comes to the Third Dynasty.'

I smiled at him, ignoring Sir Henry's grunt of derision. The fact that he was clearly in a minority at his own dinner table didn't seem to worry him.

'Can't see the point of a woman going to university, myself,' he said dismissively. 'What's she going to need all that for when she marries and has children?'

'*Varium et mutabile semper femina*, do you mean, Sir Henry?' I asked innocently.

He glared at me and Lady Faulkner moved swiftly to smooth the waters.

'Kate darling, shall we retire to the drawing room? I've got some fabrics I simply must show you and perhaps we could discuss some invitations I have already received . . . '

I stood up, resigned to an evening of feminine conversation. I knew it was very

46

kind of Lady Faulkner to undertake my season and I did feel grateful to her and also excited, but I also didn't want to leave Papa alone too much with Sir Henry. He had begun to show a tendency to dwell too long on Khaemwaset without realizing that he was becoming tedious. However I could hardly refuse Lady Faulkner and so we left the gentlemen to their port whilst we took coffee in the cosy drawing room.

I enjoyed myself more than I expected to, choosing different materials and looking at different patterns for an array of costumes for morning wear, day wear, formal occasions, even a hunting outfit, although I couldn't help wondering how much it was all going to cost. We had some money for my wardrobe, but I was well aware that the purse wasn't bottomless; I was the one who organized our budget. Something of this worry must have communicated itself to Lady Faulkner because as she put the books of swatches to one side she said:

'I hope you will allow me to make a present of this dress and this outfit, my dear. I would be so pleased.'

'Oh — really — Lady Faulkner — Papa and I couldn't — '

'Nonsense. It would be my pleasure. And please do call me Alice. I knew your dear mama. She was very kind to me when I was a girl and I would like to repay that kindness. Besides,' she looked away briefly to pour another cup of coffee, 'who knows when I'll get the chance to do this again?'

Before I could reply to this, the door to the drawing room opened and Papa and Sir Henry walked in. One look at Sir Henry's face told me he had heard more than enough about the court of Khaemwaset for one evening.

' . . . and the scripts are tantalizing, old man. They give the most maddening glimpses of directions for the burial site and several times I've been certain I know the exact location. But then the instructions peter out or they aren't preserved or — '

'Papa,' I said, going up to him and putting my arm through his. 'Forget about Khaemwaset and his treasures and come and tell me which fabric you prefer. Oh, and do you remember Lady Faulkner's cousin, Adam Ellis? He was an assistant a few years back. He's arriving next week to take up his new position as senior archaeologist at the museum. Won't it be nice to see him again?'

Grudgingly, Papa sat down next to me on the striped Georgian sofa, not looking too excited at the prospect of inspecting a book of silks. Sir Henry, by contrast, shot me a look that could almost be described as gratitude and I knew I had intervened not a moment too soon. If Papa wasn't careful, we were going to lose all our support from the museum.

'Can't say that remember the name, my dear. Was he the one with a limp?'

'Of course not, Papa. He was the one who found the twenty-sixth dynasty pendant of the goddess Maat.'

'That's right!' Papa perked up suddenly. 'Beautiful piece, almost intact too. The markings were perfect, Henry, absolutely typical of the era.'

'Hmph. Thank you, my dear,' Sir Henry said to Lady Faulkner as she passed him a coffee-cup. 'The boy *is* good at what he does. That's why we hired him. And how did you get on with him, miss?' he added suddenly and I knew he was thinking of the frogs in his bath again.

'Mr Ellis and I had reached an understanding by the end of his stay,' I admitted, grudgingly.

'Was he the one who took you into the tunnels?' said Papa suddenly.

I nodded.

'Now I remember him. Yes, useful sort of fellow. And he didn't moan about you the way the others did.'

'Didn't he?' asked Sir Henry, incredulity in his tone. I had a brief bout of nostalgia, reflecting how satisfying it had been to sabotage his bath-time with the frogs.

'I'm so glad you were friends, darling,' Lady Faulkner said, patting my hand. 'But you know of course, he's Dr Ellis now.'

Her face shone with pride as she said this and it occurred to me that she looked really happy for the first time since we'd met at the port, rather than just showing her gracious hostess face. Our conversation after that turned to more general matters like the eruption of Mount Vesuvius the year before and Mrs Pankhurst's suffragette movement, although Lady Faulkner swiftly changed the subject when it became clear I was in favour of it and Sir Henry most definitely wasn't. We moved on from politics and talked instead of the theatre and various exhibitions and galleries that Lady Faulkner had decided I must see. When we eventually retired some two hours later I was exhausted and more than ready to sink into the soft downy bed, but my enthusiasm for our trip was once more invigorated and I could hardly wait for the morning to come.

★ ★ ★

The music of the waltz finished with flourish and I bowed to Lord Elmsbury, my partner, and allowed him to lead me to the refreshment table. My cheeks felt flushed with all the exercise and I tried to catch my breath in as ladylike a fashion as possible, but I must have looked uncomfortable because Lord Elmsbury looked at me in some concern.

'I say, would you like some fresh air? You seem a little . . . ' he waved his hand at me and I nodded gratefully.

'Yes, that would be lovely. Shall we go out into the garden?'

He looked a little startled at first, but then nodded his head happily.

'Of course. What a delightful idea. Here we go, my dear,' he said cheerfully as he lead me to a door which took us out into the beautifully laid-out garden. The scent of the rose-bushes in the sultry night air seemed a perfect match for the fairylike quality of the light from the candles and the streetlamps beyond the walls. I could not help smiling in pleasure as I breathed in the night air. Despite missing the heat and the noise of Egypt I was enjoying myself immensely.

'Isn't this lovely?' I said as we walked across to a pond with a fountain gently spraying water out of a stone dolphin. A frog croaked from somewhere in the undergrowth.

'Yes, my dear and so are you, if you'll permit me to say so,' said Lord Elmsbury, fixing a monocle in his eye in a fashion I did not particularly care for. I retaliated by getting my own spectacles out of my beaded reticule and putting them on to stare at him. Ruby was right: ladies did not usually wear spectacles to formal occasions but I found I was missing so much that I compromised by taking them everywhere and wearing them whenever I could.

'Thank you, Lord Elmsbury, you're very kind,' I said and was further surprised when he took my hand and pressed it to his lips.

'Not at all,' he said. 'It's you who are kind, dancing with me and then accompanying me to this delightful garden.'

Since he had given me the impression earlier that someone had forced him to partner me and he had spoken of nothing but his horse for the entire duration, I was a little startled by this, but before I could say anything another figure suddenly appeared in the dark and called to us.

'Good evening, Lord Elmsbury.'

'What? Oh, good evening.' The expression of resentment on his face was so palpable I had to force myself not to laugh. He looked like an overgrown child deprived of a cake.

But then he took my arm rather forcefully. 'Miss Whitaker and I were — '

'Ah yes, Miss Whitaker, good evening.' The interloper turned to me now and I recognized him. His face was leaner and paler than I remembered, but the disapproval on his face took me right back to that first day on the ship.

'Mr Ellis. How nice to see you again. But I should say Dr Ellis now, shouldn't I?' I said, brightly, ignoring his expression. After all, I wasn't fourteen any more. 'I take it you know Lord Elmsbury?'

'We were at school together,' he said brusquely. 'Alice sent me. She wanted to know if you are ready to leave yet.'

'Oh, is she with you?' said Lord Elmsbury, as though I were a poodle. 'Actually, Lord Elmsbury — ' I began, but was interrupted by Adam. 'Yes she is. I believe Miss Hetherington was looking for you, Elmsbury. Perhaps you should go and find her.'

'Oh, that's right,' I said. 'You're Amelia Hetherington's fiancé, aren't you? I met her at the ballet the other day and she was telling me all about — '

Lord Elmsbury had been glaring at Adam but as I spoke he turned to me, the anger visible on his face.

'Of course, Miss Whitaker, thank you for

reminding me. Good evening.' And before I could reply, he stormed off.

'What on earth was all that about?' I said, watching him go. Adam gave an exasperated sigh.

'You know, I was hoping that in seven years you'd have grown up a bit, Kate. But I can see you haven't. Henry was saying as much yesterday.'

'Oh, was he? And how is this my fault?' I turned and glared at him myself now. 'We were getting on perfectly well until you arrived.'

'I'm sure you were. Come on, I told Alice I'd fetch you.'

' 'Fetch me'? What am I, a dog?'

He rolled his eyes as he perched on the edge of the pond, apparently unconcerned by the damp moss on his evening clothes.

'You really haven't changed, have you, Kate? You're just as ill-mannered and unreasonable as when I first met you.'

I stared at him in disbelief for a few seconds.

' 'Ill-mannered and . . . ' For your information, Adam Ellis,' I said, taking off my spectacles and placing them back in my reticule before glaring at him, 'I was having a perfectly pleasant conversation with someone who, I might add, is a great deal more civilized than you are, and then you come along and behave like a boor. Which, by the way, is exactly how I remember you were the first time we met. Now if you'll forgive me, I think I've had enough of your company for one evening.'

I swept past him and walked back into the ballroom, irritated beyond belief at his attitude. Inside, another waltz was beginning, the lilting music already sweeping couples up in its irresistible harmonies, but although my dance-book was full, I was too annoyed to want to dance. I managed to get rid of my next partner just as Alice appeared. She looked a little flustered.

'Oh! There you are darling. Did Adam find you? I was a little worried when you disappeared with Lord Elmsbury like that.'

'Yes, he found me,' I said with what I thought was admirable restraint.

Alice sighed in relief. 'Oh good. Where is he? Oh yes, over there, talking to Lord Elmsbury. Oh dear, I hope everything's all right.'

I glanced over to where she was pointing and saw Adam and Lord Elmsbury deep in conversation. It didn't look as though either of them was enjoying himself very much, but then Lord Elmsbury nodded before walking off.

'I'm sure everything's fine,' I said. 'But you really needn't have bothered sending him, Alice. Surely it's a little early to be leaving yet?'

Alice looked bewildered for a moment before her face cleared.

'Oh, is that what he told you? Oh no, we don't need to leave yet. Shouldn't you be dancing, dear? I thought your book was full?'

'It is,' I said, as pairs of dancers twirled on the floor, the startling black-and-white of the men's evening wear offset by the brilliant reds and blues and greens of the ladies' evening dresses. As the music soared around us I began to regret sitting this one out. 'I was a little warm beforehand, Alice, which is why I went out into the garden, but . . . '

Before I could get any further, Papa came up behind me.

'Kate darling, are you all right?' he asked in concern.

'I'm fine, Papa, why wouldn't I . . . ?' But I got no further as he put a hand on my forehead and Sir Henry joined us.

'How's the girl feeling, James?'

'She's very hot, Henry. I think we should leave now.'

'What's wrong, Henry?' said Alice, picking up her own reticule and taking my hand in her own.

'James and I were just chattin' with Phillips and Meredith over there when Elmsbury came over and said young Katie didn't seem too well.'

'"Didn't seem too well'?' I echoed in surprise. 'Why on — ?'

'Darling, you should have said something,' Alice remonstrated gently as she put a cool hand on my forehead. 'Henry, fetch a cab. James, take her arm.'

'Really, I'm fine,' I said as forcefully as I could but nobody seemed to be listening to me any more. Sir Henry walked off briskly to find us a cab and Papa and Alice hurried me along, ignoring all my attempts to assure them that I felt perfectly well. Just as we were about to leave, Alice explaining to our host and hostess that I was 'a little overcome with excitement', I saw Adam in the middle of the dance floor, a pretty young woman in his arms. He looked up and grinned at me as we were shown to our cab and I scowled. Suddenly I was fourteen and it was the laundry-room all over again.

★   ★   ★

I woke up next morning feeling a little groggy and it took several minutes before I could remember the events of last night. As soon as

57

we had got home, Alice insisted I went straight to bed, and my last memory as I was chivvied up the stairs was of Sir Henry and Papa walking into the smoking room, cigars and whiskies in their hands, looking very pleased with themselves. Since neither of them had been too keen on attending the ball in the first place, I had the strong impression that they were none too sorry at being given an excuse to leave. Certainly neither of them seemed to feel that my 'illness' required any more of their time.

I sat up and got out of bed slowly, still slightly dazed. Alice had insisted on giving me a sleeping draught, chosen from what appeared to me to be an astonishing array of pill bottles. The sunlight was streaming through the windows and when I looked at the little ormolu clock by my bed, I was surprised to see it was half past ten. I rang the bell for Ruby and began searching my now greatly expanded wardrobe for clothes. I had just returned from the bathroom when there was a knock on the door.

'Come in, Ruby,' I said briskly. 'Why didn't you wake me? I've got a luncheon appointment and — oh!'

It wasn't Ruby in the doorway, but Rose, with a tray in her hands.

'Begging yer pardon, miss, Ruby's busy

now, so Lady Faulkner's sent me up with yer breakfast things. She said ter say you've ter take it easy this mornin', being 'as 'ow you ain't feelin' so well.'

'Oh. That's very kind of you, Rose, but I feel fine. You must go and tell Lady Faulkner that immediately.' I paused. 'She still intends for us to visit the museum at noon, I take it?'

'I dunno, miss. 'Er ladyship was on the telephone a lot this mornin'.'

I frowned. Sir Henry had had a telephone installed in the house and although I had been thrilled at the convenience of this marvellous device when we first arrived it occurred to me now that there were some definite disadvantages to its existence. Papa had arranged for us to take luncheon with some archaeologists from the museum and Lady Faulkner's busy morning on the telephone suggested she had been in the process of cancelling it.

'Rose,' I said, thinking quickly. 'Could you just help me with these stays. I need to see Lady Faulkner immediately.'

'But — ain't you ill, miss?' Rose seemed suspicious.

'Not at all,' I said briskly.

She grunted at this, but said nothing and I began to wonder exactly what was being said in the kitchen. Experience had taught me at an early age that if one wished to know what was going on, the domestic quarters were the best place to find out.

'Rose, did I ever apologize to you for my appalling behaviour on that trip to Egypt?' I said ingratiatingly.

Another grunt. 'No miss, I don't recall you ever did.'

'Well, I hope you can forgive me now. I was a wretched little child and I'm sure Dr Ellis did quite the right thing in making myself and William help you with your work.'

I grimaced as I said that, but it seemed to be working. Rose sniffed with righteous indignation.

'Well, you was *very* naughty, miss.'

'I know.' I bowed my head slightly. 'I am most dreadfully ashamed of myself.'

Rose nodded her head. 'I daresay you was just bein' mischievous,' she said magnanimously. 'An' no 'arm was done in the end. Mr Adam saw to that.'

'Yes, he did, didn't he?' I said sweetly, between gritted teeth. I had remembered Mr Adam's part in last night's fiasco by now, as well.

'It's a good job, 'e's around really, Miss Kate, init? Ovverwise you woulda bin in a lotta trouble last night too.'

'What?' I snapped, turning round.

Rose pulled at the laces in my stays with

rather more force than was absolutely necessary. 'You nearly got yourself in trouble lars' night, Miss Kate,' she repeated, her eyes narrowing. 'It's a good job Mr Adam was there to sort it out.'

'Sort what out? What trouble?' I asked, bemused. Rose stopped tugging at my stays and looked at me shrewdly.

'Don't you remember what 'appened last night with you and Lord Whatsisname?' she asked.

'Lord Elmsbury?' I said in surprise. 'Nothing happened — at least nothing that I know of. We danced and then we took a walk in the garden. Everything was fine, until Dr Ellis turned up.'

'Miss Katie, are you tellin' me you really don't know what you done wrong?' Now Rose had given up any pretence of deference. I shook my head.

'Miss Katie, you allowed yourself to be escorted, unchaperoned, into a garden, alone, at night, wiv a man wot you're not related to. Young, unmarried ladies do not do that. Not 'ere, at least,' she added darkly.

I barely heard her last words. I was remembering Lord Elmsbury's expression when I suggested we go into the graden and the cold moistness of his lips on my hand. I shuddered.

'Do you mean he thought that — because we went into the . . . '

Rose nodded grimly.

'Good Lord.' I shuddered again. 'No wonder he was so pleased when I suggested going into the garden.'

'You suggested it?' Now Rose looked shocked and I couldn't help laughing. 'It's no laughin' matter, miss,' she continued grimly as she held out a turquoise dress with triple shoulder frills. 'Young ladies what don't know their manners get into terrible trouble.'

'Well I was hot,' I replied as I put my arm through the sleeves. 'And the garden looked cool. In Egypt we're outside all the time.'

'This ain't Egypt, miss. You're jus' lucky Mr Adam got there in time.'

'Am I indeed?' I said coolly and Rose frowned. I'd forgotten how much she liked Adam.

'Yes, you are, miss. 'E made sure that Lord Whatsisname told everyone you was ill, so's it didn't look like you knew what you were doin'. You owe 'im an apology, miss.'

I was sitting at the dressing table by now and Rose was brushing my hair, but I turned round and stared at her in surprise when she said this.

'What for?'

'Fer bein' 'orrible to 'im lars' night,' she said firmly.

'How do you know I was horrible to him?' I was trying for outraged indignation, but Rose wasn't impressed.

'Lady Wendell's 'ousekeeper told Mrs Nichollson-Jones's parlour-maid 'oo told Violet 'oo told me,' she said with absolutely no shame whatsoever. ''E's downstairs now, miss, with Sir 'Enry, in 'is study.'

I sighed. If everything she said was true — and I had no doubt it was: servants always knew everything — I realized I was going to have to apologize to him. I just couldn't forget his smirk as I'd been bustled out, like a child. It was very frustrating.

I watched Rose's face in the mirror for a few minutes, determined that I was going to get something out of this. By now I had a very shrewd idea as to why Ruby hadn't brought me breakfast this morning and it had nothing to do with work. Rose was a dragon in many ways, but she looked after her girls and she certainly wouldn't want an impressionable child like Ruby waiting on a hussy like me.

'You're right, Rose. I'll go downstairs straight away and talk to him. Um . . . Lady Faulkner and I were going to the theatre this evening. Do you think Ruby will able to dress me or will she have too much work to do?'

Rose flashed me a glance through narrowed

eyes in the glass, before pursing her lips. 'I daresay young Ruby will 'ave finished all her other work by then, miss.'

'Oh good.' I jumped up. 'Thank you for helping me, Rose. You've done my hair beautifully.' I ran out of the bedroom and went downstairs.

I hadn't had anything to eat or drink yet and I decided if I was going to humble myself I needed a good strong cup of coffee first. I knew it was Alice's habit to take a particularly fine blend in the sunny, pleasant little parlour she used whilst dealing with her correspondence, so I decided to visit her first. As I reached the bottom of the stairs, Violet, the parlour-maid, was just coming out of the room.

'Violet, would you bring me a cup of coffee in here, please,' I said, as I entered the parlour. She bobbed a curtsy and retreated down to the kitchen.

'Alice, have you cancelled our luncheon appointment yet? Because there really is no need — oh!'

I stopped. Alice wasn't there, but the room wasn't empty. Adam was perched on the window-seat, wearing a lounge suit of blue-grey tweed. He was reading a news-paper, but he looked up and grinned when he saw me.

'Good morning, Kate. I hope you're feeling better.'

I scowled. 'There's nothing wrong with me as you very well know, Adam Ellis. Thank you so much for getting me taken home like a naughty little girl last night.'

His grin grew. 'It was just like old times, wasn't it?'

'If, by old times, you mean you were despicable, then yes I entirely agree,' I said. He turned a page of the newspaper.

'So this morning I'm despicable. Last night I was a boor. Which I was quite upset about, I have to say. I thought I was doing you a favour.'

'Really?' I went over to the table where Alice kept her post and leafed through some brochures. 'Well apparently you're not the only one. Rose tells me I should apologize to you as well.'

He put the paper down. 'Please don't break the habits of a lifetime on my account. I remember your brattish manners quite well.'

I surveyed him coolly. 'And I remember your arrogant high-handedness.'

He scowled, but couldn't retort as Violet came in at that moment, bearing a tray with a coffee jug and two cups.

'I brought two cups, miss, in case Mr Adam wanted one an' all,' she said, bobbing a slight curtsy in his direction. I noticed a faint flush in her cheeks as he smiled at her. Violet was pretty young woman of about nineteen, I should add.

'How kind, Violet,' I cooed. 'Dr Ellis, would you like some coffee?'

'Thanks,' he said. As I handed him the fine bone-china cup, I smiled sweetly.

'I see you're still as popular as ever with the female staff, Adam. Rose was quite vociferous in her defence of you.'

He took the cup and we sat down opposite each other on rather stiff, horsehair-upholstered mahogany armchairs.

'And how *are* you and Rose getting on these days?' He grinned. 'Should I be checking the laundry room?'

I lifted the cup to my lips and took a sip.

'Rose and I have adjusted to the new status I enjoy in this household as a respected friend of the family,' I said loftily. 'In fact, she's becoming quite useful.'

He hooted at this. 'In other words, you grovelled, she accepted your apology and in return she's letting you in on kitchen gossip.'

I would have liked to deny this, but sadly it was far too close to the truth. So I contented myself with giving him a tight little smile instead.

'You know, I really let you off far too lightly

seven years ago,' I said. 'I can't believe I was so nice to you.'

'Nice to me?' He scowled. 'Some of those Arabic phrases you taught me would have made a camel-trader blush.'

I grinned. 'Just a little local colour. Besides, you made me clean your boots for the entire voyage.'

'You should be grateful that's all I did. *And* I forgave you and took you into the tunnels as you wanted.'

I sniffed. 'Not every time.'

'Most of the time,' he retorted. 'And even then you were still up to your little tricks.' He looked at me through narrowed eyes. 'I got fed up with constantly having to check my bed to make sure there were no scarab beetles in it.'

I couldn't help smiling. 'Ah yes. How easily one forgets those satisfying little details.' I looked at him for a moment, then put my cup down. 'But I suppose you *did* keep your end of our bargain all those years ago. And I suppose Rose *is* right.' I took a deep breath. 'Thank you very much for protecting my reputation last night, Adam. It was very kind of you. It just would have been more tactful if you hadn't looked so pleased that I was going home.'

'I wasn't pleased that you were going

67

home,' he protested.

I snorted. 'Of course you were. It was written all over your face.'

He grinned. 'Well, let's just say it was nice to see you getting your just reward for comparing me so unfavourably to that loathsome creature Elmsbury. But come, let's call a truce. Alice will be back in a moment. She's asked me to accompany you this afternoon. Do you want me to come?'

He leaned forward as he said this, a sincerity in his eyes that I had never seen before and I realized suddenly that I did want him to come with us. I wanted that very much.

'Yes,' I said. 'That would be very nice.'

We looked at each other, sharing a smile, just as the door opened and Alice came in.

'Oh, there you are, darling. Henry and your papa have just left for the museum. I told them I would let them know if you were well enough to take luncheon later on. How are you feeling, dear?'

She sat down next to me, anxiety clouding her eyes and making her pale face seem even paler. I beamed at her.

'I feel absolutely wonderful, Alice.'

'Oh good. Well in that case . . . '

She continued to talk about our appointment, but I barely heard her. Suddenly all I was aware of was Adam sitting opposite me, and the fact that he would be accompanying us to lunch. There was a strange fluttering in my stomach.

Third dynasty artefacts had never been as exciting as this.

3

Saqqara, Egypt — October 1907

'Hurry up, Adam!'

As soon as he turned towards me, I felt my heart sink. It was going to happen again. I knew it.

He came down the stairs of the something Hotel and walked over to the *calèche* that Papa had already ordered to take us to the pyramids.

'Kate, I'm sorry, but you're going to have go without me. There's a new sponsor I need to see and he's only available this afternoon.'

Papa grunted. 'Oh well, never mind. Come along, Kate. We don't want to miss the — '

'Wait a moment, Papa,' I said. 'Adam, surely you don't have to go right away? We only made these arrangements a couple of hours ago.'

'I know and I'm truly sorry.' He pushed his hair back from his forehead, trying not to frown. 'But I just got the message from the museum and it's vital I see this chap before he goes back to New York. The potential revenue is . . . '

I stopped listening at this point. It was the bit about the message he'd 'just' received from the museum that interested me. I was fairly certain I knew who'd sent it. I forced a pleasant smile on my face.

'Well, if you have to go, then you have to go,' I said lightly. 'Will we see you at dinner?'

'Of course.' He smiled at me now, before turning to Papa. The smile, I noticed, became a little strained. 'Professor, perhaps this evening we can discuss the texts you showed me last night?'

'Certainly,' said Papa. 'I'd be interested to hear what your opinion is.'

I could tell from the expressions on both their faces that this was not true at all and suddenly the idea of Adam not accompanying us to the pyramids did not seem such a bad idea.

'Until this evening then. Come, Papa.'

I took Papa's arm and we climbed into the calèche, instructing the driver to set off.

'Shame he couldn't come,' said Papa after a few minutes, as we made our way slowly through the crowded, noisy streets of Saqqara.

'Papa, that is the most insincere thing I think I've ever heard you say.'

'Hmph.' He scratched his beard and fanned himself with his battered old panama.

'I know you like him, Katie, but I'm beginning to wish Henry had never suggested he come back home with us. The boy's a pest. He questions every document I show him in the minutest detail. One would think he believes I'm making it up.'

'Well, Papa,' I said carefully, 'perhaps that's a good thing. If you can persuade Adam that Khaemwaset's tomb really exists then the museum will have no choice but to fund us.'

Papa grunted at this and I knew he was disappointed. He had expected the Cavendish to grant him the money to search for Khaemwaset's tomb before we left England and the fact that Sir Henry had demanded further evidence hurt his pride more than he was prepared to admit. He had been quietly furious when the museum board foisted Adam upon us to examine his research, but for the first time ever I found I did not agree him. I had been delighted that Adam was coming back to Egypt with us.

'Maybe,' Papa agreed reluctantly. 'Although he's very obstructive. I don't know what's got into the boy. He was never this sceptical when he was out here with us the first time.'

I held my tongue. I knew Papa had no idea how irritating he had been in London when he had constantly harangued the board members to look at his evidence. I strongly suspected that Adam had been given very specific instructions on how to deal with Papa.

'And another thing,' Papa continued, waving away the small boys who kept jumping on the *calèche* to sell us dates and figs. 'Why does he keep cancelling appointments like this? It's damned irritating.'

This I could not disagree with. Several times during the voyage over we had made arrangements for various outings only to find at the last minute that Adam was unable to accompany us due to some task telegraphed over by the museum. I was beginning to hate Mr Marconi and his marvellous invention.

'I mean to say,' Papa grumbled. 'One understands that he's fond of Alice, but does the gel constantly need jade necklaces and ivory fans and other knick-knacks sent from every blasted place we stop?'

And that was the crux of the matter. It was invariably Alice who sent these telegrams. They always seemed important at first glance, but after the third cancellation I had begun to question just how official they really were. Adam seemed to buy a lot of jewellery, although I couldn't complain, since I always got a present out of it too. At least I tried not to complain, but lately it was getting harder.

'Well,' I said, struggling to be loyal,

73

although I was beginning to wonder just to whom I was being loyal, 'Alice and Adam have always been very close. And she *is* the wife of his employer. I suppose it's only natural he should want to please her.'

Papa looked at me shrewdly. 'I should have thought he'd want to please you, my dear. After all, you're the one he dances attendance on every minute of the day. When he's not questioning my research methods and arguing with my conclusions, that is.'

'Papa! He does not dance attendance on me,' I cried, feeling my cheeks blush with embarrassment. Then I saw him smile and I could not stop myself smiling in return. 'Does he really?'

'I may be old, but I'm not blind, my dear.' Papa leaned across and patted my arm. 'The boy is besotted. And why should he not be? You're beautiful, intelligent, charming — '

'Papa!' I laughed. 'You're only saying that because you're my father.'

'Not at all, my dear. I say it because it's true. So why he allows himself to be at Alice's beck and call is a mystery to me.'

It was to me too. 'Perhaps he doesn't realize he's doing it,' I said, but without much conviction. Papa raised an eyebrow drily.

'Then it's about time he did, my girl. A man can't serve two mistresses. Ah, here we are, at last,' he continued as the *calèche* came to a shudddering halt. 'And look, it's old Jefferson. I wondered if we'd see him out here. And Andrews and Palmerston too. Jefferson! Hold up, old boy . . . '

Papa jumped down from the carriage and was immediately swallowed up by a crowd of friends. I climbed down more slowly, not at all reassured by Papa's last comment. If Adam were forced to choose between me and Alice, I had a horrible feeling I would lose.

Luxor, Egypt — November 1907

I was seated at my desk, ostensibly typing a report, but in reality straining to hear the conversation going on downstairs. This was not hard as it was rapidly becoming more heated by the minute. Eventually the door to Papa's study opened, there was a curt goodbye from Adam and the front door slammed.

I leapt up and ran to the window of my bedroom just in time to see Adam marching down the road, clearly annoyed. I picked up my straw hat, jammed it on to my head and ran down the stairs into the hallway.

'Kate — '

'In a moment, Papa,' I shouted, before

75

running out on to the street. 'Adam! Wait.'

He turned, the angry expression still on his face, but softening as he realized it was me.

'Kate. I'm sorry I left without saying goodbye.'

I walked up to him more slowly now. It was mid-afternoon and the sun beat down mercilessly on the market square, making everyone stick firmly to the shaded areas. Old men sat in cafés with tiny cups of coffee and *sheeshas* (waterpipes) in front of them, market traders called seductively for customers and the smell of *aysh* and *babaganoush* hung in the air. I took his arm and drew him under the shade of a café awning.

'My dear, you didn't even say hello.'

'I know.' He looked away briefly, unsure how to proceed. 'It seemed inappropriate when I knew your father wasn't going to be happy with my news.'

I looked down at the dirty pavement.

'Oh dear. Does that mean you're recommending the museum doesn't fund any further research into the burial site?'

'I'm afraid so.' He sighed. 'Kate, you know if there — '

I cut him off, unable to bear the look of desolation on his face. 'I know, Adam. But Papa is so convinced. Have you looked at the — '

'Kate, I've reviewed all the evidence. Over and over again. You know I have. I agree that some of the texts are intriguing and the mention of a gold statue is tantalizing, but there's no real proof that any of it exists. You know how unreliable these texts can be. And the museum can't afford to go chasing rainbows. We've spent enough time and money on this as it is.'

'But — '

'I can't justify the expense, Kate. I'm sorry.'

'What about if we — '

'No.' His tone was firm now. 'I'm overlooking the transfer of funds from the Saqqara project as it is.'

'Ah.' I felt my face flush as I tried, and failed, not to look guilty. 'You noticed that, then.'

He took my chin in his hands, one eyebrow raised drily.

'Your accounting is very persuasive, Kate, but I'm not a fool.' Then his expression softened again. 'I'm sorry. I know James will be disappointed, but I really can't justify any more money on this.'

I sighed, but I wasn't really surprised. Ever since Papa had first found the texts describing Khaemwaset's tomb and all its riches he had seemed to become almost bewitched by the notion of its existence. I had been as captivated as he had initially, but after

77

several abortive attempts to find the site even I could see it was time to concentrate on other projects.

'Never mind,' I said, putting my arm through his as we strolled along the bustling market place. 'Ahmed came by a few days ago with some information about a burial chamber of a boy pharaoh somewhere in the Valley. I know he was interested. Perhaps when you come tomorrow you could discuss that with him. But be here before nine because I've booked the carriage for ten and we need to get to the station in plenty of time for the train if we — '

'Ah. Yes. I was meaning to talk to you about that.' Now he was looking guilty and I found myself frowning.

'What?' I snapped.

'I — er — I'm afraid I'm not going to be able to come with you to the Temple of Karnak tomorrow.'

'Why not?' I was still snapping, but I couldn't help it. I knew exactly what he was going to say.

'There's a sarcophagus up river I need to examine.'

'Well, go the next day. Or the next. We've been planning this trip for weeks. You know how difficult it was for me to get Mrs Holt to come.'

'Yes, I know,' he said patiently. 'And if I could put it off, I would. But the problem is — '

'It's Alice, isn't it?' My face was flushing even more deeply and I could feel myself begin to lose my temper. 'What does she want now? A new necklace? A piece of jade that she's discovered can only be bought at auction in Cairo? Oh no, that was last month, wasn't it? It must be something different this time,' I added sarcastically.

Adam cleared his throat. 'Kate, you're being entirely un — '

'Tell me Alice had nothing to do with this,' I demanded. I could see him wondering whether he might get away with a lie and deciding against it.

'Alice did send an additional telegram to the one I received from Henry, but — '

'Oh for heaven's sake, Adam. Why must you always jump whenever Alice snaps her fingers?'

'I'm doing no such thing,' he said indignantly, his own face darkening with anger now. 'I have to go where the museum sends me and they need me in Qus to examine a new item for them. I can't help it if it interferes with our plans. I *am* supposed to be working, you know.'

Each of us stared at the other for a moment

whilst around us the market traders stopped their business to enjoy the sight of two Europeans arguing. The noise of the bazaar was often deafening, with traders in their white *galabiyyas* shouting entreaties to passers-by to stop and examine their goods, arguing with other traders over prices or quality, and donkeys braying constantly in the background. Every so often the noise would be hushed by the muezzin calling the faithful to prayer and there would be a brief respite, but generally life on the streets of Luxor was noisy and colourful and exhilarating.

Adam sighed again and took my hands in his.

'Katie, I'm sorry. Truly, I am. But I have to go.' He paused. 'Listen. This should only take the morning. If I hurry, I can be back in Luxor by late afternoon. Why don't I come to your house and meet your father, then? We can talk about the pharaoh and hopefully I might be able to persuade him to forget about Khaemwaset for a while. And then afterwards, we could go for dinner at the Winter Palace. How would you like that?'

I smiled, wanting to argue as little as he did.

'Very much. Do you think we could stop off at the garden terrace first?'

Adam put an arm around my shoulders

and drew me under the shade of a eucalyptus tree so that we were slightly out of sight of the old men in the café. The sharp, aromatic smell pricked at my nostrils.

'I don't see why not. If you ask me very nicely.'

'And how would I do that, Dr Ellis?' I said, looking up at him slightly breathlessly. I could feel my heart thumping madly in my chest as he gripped me by the elbows and drew me up close to him.

'Like this,' he said as he pressed his lips hard against mine. For a second I was startled by his intensity; our kisses up until now had been chaste and innocent, but this was something new. There was an urgency to his movements as he pushed himself against me, and although I knew it was wrong for me to be acting in this way I found I wanted the roughness of this embrace as much as he did. Suddenly he pulled away.

'You should go back home now,' he said ruefully. 'Before I ruin your reputation completely.'

I nodded. 'I'll see you tomorrow then?'

'As soon as I can manage it,' he said.

We walked back out into the baking heat and went our separate ways. As I walked the short distance back to the house I felt strangely light-headed and hot inside, my

81

stomach tingling in the same way as it had done that morning back in England when I had first realized how excited I was by Adam's presence. I felt as if I were walking on air and if someone had told me that barely twenty-four hours later my entire life would be turned upside down, I would have laughed in their face.

★ ★ ★

The next day was a busy one for me. First I had to visit Emma Holt, the vicar's wife and a great friend, who had agreed to chaperon Adam and me on the trip to the temple. I explained that we had had to cancel our plans, but she was very understanding and I rather got the impression that she was relieved not to have to waste a day in frivolous engagements when there was plenty to do in the parish.

Then I spent the rest of the morning with Papa, trying to get him to see sense over Adam's decision. He was as intractable as ever, though, and I decided in the end that the best thing to do was persuade him to visit Sayyid Ahmed Mahmud Jamal el-Mansur to see if this parallel project might wean him off the subject of Khaemwaset and his treasures. Ahmed was a wealthy Egyptian antiques dealer and Papa's oldest friend in Luxor.

So we travelled across to Ahmed's town house and spent the afternoon there, Papa in the *salamlik* (the front of the house, where the men were), drinking cups of strong, sweet coffee and discussing the boy king Tutankhamun; and me in the *haramlik* (the women's quarters), showing off my new clothes to Ahmed's wives and daughters, drinking strong, sweet tea and laughing over the foolishness of men. Afterwards I couldn't help thinking that that should have given me some kind of warning of what was about to happen.

Papa and I left the house in high spirits. He had had a long talk with Ahmed and seemed genuinely keen to take up the challenge of searching for the tomb of the boy pharaoh. As we were passing Adam's hotel, I decided to stop off and leave a message for him, so he would have some idea of Papa's new-found enthusiasm. Leaving Papa to browse through the bazaar for any interesting artefacts, I went quickly into the blessed coolness of the reception area and wrote a quick note.

'Could you give this to Dr Ellis when he returns this afternoon, please?' I asked, handing the note to the receptionist, a young man immaculate in white uniform and wearing a stiff red fez on his head.

'Certainly, ma'am,' he said, taking the note from me and placing it in the pigeonhole reserved for Adam. But as he pushed it in, his cuff became entangled between two other letters there and, not noticing this, he inadvertently pulled the whole pile out, causing them to flutter to the blue-tiled floor. As he stooped to pick them up, I noticed that one was a brochure of a forthcoming exhibition in Cairo (we had received a copy that morning too), but the other was a letter handwritten in the distinctive mauve ink that I recognized only too well. Oh Lord, I thought, not another letter from Alice. I walked back out into the sunshine, hoping this wasn't more instructions on how to ruin my romance.

⋆　⋆　⋆

I knocked on Papa's door.

'Papa! Are you nearly ready?'

'Yes, my dear. Give me five minutes. Is Adam here yet?'

'No, but it's ten to seven. We need to be able to leave as soon as he gets here.'

'Of course, my dear,' came the muffled reply from behind the door. 'Have no fear. I shan't let you down.'

Reassured, I turned and ran down the

stairs, pausing to check my reflection in the hall mirror. Just as I was patting a stray lock back in place, there was a knock at the door and I could see Adam through the screening.

'It's all right, I'll answer it,' I said as Sayeed, our solitary, ageing servant came out of the kitchen. I gave myself one last check, then opened the door.

'You're just in time,' I said chirpily, leading us through to the parlour. 'Papa will be joining us in a minute and — '

'Kate, I've got something to tell you.'

'What is it?' I asked, but already I had a terrible inkling that I knew what he was going to say.

'I can't take you out tonight. I've had some rather bad news.'

'Bad news?' I sank down on the oak settle, feeling suddenly cold, despite the heat. 'Why? What's happened?'

He threw his hat on the sideboard and sat down next to me.

'Kate, I'm really sorry. But — it's my father. I had a telegram this afternoon from my mother saying he's ill and I'm needed at home.'

'Your father — ill? What is it?'

'Mother didn't say. The telegram was very brief. I suppose she was sending it in a hurry. But it's been there all day and she must be wondering why I haven't replied already. I just stopped off here on my way to the telegraph office to let you know what was happening.' He stood up again. 'After that I've got to go into the office tonight to cancel some appointments and leave instructions for the clerks and then I have to make arrangements to get the first boat home. I'm sorry, Katie.'

'Of course,' I said, trying not to sound disappointed. 'You must do whatever you think fit. Don't worry about us.'

He smiled. 'Thank you for being so understanding. I wish this hadn't happened.' He paused, looking suddenly awkward. It was a state that didn't naturally fit him, which made it all the more endearing. 'Kate, you know how I feel about you, don't you?'

I took his hands in mine. There was a sadness in his eyes that I had never seen before and I wanted very much to erase it. I leaned up and kissed him briefly on the cheek.

'I hope so,' I said lightly. 'Otherwise this afternoon was a terrible mistake on my part.'

'It was no mistake,' he said. 'When I come back I hope to be able to talk to your father. But I really must go now, Kate.' He stood up as he said this and walked towards the door.

'Of course,' I said. His comment about

talking to Papa made me feel suddenly very excited and then guilty because of the unfortunate circumstances, so to compose myself I changed the subject. 'Oh, what did Alice's letter say?'

There were many dark days to come when I asked myself endlessly why I had to choose that, of all subjects, to remark upon. Out of all the things we could have discussed, why did I pick on that? As soon as I said it, I felt the atmosphere in the room turn cold.

Adam had turned away to pick up his hat, a rather battered panama, and as I spoke I saw his back stiffen and go still. There was a moment's dreadful pause.

'A letter from Alice? What letter?'

He turned round as he said this and in that instant we both knew he was lying. He knew exactly which letter I meant.

'The letter from Alice today. The one at the hotel.'

'How did you know I had a letter from Alice?' he asked in a tightly controlled voice. As he gripped his hat in his hands his knuckles grew white.

'I — ah — I saw it when I left my message to you this afternoon,' I stuttered, confused by the anger I could see he was trying to conceal. 'The receptionist dropped your post on the floor.'

'Oh.' He shrugged. 'Just her weekly letter. Nothing important.' But he suddenly couldn't meet my eye.

'I see.' Suddenly I was no longer confused. I did see, far too clearly. 'Adam, when did you say the telegram from your mother arrived?'

'Sometime this afternoon, I imagine.'

'No, you didn't.' I walked up closer to him, mounting anger making my face flush with heat. 'You said it had been there all day, just now.'

'All day, a couple of hours, what difference does it make?' he said dismissively. 'The point is — '

'The point is, you said it had been there all day a few minutes ago and now you're changing your story.' I glared at him as I said this.

'My story?' He glared back at me now. 'Kate, I don't think I care — '

'Alice wants you to go home, doesn't she?' I said. 'There is no telegram from your mother. There's only that letter from Alice, ordering you home for some reason and you go running because that's what you do whenever Alice beckons. Why is that, Adam?'

'Kate, I swear to you — '

'No!' I said. 'Don't lie to me, Adam. I know there was no telegram. I know Alice Faulkner is behind this as she has been right from the start. What's the problem? Am I not grand enough to be related to the Faulkner family? Does courting the daughter of an employee who seems to be losing his faculties not meet with the approval of the great Sir Henry?'

'That is absolute rubbish, Kate, and you've no right to say it.'

'No? Then kindly explain to me what it is that makes Alice constantly sabotage every arrangement we make?'

'She isn't trying to sabotage anything!' He slammed his hat down on the sideboard again. 'You have absolutely no idea what you're talking — '

Just then, Sayeed popped his head round the door, his wrinkled brown eyes wide with concern at our raised voices.

'Is everything all right, Miss Katie?' he asked.

'Fine,' I snapped. 'Please close the door on your way out.'

He looked at me in surprise, but nodded and pulled the door silently closed. I turned back to Adam.

'Stay,' I said. 'If Alice isn't trying to keep us apart, then prove it. Stay here with me.'

He looked haunted. 'I can't stay, Kate. My mother needs me.'

'I need you.'

Katie . . . ' He took my hands in his and

held them tight. 'If I could, I would, believe me, but my father is ill — '

'So is mine.'

'Kate, don't dramatize!' He dropped my hands suddenly. 'I have more pressing problems on my mind at the moment than the nonsensical fantasies of a romantic eccentric.'

I gasped. 'Nonsensical fantasies! How dare you? My father is — '

'Your father is in danger of losing sight of his priorities, which is damaging to the museum and to his reputation, but he is not ill, Kate. Mine is and I have to go home. I'm sorry you think so poorly of Alice. She doesn't deserve your low opinion of her and when you're calmer you'll probably see that too. Now I have to go. I've got a great deal to do before I leave and I don't have time to waste on petty jealousies or pointless causes.'

He grabbed his hat again and stormed out, leaving me still gasping with anger and indignation at all that he had said. As I stood there, unable really to believe that we had just had the most spectacular of rows, Papa opened the door and came in. His tie was undone, trailing down the starched front of his shirt.

'Is everything all right, Katie? Sayeed just came upstairs in a state and then I heard all that shouting. Where's Adam? I thought I heard him arrive.'

I looked at Papa in anguish for a moment, then confused us both by bursting into tears. But even as Papa rushed over to me and began patting my shoulder awkwardly, I couldn't help feeling that if Alice had seen me, she would have been pleased. She had won after all.

4

Luxor — November 1908

'Papa! Papa! Are you awake?'

I ran through the house to the parlour where I knew Papa would be sleeping. He still hadn't recovered fully from the fall into the mummy-pit and the last bout of malaria had taken a heavy toll on him.

As I burst into the room, trying to hold my books and keep from tripping over my skirt at the same time, Papa struggled to sit up; his left leg was swathed in white bandages, making him look like a partly finished mummy himself. The newspaper he had been reading fluttered gently to the floor.

'What is it, my dear?'

'A letter from the Cavendish at last! Open it, Papa. Perhaps we might be getting more money at last.'

Papa took the letter from my hands and opened the envelope. I was desperate to know what was inside, but somehow I couldn't bear to watch his face in case it was bad news. So I busied myself instead with pouring a cup of tea from the pot beside him. He read for a few moments, then put the letter down next to his own teacup.

'Well? Is it good news?'

He said nothing, merely handing the letter to me. It began with the usual trivia about the need to conserve resources and make sure that the patrons of the Cavendish museum, for whom we just still worked, were getting the best value for their money. They had had a lot of money problems lately, mainly owing to Il-Namus, the shadowy, shrewd dealer in stolen antiquities who had become the talk of the Egyptian black market over the last two years. I read on, ignoring the comments about how sorry they were to hear of Papa's fall. The letter really started getting business-like in the third paragraph.

'Wonderful, Papa! A group from the board are going to visit the site at last. I thought they'd forgotten we existed.'

'Let's be generous, darling. Henry's death in June was an unexpected blow. Poor Alice must be distraught. I doubt that we were their first priority.'

'Well may you doubt it, Papa. We've not been their priority for the last year. Ever since that snake in the grass slunk back to London and told them you were squandering their pittance of an allowance on a private obsession.'

'Kate! You're being unfair. I don't for a moment suspect Adam of doing any such thing. I know his behaviour towards you was disgraceful, but that's a different matter. Er . . . have you read the second page?'

From the way he said it I knew he was worried. But nothing could have prepared me for what I read. I couldn't stop myself from gasping and I felt my cheeks flush.

'I'm truly sorry, Kate dear.'

'I don't care,' I said but I did care, very much. 'They can send the King if it pleases them. We have a right to ask for adequate sponsorship, after all the money we've made for them.'

But the words on the letter seemed to leap up out of the page at me. His name in bold, black type. Dr Adam Ellis. He was coming to Luxor with the museum group. After one year, two months and twenty-three days of silence after our dreadful row, he was at last deigning to acknowledge us again.

'Maybe it won't be so bad,' Papa continued hurriedly. 'Alice will be accompanying him, and the new treasurer too, so at least we'll be sure that we're talking straight to the horse's mouth.'

'Can you do that?' I heard myself asking, as though from a long distance away. I still couldn't quite believe it. Adam, coming back to Egypt? It didn't seem possible. I had sent so many letters, angry at first, then rueful and eventually, to my shame, begging him to reply, but there had been nothing, apart from one curt and stinging letter nearly six months ago, which I had burnt immediately, angered afresh by his cold arrogance.

'Probably not,' Papa agreed. 'But you know what I mean. Hand me that bottle of quinine, darling, would you?'

'Papa! Are you feeling all right? Should I send Sayeed for Dr — '

'For God's sake, don't fuss Kate. I'm fine. I just need a little to go with the tea, that's all.'

There was a short, tense pause while we both tried to pretend it was normal to drink quinine with tea. During the last expedition we had managed to finance, to the burial site, we had discovered the beginnings of a passageway sloping down into the ground. In his excitement Papa had fallen into the pit and broken his leg. We had been forced to return to Luxor while he recovered, then he succumbed to a bout of malaria. It had been a worrying time.

'It says here they intend to visit the site of Khaemwaset's alleged tomb in order to see for themselves the progress that has been made,' said Papa, perusing the letter again. 'Limited monies might be available to fund the dig for a further short period of time, dependent on the result.'

'In other words, come up with something lucrative or find another sponsor!'

I stared out the window at the feluccas — the Nile fishing-boats — their graceful white sails flying in the wind like giant birds. I was angered by the tone of the letter and yet how could I blame them? We had come up with nothing at all for the last eight months, at least nothing with which any self-respecting archaeologist would be satisfied.

'Kate . . .'

I turned. Papa was struggling out of his chair now, still looking too white and thin for my liking, but I could see that he was happy.

'Kate, this is excellent news. If we can just convince the board that there is solid reason to believe Khaemwaset's burial chamber is only a matter of yards away, feet even!' He closed his eyes and clenched his fists, making the knuckles even whiter against his cream linen jacket. 'It's so close I can feel it. It's just a matter of time!'

I went over to him and knelt beside him, putting my hands over his.

'Yes Papa, I know. But that's no reason to go throwing yourself into mummy-pits. You won't get closer to him that way.'

He put a hand on my head and gently

stroked my hair, chuckling.

'Quite true, my dear. Get a message to Ahmed, would you? This will please him, too. He was telling me only the other day how sick he was of showing fat Americans around the Valley.'

He reached for his stick and laboriously levered his way up out of the chair. Even though this effort seemed to take all his energies, I could see that the flush of colour in his cheeks wasn't just due to exertion. The idea of the museum's at last paying attention to us after months of neglect had given him new life. In spite of my concerns, I felt glad for him. I took his arm to help him across the room, then cleared my throat.

'Papa,' I said diffidently. 'When they're here . . . I think it would be best if we didn't mention the Scarlet Queen.'

I looked at him out of the corner of my eye to gauge his reaction to this, but he barely flinched. Clearly he had had the same thought himself. He nodded.

'No.'

There was a slightly awkward silence, I picked up my books again and walked towards the door.

'I have to go over to the vicarage now, Papa, so I'll speak to Ahmed on my way. I should be back in time for dinner.'

'Of course, my dear,' he said absently, brushing his greying beard as he leafed through a book of hieroglyphs. Then he suddenly looked up again. 'Kate, darling, do you really mind his coming here? Because if you do, say so and we'll tell them to go to the devil. We've managed this far without them and I'm sure . . . '

I walked back over to him.

'Absolutely not, Papa. What do I care whether he's here or not? Besides, if Alice is coming too, the expedition will be much more lavishly equipped than usual and I think we're due for a little luxury. Let's enjoy it. And then, when we find Khaemwaset and his court, we'll have the whole lot of them right here, so we can gloat and say 'I told you so' and lots of other annoying things.'

Papa chuckled. 'That's the spirit, m'dear,' he said. 'Let's show 'em how a real dig is conducted.'

He turned back to his books and I walked out of the room. In all honesty, I never wanted to see Adam again. I still felt hot with shame when I thought of my last begging letter to him. But these days it was I who arranged all our finances and I knew how desperate we were. So, no matter how much it hurt, I would welcome Alice and Adam and the rest of the board here with a smile on my face and make sure they paid us everything we were owed and equipped us with everything we needed to find the burial site. Then Papa's reputation would be restored once more and we would be solvent again.

Then, and only then, I would take great joy in telling them to go to the devil.

★   ★   ★

Outside I told the carriage driver to take me to the house owned by the church of St Matthew here in Luxor. It was known as the vicarage, since it housed the vicar and his family, but it tended to be more than that. In many ways it was the centre of social life among the expatriates in this part of the city, especially the wives.

It was hard for women to acclimatize themselves when they first arrived in Egypt. For their husbands things were much simpler. British consuls had the office around which to base their lives, as did the merchants and salesmen of the various companies based in Luxor. But for the average European woman life was much more isolating. This was where Mrs Holt, the vicar's wife, came in. She was a cheerful, motherly soul in her mid-forties with a household full of equally cheerful, noisy children and dogs and servants. She took new arrivals to the heat of Luxor under her capacious wing and made sure no one felt left out or abandoned.

When we drew up outside the sprawling house I got out of the carriage and took a deep breath, mentally preparing myself for the annual ordeal of my lecture on King Khaemwaset IV of the Third Intermediate Period. As I entered the vicarage Emma Holt came to greet me.

'Kate! Wonderful timing, my dear. The last of the sandwiches are gone and everyone is getting slightly sick of everyone else. Are you thirsty? More tea, Ayad, please,' she called to a passing servant.

Mrs Holt had prevailed on Papa to hold court over her ladies and titillate them with gems on the Great Pharaohs ever since we had arrived in Luxor in 1895, and he had taken great delight in handing over this task to me on my eighteenth birthday. I remember thinking, naïvely at the time, that at last I was an adult. I did so no more. In fact for the last three years I had tried to get Papa to take this particular task back, without success. This year, of course, there was no question of his doing the talk. So here I was again, with my lantern slides and notes ready to bore a dozen or so English ladies with information on the pharaohs, which they did not care about and

100

would not listen to.

I would have cried off this year, no matter how much I liked Mrs Holt, but there was a good chance that I might obtain a little extra tuition work out of it. Ever since the museum had drastically reduced Papa's salary, hoping to persuade him to come home of his own accord, or at least start work on a more lucrative site, we had been forced to dig into his savings and I had supplemented that by work as a Latin tutor to several families. I hated it almost as much as my pupils hated me, but I was paid well. Beggars cannot be choosers.

'How many are there this year?' I asked, as we walked into the large drawing room.

The numbers seemed to grow every year as Papa's notoriety grew, and I have no doubt that I too added to the general interest. I was a young, unmarried woman who worked on the digs, wearing unladylike clothes and talking in fluent Arabic to the locals. I knew there were rumours I had been seen wearing bloomers and smoking at the site, which I'm sure sent a thrill of horror and disapproval amongst the stiffly conservative English community.

'Almost thirty,' said Mrs Holt cheerfully, while I shuddered. She took me by the hand and lead me into the arena.

101

★ ★ ★

By half past four, my ordeal was almost over. Tea had been dispensed, slides shown and all that was left was the question-and-answer session at the end, which I had found was an easy excuse for cutting down on preparation time. If they ever asked questions that I didn't know the answer to, I lied. All that childhood training was useful after all. No one ever challenged me. To be honest, I don't think they even listened after the first sentence or two. It was enough that the expatriate ladies of Luxor could say they had attended a lecture by the notorious Miss Whitaker. To have taken it seriously as well would have been ludicrous.

'. . . so in conclusion, may I thank you all for attending this afternoon. If anyone has a question, I would be pleased to hear it.'

I stood by the little table with the aspidistra beside it. The room looked exactly like any vicarage in England would have looked, with overstuffed armchairs decorated with antimacassars and dark wood panelling everywhere. If it weren't for the heat and the sound of camels bellowing raucously in the distance, it would have been easy to forget that we were in Egypt. All Mrs Holt's guests were perched on chairs, their huge afternoon visiting-hats dominating the scene. One lady wore a stunning creation with purple feathers and pink tulle. She had been nodding throughout my lecture, making me wonder whether she was asleep.

There was a short silence. There always was. I took my spectacles off and had a sip of the tea thoughtfully provided by Mrs Holt.

At last one gloved hand went up. It was Mrs Patterson, one of my regulars at these events.

'Yes?' I said, smiling encouragingly.

'Miss Whitaker, any news on the Scarlet Queen?'

And there it was. Or rather, I should say, there she was. There was a slight stirring now among the crowd. This was what they had all really come for, although they would have died rather than admit it: news on the Scarlet Queen. I loved her myself in a romantic, rather doomed way, but sometimes I wished I had never heard of her.

'Oh yes, Kate dear, do tell us if the professor is any nearer to discovering her,' said Mrs Holt, as though she had only just thought of this. I glared at her and she had the grace to look a little ashamed, but only a little. Even vicar's wives want to be seen as successful hostesses, and what was the point of having eccentric friends if you couldn't take any advantage of them?

'I'm afraid not, Mrs Patterson. My father has rather given up on her recently. Theban culture — Thebes being the ancient name for Luxor — tends to . . .'

I droned on for a bit about Theban culture, but they obviously weren't interested. Another lady put up her hand.

'Forgive me, Miss Whitaker, what you've told us this afternoon is fascinating, but who is the Scarlet Queen? I believe I've heard mention of her before today, but only in passing.'

A couple of other ladies joined in and I could tell that I had no choice. I was going to have to rehash the whole tale. Well, these were my students. Hoping fervently that I would get some more Latin students out of this if nothing else, I put my best smile on.

'The Scarlet Queen is the name my father gave to a priceless statue which is supposedly among King Khaemwaset's burial treasures. In fact, she has three incarnations. When my father first discovered the texts about Khaemwaset, his attention was riveted by the constant reference to someone called 'The Beloved'. This person was obviously a figure of great importance in the Pharaoh's household although bizarrely he or she was never named. My father surmised she was either a favoured concubine . . . ' I noticed cynically how thrilled my audience was at the use of such a word. ' . . . or a respected counsellor or priest. We were even more excited when the texts revealed that he favoured this person so much that he commissioned a statue to be made of him or her in pink-shot gold. This was an enormously expensive undertaking and showed how valued this person was.'

I paused for breath and yet another hand shot up. I nodded.

'You seem unsure whether this person was a man or a woman, Miss Whitaker. Why is that?'

'Well, as I've said, there is no mention of a name or indeed a gender, but generally in these circumstances it would be fair to assume the beloved of a pharaoh would be a woman. And this theory gains strength with the suggestion in some texts that the statue was to be carved in the likeness of Bastet, the cat goddess. Goddess, of course, suggests a female element and when you add to that the fact that Bastet was associated with giving protection in childbirth and was also the goddess of pleasure, music and dance, the feminine slant is strengthened even more. But confusion sets in when you consider the question of colour. Red is usually associated with men. So it may be that the beloved was a favoured son or counsellor. My father nicknamed the statue the Scarlet Queen, in honour of Bastet and because he fervently believes the Beloved was a woman, but we're still no nearer to discovering who this favourite was and we probably never will, because all mention of him or her ends abruptly halfway through the texts. Presumably he or she died. We know the statue was finished, but again, mention of it ends about the same time as mention of the Beloved. Whether it still exists and is placed with Khaemwaset in his burial chamber is another matter. It's just as likely to have been broken up after this person's death. Of course to find the Scarlet Queen would be a singular event indeed. Such an artefact would be extremely valuable. But most archaeologists agree that Khaemwaset and his tomb do not exist.' I paused. 'Naturally most of them agree that the Scarlet Queen doesn't exist either.'

'Why?'

I grinned when I saw who had spoken. It was Bella, the Honourable Miss Isabella Lavinia Wyndham-Brown to give her full title. She had promised she would come this afternoon, although I wasn't sure that her aunt would approve. Aunt Augusta had very definite views about what was right and

106

proper. But sure enough, there sat Lady Faversham next to her, resplendent in her second-best hat, with her pince-nez fixed firmly to her nose. She was dividing her time between frowning at me and at her mischievous niece.

'Because the place where Khaemwaset is supposed to be buried is in an area reserved for nobles rather than kings,' I replied. 'And besides, there is no evidence that tomb-robbers have made any attempt to look there, which is usually a good sign that there's nothing worth taking. Until my father began searching the site had been left untouched for millenia. It's not unknown for texts to be bogus either, so I suppose I can't really blame our colleagues for their scepticism.'

Actually, I could and did, frequently, whenever Papa was ridiculed by his peers in their lectures and in the cafés where they met. Many illustrious archaeologists had been known to flee at the sight of me walking down the street. But I didn't say that. I didn't want to frighten off any potential students.

'But there is a good reason for the local people not to search around that area.' I continued. 'They believe it to be haunted.'

A gasp went round the room. Even Aunt Augusta looked startled and I began to feel like an entertainer at a children's party.

'Really?' Bella grinned at me. 'Do tell us by what. Or whom.'

'A mysterious figure in red. There are several theories as to her existence. Some of the workmen believe it to be the ghost of a faithless wife who was murdered by her husband for her sins and who searches nightly for her lost love. Others believe she is the ghost of a dead queen who betrayed her pharaoh and cannot rest until she is forgiven. The only thing they all agree on is that she is a young woman and she is clothed in red. That was the other reason my father nicknamed the statue the Scarlet Queen. The ghost and the statue and the person in the texts seemed to be linked in some way and it seemed fitting to honour them all. After all, the lady in red has helped keep Khaem-waset's treasures safe for centuries.'

'Goodness, how exciting,' said Bella. 'I declare I should never go out there myself.'

'It's quite safe, Miss Wyndham-Brown. My father had the local imam perform a *zaar*.'

'A what?'

'A *zaar*. An exorcism. I can promise you there are no ghosts on the site now.' There was general polite laughter. 'And that, ladies, is the story of the Scarlet Queen,' I concluded, thankful to hear the clock in Mrs Holt's hall chime five times. 'I hope you've enjoyed my lecture and I thank you for your attention.'

'That was wonderful, Kate, thank you so much,' said Mrs Holt, coming up to me as I put my notes in my bag.

'Let's hope your guests thought so, too,' I said. 'I could do with some more pupils.'

'Oh dear, is it that bad?' Her face crinkled up in a frown.

'Well, we had some good news today,' I said and told her about the visit from the museum. 'But they won't be here for some weeks and I'm not going to give up my only paid employment just yet.'

Mrs Holt looked round at her guests in a determined fashion.

'Give me a little time,' she said, patting my hand. 'There are plenty of rich mothers here. I'm sure they'd be delighted to have the daughter of Professor Whitaker as tutor to their children.'

And she walked off in the direction of a particularly well-dressed lady who obviously hadn't realized that she needed a new tutor until now. I packed my belongings slowly, waiting for Bella to sneak away from her aunt. Eventually, from the corner of my eye, I saw her wander out into the garden. I picked up my bags and followed her.

'Good afternoon, Miss Wyndham-Brown.

And how on earth did you manage to persuade Lady Faversham to come?'

Bella adjusted the ribbons on her gorgeous wide-brimmed hat and put up a tiny pink parasol.

'This is educational, my dear,' she said as she accompanied me along the path up to the gate where my carriage was waiting on the street. 'Of course Aunt Augusta is going to encourage me in such a pursuit. Besides, when she knew you were giving the lecture, she was all for it. Aunt Augusta thinks you're a good influence on me.'

I loaded my projector and slides into the carriage. 'Really?' I said, not sure how pleased I was that Lady Faversham approved of me. 'Hasn't she heard about my scandalous behaviour?'

'She doesn't believe it,' said Bella smugly. 'Nobody as scholarly as you could be so *fast* in her view. Of course those dreadfully dull clothes you wear help too. You look like a governess.'

Bella sniffed as she said this, looking down her nose at my simple white blouse with its plain blue tie and piqué skirt. We had had this argument before and no matter what I said, Bella refused to accept that frills and bows and ribbons were totally impractical for everyday wear in Cairo. It was so hot, even now at the beginning of winter, and the dust got everywhere. But Bella always managed to look cool and sophisticated, no matter how frazzled others were around her. I suppose that, when you are a nineteen-year-old heiress, that sort of thing comes naturally to you.

I smiled and put my spectacles back on to complete the image.

'My dear Bella, I *am* a governess. Or at least as near to one as possible, without actually having to live in the same house as the little wretches. But that may soon be changing.'

'Really?' Her eyes lit up with interest. Bella is dreadfully nosy as well as being a terrible gossip, two characteristics, according to her, that are *de rigueur* for heiresses. 'Do tell.' But just then, Lady Faversham came into view.

'I haven't got time now,' I said, climbing hastily into the carriage. It was rather mean of me, but a little of Aunt Augusta goes a very long way and she'd trapped me before now. 'I'll see you on Thursday. Remember to practise the imperatives. Good day to you, Lady Faversham,' I called as the carriage pulled away.

Bella glared at me from under her huge pink hat, but I just smiled, relieved to be escaping in time. All in all the day had been a

111

great success as far as I was concerned. The museum was at last acknowledging that we existed after all this time, and I still had enough gainful employment to keep Papa and myself adequately fed.

Perhaps our luck was changing at last.

5

As I walked out of the driveway from the Howards' elegant house in the most exclusive expatriate district of Cairo, I glanced at the fob-watch pinned to my blouse and noticed with satisfaction that it was already ten past four. That was when the apricot flew past me, just touching the edge of my sleeve and leaving an orange stain. I looked up and saw the branches in the tree behind the wall tremble slightly. There was a muffled sound of laughter and the thump of boots colliding with the ground.

I adjusted my straw boater, deciding it was beneath my dignity to acknowledge that one of my reluctant pupils had just got his own back on me with his catapult. Even so, I couldn't help wishing the little brat had chosen another day to practise his aim. This was my best Russian blouse with blue ribbons threaded through the waistband and collar. Just as I was wondering whether I would be able to slip upstairs without being seen, to change it, a carriage drew up.

'Kate, get in and let me drive you home,' said Bella.

I hesitated.

'Come on. You surely don't want to walk home in this heat.'

I sighed. It was hot still and I didn't relish the walk home.

'All right. But tell the driver to go slowly. I don't want to be back too early.'

'Why on earth not? I thought your museum board people were coming today?'

'Exactly. That's why I don't want to be there too early. I want them to know how much extra work I have to do since they stopped sending us any money.'

'Oh I see. You want them to feel guilty.'

'I certainly do,' I said as I got up into the carriage beside her. 'I don't see why they should expect us to drop everything and dance to their tune the moment they deign to turn up. They can jolly well wait until I'm ready to see them. What?' I added, noticing the grin on her face.

'You've been arguing with your father, haven't you? I bet those are the exact words you said to him. I can just see it from the look on your face.'

I frowned. Bella knew me too well, which was disconcerting when we'd only been friends for a short while. She had been sent out here in disgrace after ruining her London season in a spectacular fashion by being

114

caught kissing the wrong man at a society ball.

'What's that stain on your sleeve?' she asked now, poking my arm and wrinkling her nose in disgust.

'Apricot juice. One of the Howard twins has just been practising with his new catapult.'

'The little beast.'

I shrugged. 'They usually throw dried camel dung at me when they think I'm not looking.'

Bella looked at me in horror. 'Kate, how can you stand it?'

'I think of it as penance for all the times I was awful to my governesses. The gods are getting their own back on me.'

'Ugh. Camel dung though. Can't you tell their parents?'

'I could. But they might decide it's proof that a mere woman isn't capable of teaching their darling boys and dismiss me. And we need the money.'

Bella sighed. 'I wish I could just give you some of mine, but Aunt Augusta grills me about every tiny purchase I make. It's a pity you're not a boy. Then you could marry me.'

'Would they let someone like me marry you?' I asked with interest. Bella still had eighteen months to go before attaining her majority and I knew Lady Faversham was determined she wasn't going to be allowed to repeat her London *faux pas*.

'Oh yes,' said Bella, as she smoothed down the folds of the primrose-yellow tea-gown she was wearing. 'You're studious and serious and even if you haven't got any money, you've got position and status. And I know Uncle George thinks digging up old tombs is interesting. He asks me sometimes if you talk about your adventures in the Valley. But to be honest, Kate, I don't want to marry anybody just yet. I want to enjoy my money myself, without having to ask someone else all the time if I can spend it.'

I patted her hand. 'Never mind. Eighteen months will soon pass. Here we are,' I added as Bella's carriage drew up outside the house. 'Thank you for bringing me home.'

'Let me come in.'

'What?'

'Let me come in with you. I can tell them how hard you work.'

'That's a kind thought, Bella, but to be honest, I don't — '

'Oh, I know I'm young, but so long as you introduce me properly they'll listen a bit if only because I might be persuaded to donate some money later on. Please Kate. Aunt Augusta's been fussing about the new curtains in the drawing-room all day and I shall go mad if I have to listen to another discussion on the comparative merits of fringed swags and ties over valances with tassels. Besides, I told her we'd arranged an extra lesson this afternoon. *Please* Kate.'

She gave me the full force of her most hangdog expression as she said this. The lesson she was referring to was in conversational French, another of my languages. It was how we had met in the first place. She had waylaid me at a tea-party one afternoon soon after arriving here and begged me to give her lessons, flattering me with compliments about how clever people said I was. Afterwards I found out she only wanted the excuse to get away from her formidable aunt for a while, but I never turn down the chance of making a little extra money. Besides, unlike the awful brats I usually taught, Bella was fun and I looked forward to our two hours a week as much as she did.

'All right,' I said, shrugging. 'But don't blame me if you're bored. All they'll do is talk about hieroglyphs and money.'

'Nothing could be more boring than curtains, Kate, believe me,' she replied as she accompanied me into the house.

From the hallway I could hear voices in the parlour and, in spite of my determination to remain calm, I felt my stomach start to flutter. I took a deep breath and opened the door.

Papa was seated on the most comfortable, least dilapidated sofa, his leg with its ludicrous bandages propped up on a stool. Next to him sat Alice. She was exactly as I remembered her from that first day eight years ago, elegant and graceful-looking, even in her widow's weeds, the black crape skirt and high collar only serving to accentuate her fair beauty, her blonde hair drawn up in ringlets around her ears.

'Darling! How lovely to see you,' she said as she stood up and kissed me on the cheeks. 'And you look so well. I swear the heat of this country seems to make you bloom.'

I smiled heroically, trying my best to forget that this was the person who had ruined my wonderful romance and to remember instead that she had just lost her husband. Bella told me afterwards I looked as though I had sucked on a lemon.

'Alice. It's lovely to see you too. We were so sorry to hear about Sir Henry.'

Her eyes lost some of their sparkle for a moment.

'It was very quick. And he died doing something he loved. I was just telling James, he was in the conservatory repotting some orchids when it happened. He'd been so weakened by the last two attacks, but we thought he was getting better. Thank you for your lovely letter, darling.'

'Not at all,' I said stiffly. I was desperate to ask where everyone else was and by everyone I meant Adam, but I didn't want to sound as though I actually cared and besides, Alice was looking at Bella. I made the necessary introductions and everyone professed themselves charmed.

'Adam should be here soon,' Alice said. 'He had to go back to the hotel to pick up a paper he forgot.'

'Oh. I hope you're settled in comfortably.' I felt rather proud of how careless I sounded at the mention of Adam's name.

'Of course, dear. The Winter Palace is always so pleasant. I — oh, here's Mr Tillyard,' she said breaking off as a carriage pulled up in front of the window. 'He's our new treasurer. Such a charming, hard-working man. He decided to leave England before us as he had some sites to visit in Giza and he was only due to arrive in Luxor today. Run outside and help him, would you darling?' She turned to Papa. 'He hardly speaks any Arabic and the cab-drivers take such terrible advantage.'

Papa snorted. He didn't think much of

foreigners who came to Egypt and who didn't bother to learn at least a few phrases, but he was very fond of Alice. I left the room and hurried into the street, expecting to have to fight off beggars demanding *baksheesh* as well as haggling with the cab-driver over his fare. But by the time I'd reached our guest, he'd already paid the driver and was at the gate.

'Mr Tillyard? How do you do?' I said, putting my hand out. 'I'm Katharine Whitaker. I believe you're looking for us. Lady Faulkner is inside.'

'Miss Whitaker.'

He took my hand and surprised me by bowing slightly over it, before putting it to his lips. He was a tall, dark-haired man in his mid-thirties, rather handsome in a studious kind of way and there something vaguely familiar about him, but I couldn't quite put my finger on it.

Back inside the parlour Sayeed had just come in with the tea and I began to serve as Alice introduced our new guest. Papa shook his hand.

'Pleased to meet you, Tillyard. Alice was telling me you were there when she found poor Henry.'

'Sadly yes,' said Mr Tillyard. 'I'd been hoping to discuss the new Persian room we were thinking of opening at the museum. If only I'd been a little sooner, perhaps I could have prevented his passing.'

Alice patted his hand. 'I don't think there was anything anyone could have done, Richard, but you're kind to say it. Richard has been a blessing to the museum ever since we first appointed him. He works so hard. Always making trips here, even in the heat of the summer.'

Mr Tillyard bowed slightly as he sat down on one of the less shabby armchairs. 'You flatter me unduly, Lady Faulkner.'

'Not at all . . . ' she started to say, but just then we heard the sound of another carriage drawing up outside the house.

'It must be Adam,' said Alice as Bella got up to look. But when she turned back from the window, there was a wicked grin on her face. 'I do believe it's Mr Bennett, Kate,' she said happily.

My heart sank. Peter Bennett was the local inspector of the Antiquities Service and, much as I liked him, he had an unfortunate habit of saying the wrong thing at the worst possible moment. This was a dreadful handicap in a job where diplomacy was of paramount importance and consequently he was not advancing as quickly as might be expected. I felt sorry for him because he was actually good at his job, being diligent, hard-working and honest. But this afternoon was going to be hard enough as it was. The last thing I needed was to have to keep an eye on Peter in case he offended our guests before they gave us money. I excused myself and left the parlour. My only hope was to get him to come back later.

'Good afternoon, Miss Whitaker,' he said as I opened the door to the heat of the afternoon. 'May I come in?'

'Peter, how lovely to see you,' I began desperately, barring his way. 'However, we are rather busy at the moment and — '

'I know, Miss Whitaker. Your sponsors from the Cavendish are here. That's why I've come. It's imperative that the Service is kept appraised of your latest venture now that real progress is being made.'

'Real progress?' I echoed, somewhat surprised. 'Who told you that?'

'Naturally the Service is privy to all sorts of information regarding the current status of each dig,' he said bombastically. Then he relented, since it was me, and added with a shy smile: 'I'm really pleased that you and your father are experiencing success at last Kate.'

'Thank you, Peter. That's very kind of you to say so. But could you possibly come back

122

later? We'd really like to speak to them alone first.'

'Erm, sorry, Kate. I was given specific orders to see them today. Monsieur Chouan was very insistent.'

I resisted the unladylike urge to curse. Monsieur Chouan was Peter's immediate superior at the Service. He'd probably got some important people coming to the office too and was using this as an excuse to get Peter out of the way.

'Peter,' I said as emphatically as I could. 'We really need the museum to give us more money.'

'I know, Kate. I promise I won't do or say anything to jeopardize that. Please let me in,' he begged. 'It's jolly uncomfortable out here in the heat.'

I gave it one last go. 'Peter — Bella's here.'

He flushed deeply. Peter has pale gingery hair and the almost lily-white complexion that often goes with that colouring and he embarrasses easily. And since he has the most enormous crush on Bella, whenever he is in her presence he spends the entire time looking like a huge beetroot and sounding like a stuttering fool. But he took a deep breath, determined not to shirk his duty.

'I'm sure Miss Wyndham-Brown's presence is most pleasant, Miss Whitaker, but I must

123

insist that you allow me to speak to
. . . er . . . '

Here he began to falter, no doubt thinking
about Bella already. I sighed and opened the
door, careful not to let in too much dust from
the street.

'Very well, Peter,' I said gloomily. 'Don't
say I didn't warn you.'

Inside the parlour I introduced him to
Alice and Mr Tillyard. To be fair, he was fine,
if a little stiff, until he turned to Bella.

' — and of course, Miss Wyndham-Brown
you've already met,' I said, wanting to cover
my eyes at the débâcle I knew would ensue.

'Oh . . . um . . . yes . . . Miss Wyndh — '

'Mr Bennett, how lovely to see you again,'
Bella said, the evil smile still on her face.
'Oh dear, you've dropped your hat on the
floor. Oh and now your gloves.' She turned
to the others. 'Mr Bennett is always
dropping things. I declare I wonder how safe
it is sometimes to have him on a dig. Kate,
would you allow him to handle any of those
old pots and things you find? They are
valuable, aren't they? Although I suppose
since they're all broken up anyway, a few
more cracks wouldn't make that much
difference.'

Bella isn't mean really, but as an heiress,
she's used to the attentions of older, more

sophisticated men. The stuttering hopeless-
ness of a gauche twenty-something boy was
little more than a game to her, although poor
Peter felt it dreadfully when she made fun of
him. I glared at her. Meanwhile, Papa was
studying Peter, a cynical expression on his
face.

'What can I do for you, Bennett?'

Peter turned gratefully to him.

'I believe you've had some success of late
with the site at the Temple of the Nobles,
Professor Whitaker. Is this true?'

Papa nodded. 'Indeed we have, my boy.
And now I suppose, the Service wants to
know when we expect to make the big
discovery?'

Peter smiled. 'Well, you know that the
Service has a responsibility to make sure any
treasures found are divided fairly between
finder and the people of Egypt. These days
it's not such an easy task to perform.'

He was referring to the rule that any
treasure found must be divided equally
between the excavators and the authorities. It
was a rule which was difficult enough to
enforce at the best of times, but since the
appearance of Il Namus and his shady
dealings on the thriving black market of
antiquities, it had been proving almost
impossible to police recently. Most of the

125

local inspectors suspected that the archaeologists and other amateur Egyptologists who came here to dig were spiriting their finds away before the Service was properly informed, but they couldn't be everywhere at once and they had to rely on the integrity of the museums who sponsored the digs or bought the finds to help them. Unfortunately, not all museums felt they had a duty to honour this rule.

'You've got a hard job, Bennett,' said Mr Tillyard sympathetically. 'I doubt these rogues who skulk about in the bazaars have any idea what sacrilege they're performing.'

'Quite, sir. But our task would be much easier if the museums back home and on the Continent and America did not continually buy from them, then profess themselves amazed to hear that the items they buy have been illegally obtained.'

I cringed. This was exactly the sort of tactless comment that got Peter into so much trouble and I could see our sponsorship money flying out of the window. But miraculously Mr Tillyard just smiled.

'Steady on, old chap. I'm on your side. We've been losing out badly to this beggar Namus ourselves recently, haven't we, Lady Faulkner?'

Alice smiled. 'Indeed we have, Richard.

The Cavendish has taken quite a few losses in the past year, thanks to the actions of this dreadful man. When you eventually manage to identify him, Mr Bennett, no one will be more pleased than us.'

'And that will be very soon, won't it, Mr Bennett?' Bella added, handing him a cup of tea. 'Weren't you telling me the other day that Mr Bennett was the scourge of all scoundrels in the bazaar, Kate? Oh dear Mr Bennett, I do believe you've spilled hot tea on your lap.'

'Peter! Are you all right?' I cried, seeing his face turn purple with pain as he upended the cup into his lap.

'No, no, it's fine, Miss Whitaker,' he gasped, dabbing frantically at the hot liquid with the towel I passed him. 'Just a slight spill.'

'Oh, what a shame, Mr Bennett.' Bella was enjoying herself immensely. I could have shaken her. 'Your trousers will be ruined now. I hope they weren't new.'

Peter turned almost apoplectic at the thought of having a conversation with Bella about his personal wardrobe, so whilst Alice was quietly handing him more napkins, I took her firmly by the arm.

'Bella, go and fetch Sayeed, would you? And ask him to bring some towels,' I said loudly.

'Of course, Kate.'

'And if you don't stop being mean to Peter,' I hissed, 'I'm packing you straight off back to your aunt and cancelling our lessons.'

I tried to sound as harsh as possible, but my threats had as much effect on Bella as they do on my other pupils.

'No, you won't.' She grinned as she said this, sounding exactly like one of my pupils. 'You need the money.'

'Try me,' I suggested. The expression on my face must have at last convinced her that I meant business. At any rate, she shrugged.

'Oh, very well, if it means that much to you,' she said grandly. Then she turned, hearing a sound from the garden. 'Now who's this?'

I turned too, still with the scowl on my face, and felt the blood rush to my cheeks. Bella told me afterwards I looked positively ferocious and although I had retaliated, not unreasonably, that it was all her fault, by then it was far too late. For there, walking through the French windows at last, was Adam.

He looked tanned and fit, his hair slightly longer than Mr Tillyard's or Peter's. He was also dressed comfortably in white linen, in contrast to the high, tight collars and black tail-coats that they were both wearing, despite the heat.

'Adam, darling, here you are at last. Where have you been?' said Alice.

'Sorry,' he said, walking across to Papa and handing him a newspaper. 'I'd forgotten how difficult it is to get a cab at this time of day. Here you are, sir. The article on Khaemwaset's on page thirteen.'

I was aware that Papa and Alice were staring at me rather nervously, clearly worried about how I was going to react. I walked back into the room.

'Dr Ellis,' I said coldly.

'Miss Whitaker. How are you?'

It was on the tip of my tongue to ask him how he thought I was after he had abandoned me a year ago and turned the museum against my father out of spite. But good manners and the fact that we just might get some money out of the board now that Alice and Mr Tillyard were here restrained me.

'Very well thank you, Dr Ellis. Teaching Latin to nine-year-old boys is immensely rewarding. It's what I've always longed to do rather than be spending time in the Valley with Papa — '

'Kate darling, I've just realized I haven't told you the wonderful news yet, have I Alice?'

'No, you must tell her straight away.'

At any other time I would have been

amused at the sight of both Papa and Alice straining to avoid a scene but not today. I scowled as I sat down on the sofa, Bella beside me, both of us having forgotten all about poor Peter and his sodden trousers now.

'Kate, Alice is temporarily the new chairman of the board. Henry left instructions in his will that all his voting rights should be given to her, until a new chairman could be elected. That's how she managed to persuade the board to send a team out. Now we'll be able to show them everything.'

'Why are you teaching Latin to nine-year-old boys?' asked Adam, frowning.

'Well, ever since your last trip here, which we all enjoyed so — '

'And what's more, Adam and Alice are going to come out with us to see the site. Isn't that wonderful?'

'Absolutely super, Papa,' I said. 'By the way, will the board be paying the expenses for this trip? Because we are somewhat embarrassed financially at the moment, since we haven't been paid for the last three months.' I glared at Adam, who still looked confused. 'That's why I'm teaching.'

'Kate, I don't think this is the time to discuss finances . . . ' Papa began, but before he could say anything else Mr Tillyard spoke up.

'Of course all expenses will be met by the board, Miss Whitaker. But what do you mean, you haven't been paid?'

I turned to Mr Tillyard, confused.

'I mean we have received no money from the museum since June, Mr Tillyard.'

Mr Tillyard looked equally perplexed.

'This is most irregular. There was no reason for you not to be paid.'

I frowned. This was not the answer I had been expecting.

'But I wrote to you many times, Mr Tillyard. I even telegraphed you once.'

'Indeed. And yet I've received no communication from you since July. I must say I was somewhat surprised when your usual reports didn't turn up.' He took his spectacles off and began polishing them. 'Lady Faulkner, we really must look into this matter when we return. I have suspected before now that not all the post is getting through to the proper departments.'

'Of course, Richard.' Alice took a delicate sip of tea. 'I'm sorry about this darling. I was so busy after Henry's passing, sorting out all his other affairs. I've only recently managed to start spending more time at the museum.'

'I'm sure you've been very busy, Alice,' I said, frostily. 'But ever since the museum was persuaded that Khaemwaset wasn't a good

131

enough risk, we've been forced to rely on our own resources.' I glared at Adam.

'Yes, dear. Henry didn't — '

'Wait a minute, Alice. Do you think I'm somehow to blame for the museum's not supporting you, Kate?'

I laughed nastily. 'Why on earth would I think that, Dr Ellis? Just because we happened to lose all support from the museum the minute you returned home — '

'Kate darling, do you remember Mr Tillyard at all?'

Alice spoke so loudly, I couldn't in courtesy ignore her, although I was tempted to; her cousin wasn't the sole culprit in this situation. But she was the new chairman of the board, even if it was only a temporary position, and we desperately needed the money, so I looked briefly at Richard Tillyard. He seemed uncomfortable, but then they all did, with the exception of Peter, who was taking advantage of the fact that he was being ignored to try and dry his trousers.

'I'm sorry, I'm afraid I don't. As I was saying — '

'Oh, that's right. You were out here in '97, weren't you, Tillyard,' Adam said, the confusion now replaced by a worrying grin. 'Or was it '98?'

'That's very interesting, Mr Tillyard, but

132

I'm sorry I still don't recall you. But as I was saying — '

'Let's see,' said Adam. 'Would that have been the mosquito net? Or the glue on the saddle? Or would it have been — '

'The what?'

Suddenly I had a horrible feeling that I knew why Mr Tillyard had seemed faintly familiar. Mr Tillyard smiled gently as he poured a little more milk into his cup. Outside, a donkey was making its ugly braying noise, protesting at being moved on.

'Dr Ellis is teasing you I fear, Miss Whitaker. I was your father's assistant in 1897. I'm not surprised you don't remember me. I think you would have been about twelve then.'

I groaned. Now I *knew* where I had seen Mr Tillyard before. He was a good ten years older and his hair was a little greyer and he hadn't worn spectacles when I'd known him, but of course he was one of Papa's old assistants. I felt myself blushing with shame.

'Of course I remember you now, Mr Tillyard. And I can only hope you've forgotten me. Or least forgiven me. I was a horrible little girl.'

Mr Tillyard's smile grew. 'You were delightful, Miss Whitaker. Simply high-spirited.'

'You're making me hot with shame Mr Tillyard . . . '

'Yes, don't spare her any blushes, Tillyard. Here's your chance to get even,' Adam said happily. 'After all, it isn't — '

'Adam darling, I've just realized you haven't been introduced to Miss Wyndham-Brown,' said Alice desperately. 'Miss Wyndham-Brown, this is my cousin, Dr Adam Ellis.'

'How do you do, Dr Ellis,' said Bella brightly, holding out a white-gloved hand. 'It's a pleasure to meet you. You and Kate seem to know each other so well.'

I could have cheerfully strangled her, but Adam just grinned.

'Very well, Miss Wyndham-Brown. In fact, we — '

'And, of course, Mr Bennett,' Alice interrupted again, even more desperately. 'Darling, this is Mr Bennett, the local Antiquities Service inspector. Mr Bennett, my cousin and fellow board member, Dr Ellis.'

Peter looked up from the piano where he was still quietly brushing at the damp patch on his trousers.

'What? Oh, yes. How do you do, Dr Ellis,' he said, giving up with the napkin and coming forward.

'Bennett?' said Adam suspiciously, as they shook hands. 'Isn't that the name of the

134

fellow who you said keeps writing and accusing us of selling our finds on the black market, Tillyard?'

'Ah, well, I'm not entirely certain I used the word 'accused', Dr Ellis,' Mr Tillyard said.

'Yes, that's me,' said Peter, ignoring him. He looked at Adam squarely. 'I find it too much of a coincidence that so many of your sponsored digs find little or no treasure worth speaking of, but items of the period they have been searching for appear in wealthy collections soon after, Dr Ellis.'

'Yes, so do I. But that doesn't mean it's we who are embezzling them,' said Adam.

Both men looked at each other unflinchingly for a few minutes, whilst Alice's complexion grew pale, as though she expected them to start punching one another any second. But Adam merely nodded.

'Well, you and I must talk about this again at a more appropriate time.'

'Certainly, Dr Ellis. I think I should be going now, Miss Whitaker,' said Peter. Bella was staring at the stain on his trousers and I don't think he could bear it. 'Good luck with your dig, Professor. I look forward to hearing from you very soon. Lady Faulkner, Miss Wyndham-Brown.'

'Goodbye, Mr Bennett,' said Bella, but she

was looking at Adam with much more interest. Peter looked crestfallen as I escorted him to the door. I wanted to say something encouraging, but I was too tense myself to be of much comfort and the pair of us parted in very low spirits.

'What a pleasant young man,' said Alice as I re-entered the room. 'And now I really think we should be discussing the trip. There's a great deal to be decided and we don't want to tire poor James any more than we have to?'

With her impeccable hostess skills, Alice eventually managed to steer the conversation away from inappropriate subjects. Soon everyone had retired to Papa's study and all the talk was of lists and maps and studies of the area. Then Papa realized that he had left a schematic of a tomb in the drawing room and I went to look for it.

I found it behind the aspidistra. I was on my knees trying to retrieve it when I heard someone follow me into the room. Thinking it was Sayeed, I looked up.

'Ah, Sayeed, could you — oh!'

It wasn't Sayeed, it was Adam. He crouched down beside me.

'You and I need to talk, Kate.'

'No we don't,' I snapped, standing up again. 'I've got nothing to say to you.'

'Really? You sounded as though you had a

136

lot you wanted to say just now.'

'Well I haven't. Now if you don't mind, I'm very busy. Give these to Papa, would you, please?'

I thrust the notes in his hand and swept back into the parlour, where I began clearing up teacups, furious with him, and with myself for still allowing him to affect me this way. I clashed the crockery together and smashed a saucer, then swore in a very unladylike fashion.

'May I help you, Miss Whitaker?'

I turned. Mr Tillyard was standing next to me, the gentle smile still on his face.

'Please don't bother,' I said, flustered that he'd heard me be so indelicate. 'I already feel bad enough about blaming you for not paying Papa, when clearly it wasn't your fault. And of course I still feel dreadful about . . . ' I tailed off, not really too sure what trick it was I had played on him all those years ago.

'About starching my underwear?' His smile grew, as I blushed. 'Please think no more of it. I'm sure we assistants were an irresistible source of amusement to you.'

'You really are far too kind, Mr Tillyard,' I said as he held the door open for me and we made our way to the kitchen.

'I'm just glad to be here, Miss Whitaker. I had been reading your reports on the excavations for the past year before they seemed to go astray, and may I say I have always been impressed by their clarity and attention to detail. I might even add I feel as if I know you.'

'You're very kind,' I repeated. 'I didn't realize you had been with the Cavendish Museum for so long.'

'I was the assistant treasurer before taking up my present position, Miss Whitaker. And as I said, I've long been privy to the work you and your father have been doing here in Egypt, but unfortunately my influence has not been very great up till now. I'm only glad I was at last able to help Lady Faulkner persuade the board how important your work out here is.'

'I'm flattered, Mr Tillyard. Of course I knew Sir Henry wasn't happy with the direction Papa's research was taking, but I can't help feeling he was listening to outside influences.'

Of course, by this I meant Adam. Mr Tillyard looked at me speculatively.

'Might I give you some advice, Miss Whitaker?'

'Of course,' I said, stopping by the kitchen door.

'Be careful about whom you take into your confidence. And warn your father to do the same. I know he has had to endure a great deal of mockery over the last few years because of his interest in Khaemwaset and his Scarlet Queen, but the recent discovery of the mummy-pits caused quite a stir in certain circles. The news even travelled as far as London. It would be a mistake to think that nobody is taking you seriously.'

I met his gaze, looking for mockery, but finding only sincerity instead. I nodded.

'Very well, Mr Tillyard. Thank you for your advice.'

I took the tray into the kitchen. As I returned I noticed Bella's carriage still waiting outside. I looked quickly at my watch; it was five minutes to six. I hurried back into the study and found Bella seated by the window, talking animatedly to Adam. As I approached them she looked up at me, giggling.

'Kate! Dr Ellis has just been explaining to me about your father's assistants and the glue on the saddle. Did you really do that to poor Mr Tillyard?'

'No,' I said crushingly. Adam's smile was unbearably smug.

'Well then, it must have been the time you sabotaged the mosquito nets. Or was he the one whose bootsoles you cut so they let in mud from the Nile? Or perhaps . . . ' Bella's eyes were growing rounder as he catalogued my litany of mischief.

'If you must know,' I snapped at last. 'I starched his underwear. Bella, I hate to drive you away, but it's six o'clock and I don't want you getting into trouble with your aunt.'

'Oh. Yes, of course.' Reluctantly Bella stood up. I could tell she was insatiably curious, but I had no intention of entering into a discussion with her now. I hustled her away from him and out into the street.

'You are going to tell me everything on Thursday, you horrible girl,' she said, as she climbed into the carriage.

'There's nothing to tell.'

'Nothing to . . . Kate, you've been spitting venom at that man from the moment he walked through the door! What on earth happened between you?'

'Nothing. I — we — nothing. Bella, I can't discuss it now. I have to get back.'

'All right,' she conceded reluctantly, pecking me lightly on each cheek. 'But I want to know everything next time.'

'Bella, you're a dreadful gossip.'

'Of course I am. That's what we heiresses live for. See you on Thursday,' she cried as the carriage pulled away at top speed. The driver had been relieved to see her and I suspected he was contemplating Lady Faverham's ire at her niece's late arrival.

I returned to the house and went back to

the parlour, hoping to escape and have a few moments' peace. I sat down in Papa's chair. A faint aroma of cigar-smoke clung to the upholstery and I found it very comforting.

'You've still got a wicked tongue, Kate.'

I jumped as Adam appeared at the door. He came and sat down on the sofa beside my chair and I considered getting up and walking out, but only briefly. After all, if we were going on an expedition together, we were going to have to get used to one another. Besides, wasn't this what I really wanted?

'And you still have a childish sense of humour.'

He grinned. 'You used to like my sense of humour.'

'That's because I was a child too. I've grown up now.'

'Yes you have, haven't you? Somehow I can't see you putting glue on anyone's saddle anymore.'

'Why *did* you come out here, Adam?' I asked coolly.

'I'm the new secretary of the board, Kate. If you want money out of us, you've got to expect to be able to justify your needs.'

'Really? Well, I'm amazed *you'd* bother coming. You made it perfectly clear what you thought of Papa's theories last time. Let me see; 'the nonsensical fantasies of a romantic eccentric'. I seem to recall that was how you phrased it last time. Or what about 'the last desperate efforts of a once respected scholar in his decline'? I was particularly struck by that one.'

'I shouldn't have said those things — '

'No, you shouldn't. But you did, Adam. And you have the nerve to accuse *me* of having a wicked tongue.'

He sighed and sat forward, rubbing his eyes.

'I seem to remember you said a few things that didn't do you any credit either.'

'If I did, then I apologize. But you had no call to just abandon me, Adam — '

'Abandon you! Do you know how many times I tried to see you during that last week? I had to go back to England. My father was ill and my mother needed me — '

'I needed you.'

'It wasn't the same. I — '

'No, it wasn't, was it, Adam. I didn't have Alice to snap her fingers for me.'

We glared at each other, then Adam gave a curt laugh.

'Still jealous of her, Kate? After all this time?'

'You gave me plenty to be jealous about, Adam,' I said, feeling myself becoming as heated as if the years had never happened and

142

we were back in the same room having that same argument all over again. 'You could have stayed and helped Papa. Even to make him see sense if that was what you truly believed. You could have stayed to be with me. But when Alice wrote to you that last week, calling you back, you just left without a second thought. Because whenever Alice beckons you come running, don't you?'

He was glaring at me now, all traces of condescension gone. We were very close to one another, so close that I could see the faint hints of green in his dark-brown eyes, smell the familiar scent of the cologne he always used.

'How many times do I have to say it before you believe me? I never received any letter from her. I got one from my mother and — '

'You're lying!'

He glared at me, his fury just contained within his control. 'I can't have this conversation with you again,' he ground out and strode out through the door, slamming it shut with alarming force.

Left alone, I sat down on the sofa again, as confused as I had been over a year ago. He was lying, I knew this for a fact. But why?

I sat and thought. The answers I had waited fifteen months for seemed as far away as ever. But this time I was older and wiser

143

and, despite that inauspicious start, I was no longer so angry. I was more in control now and determined to find out why he had lied.

I took a deep breath. One way or another, before Adam returned to London, I would know the truth of what had happened that summer.

6

Dr Murray looked at me and nodded grimly.

'Well, Papa,' I said with a cheerfulness I did not feel. 'We'll just have to hope that Adam and Mr Tillyard remember everything you've taught them.'

'They will do with you there,' he replied, his voice little more than a husky whisper.

I frowned. 'Don't be foolish, Papa. I'm not going.'

'You must, dear girl. You must,' he said, then stopped, interrupted by a sickening bout of the shakes.

It was now ten o'clock in the morning, almost five hours since Papa had woken up feverish and delirious. At first we had both clung to the hope that it was simply a reaction to the excitement of the trip and the renewed interest in the museum, after so long being ignored. But when the tell-tale chills had returned and he grew pale and listless, we had no choice but to call for Dr Murray once more. He had just confirmed what we already suspected. Papa had succumbed to a second bout of malaria.

'Of course I'm not leaving you like this,

145

Papa' I said, as I piled more blankets on his bed. 'I'll send Sayeed over to the hotel straight — '

'Kate, you have to go.'

'Rubbish.'

'You *have* to.' He struggled to sit up in the bed. 'Do you think for one minute I'm going to allow those — those *parvenus* to turn up and claim all the glory after all the work I've done! Never! You're going, my girl. You're going to dog them every step of the way. You have to go, Kate!' For a moment he'd been strong, but suddenly the fever took its grip again and he had sunk back on his pillows. 'You have to go, Kate,' he repeated in a whisper. 'Otherwise — otherwise . . . '

'Ssh, Papa, ssh. I'll go. Of course I'll go, if that's what you want.'

He nodded, his eyes far too bright and Dr Murray and I tiptoed out of the room.

'How long do you think this will last, Doctor?' I asked, as I escorted him to the door. Dr Murray looked at me with compassion, but his voice was firm.

'I know what you're thinking, Kate, but it's no good. He won't be going with that expedition out to the Valley, unless they're prepared to postpone it for at least three months. And they won't do that, will they?'

I shook my head. 'No, I'm afraid not.'

146

'Then your choice is simple, my dear. Either you go with them or you stay here with him. I'll be back this evening to see how he is. Good day to you, Kate.'

I spent the rest of the morning in the sick-room, trying to keep Papa calm as I dosed him with the almost useless tonic. When he eventually dozed off into a fitful sleep, I sent a message to the Winter Palace, apprising Alice and Adam of Papa's condition. Then around five o'clock I had a visitor.

'Sayeed, is Miss Whitaker in? Please tell her I must speak to her immediately.'

I stared over the banisters.

'Is that you, Bella?'

Bella looked up, her face alight with excitement.

'Kate, wonderful news! Do come down here! I have to tell someone before I burst.'

I walked slowly down, my hands full with a basin of water and linen flannels. I was absolutely exhausted, but Bella seemed not to notice. I followed her into our drawing room, left the basin on the sideboard and flopped down into an armchair.

'Uncle George has arranged for us to accompany you out to the tombs! Isn't that marvellous?'

'You're accompanying us?' I echoed. 'Out to the tombs?'

'Yes! You know I told you the other day how Uncle George was always asking me about your trips? Well, last night, we happened to be dining at the Winter Palace and we met Lady Faulkner and her cousin — who I think is delightful and you still haven't told me why you were so angry with him — and we talked for absolutely ages about the trip and Uncle George was completely *consumed* with the idea of going as well. So this morning he met Lady Faulkner and Mr Tillyard and they agreed we could accompany you in exchange for part financing the trip. Isn't it wonderful?' She ended at last, unpinning her broad-brimmed primrose chapeau and sitting down opposite me.

'Wonderful,' I said faintly. 'And how is Lady Faversham taking the news?'

'I think she's quite glad to be rid of us for a while. She's already talking about refurnishing the parlour whilst we're gone,' Bella said, frowning. 'I must say, Kate, I thought you'd be more excited about this. Don't you want me to come with you?'

She sounded so forlorn, that I couldn't help smiling just a little.

'Of course I do, Bella. Forgive me. It's just that Papa has had another attack of malaria and I've been up since five with him.'

'Oh darling!' She leapt up, her face contrite as she took my hands in hers. 'And here I am, babbling like an idiot. Is there anything I can do? Oh!' Suddenly she gasped. 'Does this mean you won't be coming after all?'

I sat up, and began folding the linen flannels into squares.

'I really don't know. Papa can't, of course, and he's absolutely adamant that I must go, but I don't see how I can leave him. I've asked Mrs Holt if she knows of anyone suitable to stay with him, but I have to say I'm not hopeful.'

'Oh dear, how dreadful for you, Kate. And poor Professor Whitaker too. To miss out on this trip after all your hard work.' She stood up. 'Let me speak to Aunt Augusta. She knows all the best servants in the English community and no one will dare deny her. If she can't get you one, there isn't one to be had.'

I smiled at the thought of Lady Faversham marching round the ex-patriate community in Luxor, demanding the use of a nurse until further notice.

'Really, Bella, you mustn't concern your-self — '

'Don't be ridiculous, darling. What's the point of having a ferocious harridan of an aunt if she isn't useful occasionally?' said

149

Bella, pinning her hat back on and preparing to go back out into the heat of the afternoon. 'Anyway this is the sort of crisis Aunt Augusta loves. She'll be in her element. Besides,' she added, honestly, 'if you can't go, she might decide I can't. And I am absolutely not going to allow that. I'll be back later.' And she marched out of the house, in a most determined manner.

I stayed where I was, letting my head rest against our ageing antimacassars, intending to rest my eyes for just a few moments before I went to the kitchen to find something that might tempt Papa's appetite. To be honest, I did not expect to see Bella again for a couple of days; I certainly didn't expect her to concern herself with my staffing problems. So I was astonished when the doorbell rang and I looked up, startled, at the little clock on the mantelpiece. It showed a quarter to eight and I realized I had been asleep for nearly three hours.

'Miss Katie, you want to see anyone?'

I rubbed my eyes. Sayeed was peering round the door.

'Who is it, Sayeed? Is it Dr Murray?'

'No. It's Miss Bella. With a fat old woman.'

I stood up. Before I could answer, Lady Faversham sailed into the room, resplendent as ever in grey mousseline-de-soie, a lorgnette in one hand, with Bella behind her. Not for the first time, I was glad that most expats didn't bother learning Arabic.

'Good evening, my dear,' she said regally, sitting down on the oak settle and drawing a portfolio out of the capacious bag she was carrying. 'Isabella tells me your poor papa is ill and you need a good nurse to take care of him whilst you are away. Hmm — you look a little pale yourself. It's a good job I brought Elliot round with me. She'll stay here tonight to help you until we can find someone suitable. Now, I have a list here of several women who I consider would be acceptable for your needs.'

I looked over at Bella, seated demurely opposite her on the armchair. She smiled mischievously at me, winked broadly, then turned her attention back to her formidable aunt once more.

With a mixture of relief and defeat, I did the same.

⋆   ⋆   ⋆

So that was how Bella and I came to be standing on the top deck of the Nile ferry some two weeks later, watching the scene below. Enterprising locals jostled each other, ready to sell their wares at grossly inflated prices to the unsuspecting tourists who flocked out to see the Valley of the Kings. Women in brightly coloured *hijabs* — long dresses which covered all the body and the hair, but left the face uncovered — offered the Egyptian version of breakfast, made up of cooked *ful*: fava beans spiced with garlic and lemon-juice and the flat round bread called *aysh*. There was *hummus*, *babaganoush*, made from eggplants, and apricots and figs and pomegranates and, to drink, thick, black, syrupy coffee. I felt suddenly hungry and bought two apricots and some *aysh* from the nearest vendor.

Beneath us the Nile flowed, thick with water-hyacinth, the beautiful blue flower that grew so fast and was considered such a pest because it clogged up the river. I could see herons wading along the banks, taking care not to get too close to the crocodiles that slithered in and out of the water.

'Isn't this exciting!' yelled Bella above the noise. 'I can hardly believe I'm here!'

'Neither can I,' I said with feeling. 'I do hope Papa will be all right.'

'He'll be fine.' Bella patted my arm. 'Aunt Augusta wouldn't have recommended Miss Hopkins if she hadn't approved of her. Besides, she promised to visit every day. He's in the best possible hands.'

I nodded, knowing this was true. Miss Hopkins, a thin, efficient-looking woman, late of the Ffolkes-Jones household, was now resident in our guest room. She had trained as a nurse at St Thomas's in London and was much better than I at getting Papa to eat and rest and take his medicines.

I offered her an apricot and we walked arm in arm along the deck, letting the heat of the sun warm our faces.

'Oh look,' said Bella suddenly. 'There's Dr Ellis down there.'

I followed the direction she was pointing in. He was on the lower deck, talking to two boys aged about ten. They were dressed like miniature English gentlemen, complete with starched collars and Norfolk jackets.

'Aren't they the Howard twins?' asked Bella.

'That's right. After I told their mother I wouldn't be able to tutor them any more, she confided in me that they were going to send them back to England soon anyway. Time for them to be educated properly.' I grimaced. 'Poor little wretches. I almost feel sorry for them now.'

'I don't,' said Bella callously. 'Anyway, what are they doing here?'

'Their father promised them a trip to the Valley of the Kings before they left, so I suppose this is it. They're going to be roasted in those clothes.'

Bella turned towards me now, fanning herself with a travel book.

'So when are you going to tell me what happened between you and him?'

'There's nothing to tell. Really,' I insisted as she looked at me disbelievingly. 'Nothing you couldn't guess anyway. He came out here eight years ago to be Papa's assistant, but it wasn't until Papa and I went to London last year for my season that I got to know him really well.'

'You had a season?' Bella looked astonished.

'Yes, I had a season,' I said. 'We might not have as much money as you, my dear Bella, but we're not exactly paupers. At least, we weren't then. Anyway, I met Adam at one of the balls.'

'And?'

I shrugged. 'We became friends.'

Bella stopped walking and frowned at me.

'Kate, you're impossible. You fell in love, didn't you? It was love at first sight, hopelessly romantic and all you can do is say you became friends.'

'It could hardly have been love at first sight since I'd met him seven years previously.'

She frowned, determined not to have her

154

fairy-tale notion of romance ruined by anything as dull as reality.

'Very well. It was love at first sight seven years previously. I can just see it,' she continued, waving a hand languidly as though to indicate the scene was unfolding in front of us. 'The long, hot nights, the heavy scent of jasmine in the air; you, sweet sixteen and struck by Cupid's arrow for the very first time; he, young, handsome and intoxicated by the exotic — what?' she said, frowning, as I began to laugh.

'If you must know, Bella, I was fourteen and obnoxious and he was an arrogant, condescending bully. I sabotaged his work, taught him bad language in Arabic under the pretence that it was polite, drawing room conversation, and spread rumours among the diggers that he was afraid of the dark.'

Bella looked at me uncertainly for a few moments.

'Did you really do all that?'

'Absolutely, but before you start feeling sorry for him, he forced me to work in the ship's laundry for hours on end, got Alice to believe I enjoyed copying out dull passages of Cicero and made me clean his boots for weeks after the Egyptians had forgiven him for cursing them in Arabic.'

She thought about this, then chuckled.

'You really were a very bad little girl, weren't you, Kate? I thought he was making those stories up back at your house. Why were you so mean to your father's assistants?'

'Why not? They were all so smug, thinking that they knew everything. Every season I had to watch while they forgot to label their specimens or crushed important pieces of evidence because they couldn't be bothered to look where they were going. And whenever I tried to point out what they were doing, they'd either ignore me or ask me why I wasn't with my nanny. It was infuriating. I tell you, Bella, by the time I was ten, I was heartily sick of Papa's stupid assistants.'

Bella laughed. 'But they're men, my dear. What else do you expect of them?'

'I expect them to have some basic knowledge of their subject when they get out here and the common decency to be able to admit when they're wrong,' I said, but Bella was unimpressed.

'Good heavens, Kate, what odd ideas you do have.'

'And what cynicism you have for one so young.'

'I've been worth ten thousand a year since I was five, darling, and it's due to go up soon, so the trustees tell me. Believe me, there's very little nonsense I haven't already heard. But anyway, you were telling me about Dr Ellis. If he was so awful, how did you become friends in London?'

'I was seven years older by then, Bella,' I said, smiling. 'I like to think I'm a little more sophisticated now.'

'Of course.' She put her arm through mine again. 'I can just imagine it. After seven long years you meet up again, only this time, instead of the gawky tomboy he sees the beautiful young woman and falls madly in love with her.'

'Bella, how can you be so cynical one moment and then so appallingly sentimental the next?'

Bella shrugged. 'Very well, Miss Sensible, what was it really like?'

I began to stroll along the deck, feeling the hot sun on my face and neck. I had absolutely no intention of telling Bella or anyone else how I had fallen so desperately in love with Adam that summer. It was still too raw and painful.

'Well. Papa and I were staying with Sir Henry and Lady Faulkner and he'd got the post of senior archaeologist at the Cavendish Museum and had been intending to meet us anyway, to discuss Papa's work with him. And when it was time for us to go back home, the

157

museum decided he should accompany us.'

'The museum decided?' Bella's tone was sceptical.

'Of course. Papa was convinced he had a good case for them to give us extra funds to search for Khaemwaset's tomb.' I forbore to mention what a nuisance Papa had made of himself in London. 'It was entirely reasonable that the Cavendish should send a representative out to verify Papa's claims.'

'I see,' said Bella, but there was a waspish look in her eye as she studied me. I had no chance to comment further though, because just then the subject himself appeared.

'Good morning, ladies.'

'Dr Ellis, Kate and I were just talking about you,' said Bella. I could have cheerfully strangled her.

Adam looked at me rather bleakly. We hadn't spoken since our argument, each of us being too busy with our preparations for the trip and, for me, there had been the added concern of Papa's illness.

'Well,' he said. 'That would explain why my ears were burning.'

'Kate was just telling me about her London season. Tell me, Dr Ellis — '

'I left some receipts at the hotel for you yesterday, Dr Ellis,' I interrupted, giving Bella a glare. 'Did you receive them?'

'Yes, thank you. You're as efficient as ever, Kate.'

'Well, I wouldn't want the museum to think they were wasting any unnecessary resources on us,' I said frostily.

'I wouldn't be here if I didn't think it was worth while.'

'Of course you wouldn't. Dr Ellis is a demon of efficiency too, Bella,' I said, turning to her. 'He would never dream of wasting his time on pointless causes. That was another of your opinions on Papa's theories about the Scarlet Queen, if I remember rightly.'

Adam leaned against the rails of the deck.

'You must have written down everything I said that day, Kate,' he said. 'I never imagined you hung on my words so devotedly.' Before I could reply, he looked at Bella. 'You look very businesslike too, Miss Wyndham-Brown. Those clothes suit you.'

Bella preened, lifting the blue material of her divided skirt bought especially for this trip. Despite her contempt for my wardrobe, she had been amused at the idea of wearing such unladylike clothes and relished the freedom of movement. Meanwhile I scowled at him. Hanging on his every word, indeed! I looked down and noticed the Howard twins rushing along the deck below us, despite the unsuitable clothing they were wearing.

159

'Oh look,' said Bella, suddenly seeing them too. 'It's those little boys you were talking to. They're pupils of Kate's, you know, and they've been horrible to her. I hope you weren't being nice to them.'

He looked down to where she was pointing.

'Actually I met their parents the other day and Mrs Howard was telling me they're going to my old school in Bath. I was just having a chat with them about it.'

'How kind of you,' I said disagreeably and he looked at me and grinned.

'Well, schooldays are the best days of your life, aren't they Kate? Oh wait, I forgot. Not for you they weren't. Kate ran away from school,' he informed Bella.

'You ran away from school?' She looked at me, astonished.

'Three times,' said the ever helpful Dr Ellis. 'School life apparently didn't agree with Kate.'

Bella laughed. 'Kate! You really are my absolute hero,' she said, putting her arm through mine and hugging me. 'I wish I'd had the courage to do that at my school. I loathed every minute there.'

'It really wasn't courageous at all,' I said. 'I just wanted to be back in Egypt.'

'And who wouldn't, when your life here is

160

so much more exciting? Well, my dear, I can see Uncle George down below looking a little lost. I'd better go and rescue him. I'll meet you when it's time to disembark,' she said and disappeared down the stairwell.

I turned and began walking along the deck in the opposite direction. Adam fell into step beside me.

'I'm sorry about your father. I know he must be disappointed not to be able to come.'

'Thank you. I'll be sending him daily reports of our findings, so he'll know exactly what's happening.'

'That's nice.' He sounded a bit surprised by this. 'You know Tillyard's brought a couple of secretaries from the museum. They'll be making daily records of our activities too. I'm sure he'd be happy to let them give you copies.'

'No thank you, Dr Ellis. I prefer to write my own reports.'

'For the love of God, Kate, will you stop calling me that? You sound ridiculous.'

'I don't care. I'd prefer to keep some distance between us. And while we're on the subject, I'd prefer it if you didn't call me by my first name. People might get the wrong impression about us.'

'Like what? That we've known each other for a long time, perhaps, and don't feel that we have to keep up some farcical society charade?'

'No.' I stopped abruptly and he nearly bumped into me. We were very close. 'They might think we're friends and in case you hadn't noticed, *Adam*, we're not.' I began walking again.

'Kate, I'm sorry about the other day — '

'I'm not. There's no longer any relationship between us, Dr Ellis. We are merely colleagues working together on a project that happens to be very important to my father and is therefore very important to me. As the secretary of the board and the senior archaeologist on this team, I'm prepared to listen to your views on Khaemwaset and the dig. Beyond that, I'm afraid I have nothing more to say to you.'

I felt rather than saw him stop walking beside me and before I could stop myself, I had stopped and turned round too. He was leaning against the railings again, clapping his hands very slowly. We had stopped in a part of the ferry that was populated almost entirely by native Egyptians and they were all watching us curiously, no doubt entertained by the strange behaviour of the *khawagas* (foreigners). A light breeze blew across the deck, bringing with it a mixture of citrus fruits and hot *ful*.

'Well done! Very impressive, Kate. If you didn't look so angry I could almost believe you.'

'Believe what you like. I don't care.'

'Yes, you do. You care so much you can hardly stand it.'

I whirled round to face him.

'What I can hardly stand is the fact that I was so childish and stupid as to believe you were ever a good friend. Just because we argued, Adam, there was no reason to take it out on my father.'

'What? Take what out on your father?'

He looked genuinely puzzled at this, but I wasn't going to be fooled by his act, no matter how good it was.

'Oh well done, very impressive,' I said deliberately imitating him. 'If I didn't know the truth, I could almost believe you had nothing to do with making sure the board refused to give Papa the help he needed.'

'You keep saying that but I have no idea what you're talking about. I had nothing to do with any of the decisions the board made after I left Egypt.'

'Oh really?' I was scathing with sarcasm. 'The secretary of the board had no say over how the budget was spent? Do you take me for a fool?'

'I've only been secretary for the last two

163

months. I know I'm resourceful, Kate but even I can't supervise the museum from thousands of miles away.'

'What?'

'I was only made the secretary on Henry's death. Before that I was still senior field archaeologist. I've been in Persia for the last year.'

'What?' I almost fell into one of the white wicker chairs placed on the deck for the passengers. Adam sat down beside me.

'Didn't you get my letters? I wrote to you half a dozen times.'

'Half a — ' I stared at him. 'I got one. You said you couldn't see any point in continuing our relationship since I was obviously determined to be so obstinate.'

'That was the last one I wrote after all the others. When you didn't reply to any of them, I thought — '

'But I wrote to you hundreds of times! Well, six or seven anyway. You were the one who didn't write back.'

We looked at each other in confusion for a few moments.

'Well, it looks as though Tillyard's not the only one who's been having problems with the post,' he said at last, breaking the silence. 'I suppose it was inevitable that there would be some problems with letters getting to

Persia. Although I got most of the ones the museum sent.'

'What were you doing there?'

'In Persia? Snooping around trying to find a back way into Mount Ararat. There've been reports over the last few years that remains of a fossilized boat have been found in the mountains and quite a few of the bigger museums have sent people out there?

'Really? Noah's Ark?' For a brief moment I forgot I was angry with him and thought instead of how it would be if he found the fabled boat. He smiled rather forlornly.

'Unfortunately the Turks aren't over-keen to help the West to further the cause of archaeology. And the Persian government has little control over their mountain regions. I've spent most of my time in government offices, arguing with minor bureaucrats over which documents I needed for every five yards I want to travel.'

I frowned. For over a year I had been harbouring a grudge against this man, sure he was at the bottom of the seemingly personal vendetta the board appeared to be waging against Papa, and apparently he hadn't even been in the country at the time. Something wasn't making any sense, but I couldn't work out what it was. I got up from the chair and walked towards one of the coffee-sellers.

'Do you want a cup?' I asked Adam and he nodded, following me. As the man handed over two tiny cups of the steaming, thick liquid with its sweet, pungent smell, he grinned at us. We had obviously been amusing the Egyptians greatly with our argument.

'How long have you been back?' I asked, sitting down again.

'About five months. Alice wrote to me and told me about Henry's last two strokes and since I wasn't doing any good in Persia I thought I'd better return. And if you say anything about Alice snapping her fingers and me coming running, Kate, I swear I'll put you across my knee,' he added, as I opened my mouth to speak. 'I was the senior archaeologist and Henry's health was failing. I had to come back and it had nothing to do with Alice.'

'Of course not,' I said sweetly. 'That was just a bonus, wasn't it?'

He stood up abruptly and I jumped, slightly startled.

'Getting a bit worried, Kate?' He grinned, leaning over me in the chair as he said this.

'Don't be ridiculous.' I got up too. 'Touch me just once, Adam Ellis, and you'll never get within a hundred miles of Khaemwaset's tomb.'

'If it exists.'

He had stopped by a tobacco vendor now and was buying a fat cigar. As he lit up, wafting the smoke around to discourage the mosquitoes, I could see from the look in his eyes that he was deliberately trying to provoke me, but two could play at that game. That was the trouble really. We both knew too well how to wound each other.

'If you don't think it exists, why are you here? Oh, wait a minute, I know. Because Alice asked you to come.'

'No,' he said with sweet patience. 'I came because there seems to be some genuine reason at last to believe that your father's right. You really have no need to be jealous of Alice, Kate.'

'Really? How comforting. If only you hadn't given me so much to be jealous of in the past.'

He followed me as I walked along the deck.

'You keep saying that as well. But what did I do that was so terrible?'

'You mean apart from running out on me the moment we disagreed because she decided she needed her lapdog back?'

His expression hardened but he kept his temper this time.

'I am not having that argument with you again. And is that really all there is to it? Are

167

you really so petty as to remain so annoyed over just that one thing?'

'Petty!' My eyes narrowed. 'Well, if you really want to know what else annoyed me, Dr Ellis, let's see. What about that time in London when you promised to take me out to the theatre and then Alice realized she needed an escort for Henry's cousin at a dinner party instead? So naturally you cancelled our arrangements — '

'I apologized for that. It was an important dinner.'

'Of course. And that's what I told myself too. And then when we got to Cairo you and I were going to take a trip on the Nile and I had made lots of complicated arrangements to get Professor McNulty and his wife to chaperon us which was very kind because they really didn't have the time to spare and everything was ready and then you got a telegram from Alice asking if you could go straight to Alexandria because there was a valuable shipment waiting to be sent on.'

'It *was* valuable! And Henry was asking too!'

'But it was Alice who sent the telegram, Adam. And then twice you promised me — '

'All right!' He frowned as he leaned back on a railing. 'Perhaps sometimes I was a little inconsiderate — '

'A little!' I glared at him for a second before walking briskly down the stairs to the passenger lounge. As I left, I heard one of the Egyptians say something to Adam. After a few minutes, he caught up with me again.

'The coffee-seller was impressed with you, you know.' I'd forgotten Adam's habit of picking up a conversation two minutes after we'd had an argument as though nothing had happened. I'd always found it immensely irritating and time hadn't changed anything. 'He said you'd make an excellent wife once you'd been beaten soundly.'

'I'm sure you found that very amusing.'

'I told him you were a Western woman and unfortunately I wasn't allowed to do anything like that.'

'How very entertaining. Why don't you go back and talk to your new friends? I've got nothing more I want to say to you.' I began to walk a little more quickly, then changed my mind. 'Actually I have got something more to say. You tell me you've been in Persia for a year and have had very little contact with the museum, which is all very well, but it still doesn't explain why the board was so reluctant to fund us. If you weren't poisoning them against us, why didn't they help? It makes no sense.'

'Well, it probably had a lot to do with your

terrible reports,' he said, still puffing on the cigar and sounding appallingly smug.

'My what?'

'Your reports. They were awful. You can't expect a national institution to take you seriously if you can't even be bothered to file proper reports, Kate. If it hadn't been for the article in The Times that one of the board members happened to read a few months ago I doubt even now that we'd be out here.'

Now at the risk of sounding arrogant, I am very proud of my report writing and typing abilities. I know it's considered a mere woman's job and people look down on the actual mechanical skills, but I always take a great deal of care over my work and if I do say so myself, there's no one faster than me on a keyboard once I get started. I bought a typewriter in London, a little Oliver and I am a very good typist and documentarian. And here was this arrogant wretch telling me I had been the cause of our problems! I saw red.

''Can't even be bothered to file proper reports!' How dare you! How would you know what my reports are like? You're supposed to have spent the last year in Persia. My reports have been perfect! They have been clear, concise, detailed and beyond reproach. Just because your stupid museum refuses to support its most expert, senior and

170

faithful archaeologist, don't dare to try to — '

'Calm down, Kate. If I've offended you, I apologize.'

It would have sounded more sincere at this point if he hadn't obviously been fighting back laughter and I was so incensed I could barely speak.

'You really are the limit, Adam Ellis. You come out here and — '

'Very well, I beg your pardon, Kate. You're quite right. How would I know?' He frowned, doing his best to look grave now and took my arm as we walked through a small rush-woven door into the first-class passenger lounge. 'Look, there's Alice with the others. Let's join them and see if everything's ready for disembarkation, shall we?'

I glared, but before I could say anything else the two little Howard boys appeared in front of me.

'Hello Miss Whitaker,' they piped in unison, talking as though they were two voices with one brain. I always found it eerie.

'Hello boys,' I said. Adam walked on ahead.

'We've just come to wish you good luck on your expedition, Miss Whitaker,' said Hugh, or it could have been Charles. I was useless at telling them apart.

'That's very kind of you. And good luck at

your new school. I'm sure you'll enjoy it,' I lied.

'Thank you, Miss Whitaker. We'd also like to say we're sorry for our bad behaviour during our Latin lessons. We hope you'll forgive us.'

'Oh — of course.'

I was amazed. They'd never shown any remorse before and in fact I'd got the distinct impression they'd enjoyed every evil trick they'd played on me. As they walked away, smiling angelically at their good deed, I realized that Adam was watching them. Then he turned towards me. As we looked at one another his face broke into a smile and he winked.

Something told me the Howard twins' change of heart wasn't entirely voluntary.

7

The sun was setting, its blood-red colour staining the plains as though a great god had died there. I shaded my eyes with one hand and watched as the shadows grew longer; the worst heat of the day was past now, but to compensate for this the mosquitoes were out in force pestering us with a never-ending whine.

Behind me our little camp was spread out among the lush plains that made up the fertile river-country of the Nile. I say little, but in fact it was the most luxurious campsite I had ever been in. When Papa and I came here, it was usually only us and whomever visiting archaeologists or historians we had with us at the time, although for the last year they had been precious few.

But now I was getting a glimpse of how the truly wealthy travelled. Besides myself and the other five immediate members of the group, Mr Tillyard had brought with him from London two secretaries to transcribe any texts found and a skilled watercolourist. There was also a cook, a couple of general servants, a boy employed exclusively to fetch and carry water and grooms to see to the donkeys and horses.

It had taken us all day to travel from the river to the plains and then set up this small canvas town, so by the time there was some semblance of order evening was coming on and there was no chance of doing anything more constructive than to have our evening meal. I had enquired rather sarcastically of Bella whether we were expected to dress for dinner and she had seemed surprised that I even remarked on it. So I had hurriedly searched among my meagre wardrobe for something that might just pass as evening wear. The only thing I had that looked even remotely suitable was a blue muslin tea-gown. Hoping it would do, I had quickly put it on and left Bella to complete her own evening toilet with the inexpert attentions of the little Egyptian girl whom Lady Faversham had insisted should accompany us. As Bella and I had already agreed to share a tent before we left, I had wondered what function this child might serve and now I knew. Karima had many talents, I've no doubt, but as I left Bella with her that first evening, I had the feeling being an English lady's maid was not one of them.

One glance at the cooking-tent and the ridiculously large table that had been set up told me that dinner was not yet served, so I wandered away from the site and climbed a small hillock, settling myself down to await the call to dinner, enjoying the smells of cinnamon and saffron that wafted across from the kitchen. I wouldn't have been surprised if a gong had sounded. Looking down on the scene before me there was something almost surreal about the dinner table laid out among the tents. I couldn't help laughing. English people abroad were truly insane.

'Kate, can I join you?'

I looked up and saw Alice. She was elegant and sophisticated as always, in a gorgeous evening dress of black crape clinging to her trim waist before flowing out into a wide, circular skirt. Her décolletage was low with triple shoulder-straps and her hair was dressed with jet beads, which also adorned her ears and throat. She looked sumptuous and beside her I was just a provincial bookworm with no money or prospects.

'Hello Alice,' I said, trying to sound pleasant. After all, we needed the museum. 'You look lovely.'

She laughed. 'We both know I'm completely overdressed for a camping trip by the Nile. But I can't get out of the habit. I've been doing this for too many years to feel happy in anything other than a proper

175

evening gown at night. You look just right for this place,' she added, coming to sit down beside me and putting an arm through mine.

I shrugged. 'Usually Papa and I just sit by the fire in the evenings with blankets round us, writing up our notes. We save on water by eating out of the tins.'

'Don't be naughty,' she laughed. 'You do no such thing.'

I smiled, aloof but curious about Alice. Her manner mystified me. A year ago she had done everything she could to ruin my romance with her cousin for reasons I didn't understand, and yet here she was, behaving as though she had nothing but the warmest feelings towards me and expected the same in return. And now I thought about it, she had been just as gracious when she arrived at our house last week, showing me the same kindness and compassion that she had displayed eight years ago in escorting home an obnoxious little schoolgirl. It made no sense at all.

'It really is such a pity poor James can't be here,' she continued, waving a folding silk fan with ivory sticks. 'I hope he gets better soon.'

'Thank you,' I said. There was a slight pause, while we watched the groom begin feeding the horses and donkeys. 'We were sorry to hear about Sir Henry, Alice. Didn't you say in your last letter that his health seemed to be improving?'

'That's what the doctors said and we all thought the worst was over. But apparently more heart attacks are not uncommon and of course the nearer they are to one another the more dangerous it is.' She sighed. 'He died instantly for which I'm glad. There was no pain. I know things weren't at their best between James and Henry during the last two years, but believe me Kate, he always wished for the best.'

'I'm sure he did.' What else could I say?

'Miss Wyndham-Brown is a delightful person,' Alice continued, changing the subject in her best society hostess manner. 'And she seems very fond of you.'

'Well, it's nice to know one has some friends.'

My tone must have been more bitter than I intended, because Alice looked at me keenly for a moment before taking my hand.

'Oh dear. Does this mean you and Adam still aren't talking?'

'I'm sure you know exactly how things are between Adam and me, Alice,' I said, coldly. 'If I remember correctly, Adam used to tell you everything.'

She looked away in the direction of the setting sun. The shadows were getting even

177

longer now and it was becoming harder to distinguish between tents and rocky outcrops. Still holding my hand, she said:

'Yes, he did, didn't he? And I wasn't always as considerate as I could have been, Kate. I — regret that.'

She looked so forlorn as she spoke that for a moment I almost felt guilty for the sharpness of my tone. Then I remembered all the letters and telegrams she had sent from England, causing Adam to go scurrying to and fro on her errands. This was a woman who knew how to manipulate people. I decided to take the bull by the horns.

'Alice,' I said. 'Why *did* you write last summer, asking him to return home?'

She stiffened almost visibly. Behind us the camels and donkeys were being fed now and their noisy appreciation of their evening meal echoed around the valley.

'I don't know what you mean, dear. I didn't write to him asking him to return. It was his mother who wrote. I think we should return now. Dinner must be ready.' And she got up abruptly and made her way back to the campsite.

I watched her go, my eyes narrowed coldly in suspicion. First Adam had lied to me and now Alice had too. Suddenly I began to wonder just exactly what was going on between Adam and Alice. I had always assumed that Adam's slavish hero-worship of his older cousin was just a hangover from his youth, something that Alice took advantage of because she was so used to it and she barely noticed what she was doing any more. I had been jealous of her, certainly, and irritated that she had amused herself with him as she did, but up until this moment, I had always assumed their relationship was entirely innocent. Now for the first time I began to have my doubts.

As I mulled over these thoughts, a gong did indeed sound, the hollow, tinny echo faintly ludicrous in the balmy heat of an Egyptian evening. I walked slowly back to the camp.

''Ere, Miss Kate. Can you 'elp me a minute?'

I looked over in the direction of the speaker and smiled. One of the few genuinely pleasant surprises of this trip so far was the presence of Ruby, my little friend from London. I knew that for the last few years Alice had travelled without a lady's maid, having learnt the hard way that English servants and hot, foreign countries don't mix. When Rose had come out eight years ago, she had been sick so many times that Alice had had to employ a servant to look after *her* in the end. Rose had spent the few hours when she wasn't ill vowing she would starve on the streets before following her ladyship out of England again and I remember, at fourteen, being vastly impressed at the seemingly endless hours she could devote to vomiting, despite appearing to eat hardly anything. By the end of the trip, Rose had lost two stone in weight and Alice nearly lost a good lady's maid.

But Ruby had managed to persuade Alice that she would not succumb to the same condition and so far the experiment seemed to be working out well. Indeed the Egyptian heat seemed to agree with her, she looked so tanned and fit. At the moment she was standing beneath a huge palm tree, scowling at the water-boy.

'What's the matter, Ruby?' I asked, walking across to them.

'I need some water to do some washing fer 'er ladyship, miss, an' I can't get this 'ere imp to understand a blessed word. 'E's bein' very uncooperative,' she added darkly, as Naguib turned his back on her.

'I see. Naguib, Ruby needs some water for her mistress's laundry. Could you take some across to her tent, please.' I made sure to speak politely in the hope that Ruby might notice.

'Yes, Miss Katie. She doesn't need to shout

at me,' Naguib said, clearly offended.

'Thank you, Naguib,' I said. He turned and bowed slightly to me before taking a large jug across to Alice's tent.

Mollified by the sight of Naguib doing my bidding, Ruby was fairly receptive to my suggestion that learning a few words of Arabic might help and I spent the next five minutes schooling her to pronounce *minfadlak* and *shukran*; 'please' and 'thank you' respectively. I watched for a while as she dipped a delicate silk stocking into the now soapy water and tried not to laugh as she screwed up her face in disgust at the strong smell of incense coming from the Egyptians' tents. I loved its pungency myself but I knew many English people did not. Then something suddenly occurred to me. Ruby would almost certainly have been at the house the day Adam returned.

'Ruby, do you remember Dr Ellis coming back to England last summer?' I asked.

''Course I do, Miss Kate. We was all so glad to see 'im.' Ruby rubbed gently at the clothes. ''Specially 'er ladyship. It did 'er the power a' good.'

'Did it?' I said acidly.

'Oh yes, miss. 'Er ladyship's very fond of Mr Adam. You know, she really missed 'im while 'e was away wiv you and the professor.'

Ruby squeezed hard on the stockings, making her face go red and for a moment I wanted to tell her to be careful. Then, maliciously, I decided I liked the idea of Alice having ruined stockings. 'When 'e come back,' Ruby continued, chattily, 'Cook said ter me: 'Mark my words, Ruby, it'll — '

I never did find out what words of wisdom Cook imparted to Ruby, because just then Bella found me.

'Kate darling, we're waiting for you. Didn't you hear the gong?'

'Yes, of course. I'm so sorry,' I said, picking up the skirt of my dress to hold it clear of the dusty red soil as I followed her to the table. Actually I wasn't a bit sorry. Now I knew that when Adam had returned to England last year, Alice had been visibly elated. It was just a little bit more evidence against the two of them.

The meal itself was every bit as unreal as I had imagined it would be. Adam and Mr Tillyard were polite when they remembered to be, but they were clearly too excited by what they had already seen of the tomb to be able to do more than answer questions put to them briefly before returning to their almost exclusive conversation about digs and equipment and methods of extraction, which peeved Bella, who wasn't used to being ignored at the dinner table. I tried to keep her entertained but I had my own demons to wrestle with.

Also it had been a long time since I'd sat at such a sumptuous dinner table and it took me a while to work out which pieces of cutlery went with which dish. There seemed to he endless courses set out on fabulously coloured platters of *Muski* glass, in turquoise, aquamarine and purple, and if we were to dine so fabulously every evening I couldn't see us accomplishing anything other than getting very fat. I'd also drunk more wine than I was used to, making me feel even more sluggish. So when Alice got up and announced that we ladies would be leaving the gentlemen to their port and cigars, I was caught unawares and found myself halfway across to the tents before I even knew what was happening.

'Alice, where are we supposed to go?' I said as we stood by her tent. 'This isn't a house in Surrey, you know.'

Alice put one hand on the canvas, rubbing her forehead distractedly with the other.

'I'm sorry, darling. Force of habit. Actually I've got the beginning of a headache. Would you think me a terrible bore if I retired for the evening?'

'Not at all, Lady Faulkner,' said Bella with

concern. 'Would you like some eau de cologne? I have a — '

'That's very kind of you, my dear but no, thank you. I have some medication with me. Goodnight.' She smiled and disappeared into her tent.

'Let's go up and sit by the tombs,' I said to Bella. 'It's too beautiful a night to go to bed yet.'

More than willing to comply, Bella went off to fetch a couple of shawls from our luggage, while I found a lantern and then raided Adam's tent for his cigars. I knew where he kept them and didn't feel at all as though I was stealing. After all, he had walked out on me a year ago. It was the least I deserved.

Very shortly we were sitting halfway up a dry, limestone hill by an abandoned tomb, the bleakness of our surroundings softened by the veil of night. The cicadas chirruped their familiar soothing song. For a while we sat and listened to traditional music being played by some of the servants on dulcimers and drums. Then, to Bella's surprise and obvious delight, I took out a cigar and lit it. She grinned.

'So you *do* smoke. I heard Mrs Fotheringay telling Aunt Augusta you'd been seen smoking before, but I didn't believe it. Neither did Aunt Augusta.'

'Why not?'

'Aunt Augusta thinks you're a much maligned character. She was very impressed with your lecture on Khaemwaset. I think you remind her of herself when she was young.'

'Good grief, I hope not,' I said, as I wafted the smoke around us to ward off the mosquitoes. 'To be honest Bella, I just use it as an insect-repellent.'

'Really?' She sounded disappointed but it was true. Papa had allowed me a puff on his cigar when I was twelve and I had been violently and copiously sick.

'Really. I love the smell of cigars, but they taste vile. So now I just use them to keep the midges away.'

To demonstrate, I waved the cigar around and Bella watched as the tiny, black smudges in the air around us danced away from the smoke like iron filings being repelled by the anti-polarity of a magnet.

'Kate, I'm disappointed in you,' she said mildly. 'And here was I thinking you were such a *fast* girl.'

I grinned. 'Sorry. I won't tell anyone else if you won't. Would you like me to point out some constellations?'

'Certainly not,' she said, settling the full skirts of her shell-pink silk dress around her feet. 'That would be incredibly dull. What you can do is finish off telling me the story of why you and Dr Ellis are no longer friends.'

I blew on the ruby-red tip of the cigar to keep it alight and softly blew its pungent aroma into the sharp night air. I didn't want to tell even Bella about my suspicions regarding Adam and Alice. No matter how hurt and angry I was, even I couldn't be that malicious. But I did want to talk to someone. I was so tired of having to pretend I didn't care. I sighed.

'He betrayed me.'

Bella's reaction was satisfyingly aghast. 'No!'

'Well — I think so.'

Now she stared at me, less aghast.

'You think so? What do you mean, you think so?'

I pulled the shawl tighter round my shoulders.

'It's rather hard to explain.'

Bella looked unconvinced.

'Well, my dear,' she drawled in her best heiress voice. 'Usually it's considered good manners to be absolutely certain about that kind of thing.'

'Well I am certain. At least — that he lied to me.'

'How?' I could tell from the tone of her

voice that she was rapidly becoming less sympathetic.

'Because he told me he had received a letter from his mother begging for his return when I knew for a fact that he hadn't and that it had come from someone else entirely.'

'How do you know?'

'Because I recognized the handwriting,' I said.

'Oh.' She raised her finely marked eyebrows. 'I see.' And I knew that despite her youth, Bella *did* see. 'And did you confront him with this?'

I laughed shortly. 'Of course I did. And he denied it and we had a blazing row and said the most awful things to each other and he left a few days later. And of course, after a while I was so miserable I wrote asking him to forgive me. Several times in fact, which just goes to show how foolish I can be, but he never wrote back except for one dreadful letter, accusing me of being obstinate and vindictive. I was so angry I swore I would have nothing more to do with him.'

'I see,' she said again. 'And what was his explanation of the letter?'

I dropped the cigar on the ground and stamped it out.

'He insisted it came from his mother. Absolutely. In the end I began to wonder if I

187

had gone mad and imagined it.'

'But you don't really think that?' She took my hand as she asked me this and I shook my head.

'No.' I sighed. 'I know that particular handwriting too well.'

She continued to pat my hand for a few moments.

'Men can be very cruel, Kate. You have to protect yourself against them.' There was a bitter note in her voice as she said this and I must have looked surprised, because she smiled coldly. 'You'd be amazed at how many I've met already. When you're worth as much as I am, darling, you either learn to spot them very quickly or you have get used to being constantly disappointed.'

I pressed her hand in mine and wondered for the first time what had been wrong with the wrong young man at the ball. But before I could ask there was a noise in the distance, We heard the crunch of stones beneath boots and then Adam appeared. He still had on his evening clothes, but over that he wore a thick coat against the evening chill. Evidently he had not forgotten everything about real life in Egypt.

'Ah. I wondered where my cigars had gone. I see you haven't lost your touch, Kate.'

I looked at him coolly.

'Well, since we were banished from the dinner table so that you men could enjoy yourselves, I thought lending us some cigars was the least you could do.'

'Don't blame me,' he said as he sat down next to me. 'I don't make the rules. Although you know, Kate, many people consider it unbecoming for a woman to smoke.'

'Do they really?'

I took a deep pull on the cigar and managed to blow a respectable cloud in his direction. The pompous look left his face and he smiled mischievously as he turned to Bella.

'I love doing that. Kate's so easy to tease. Do you know, sometimes I think about telling her I disapprove of women jumping off mountains just to see if she'd do it to spite me.'

I opened my mouth to snap back at him, but unfortunately there was still some smoke in my mouth. I inhaled by accident and began a fit of coughing instead. Ever helpful, he patted me on the back and said kindly, 'You know, you really shouldn't smoke unless you know what you're doing.'

'What are you doing here, Adam?' I gasped. 'Did the after-dinner talk get boring? Or did you run out of port?'

'You should be more grateful. I've just

headed off a major search party on your behalf.'

'What are you talking about?'

'Karima got worried when Miss Wyndham-Brown went off into the night, apparently on her own. It seems Lady Faversham gave her express instructions never to let the young miss out of her sight — '

'Oh Lord,' said Bella in exasperation. 'I *thought* she was being very nosy. I told her to go to bed.'

'Well, she didn't. She went straight to Sir George just as she'd been told to do and when it was discovered you were missing too, Kate, Sir George and Tillyard started to get very anxious.'

'But *you* didn't, of course,' I remarked.

He grinned. 'I know what you're like, Kate. I told them you'd both be fine. Sir George seemed reassured, although Tillyard insisted on searching the main site. I think you've got an admirer there, Kate.' He paused. 'Anyway, what *are* you two ladies doing out here?'

'I was pointing out the different constellations to Bella,' I said, waving vaguely at the night sky. 'Orion's belt is very clear at this time of year.'

Bella tilted her head back obligingly to stare at the stars.

'Yes, very pretty,' she said. 'But perhaps we

should go and find Mr Tillyard to let him know we're safe.'

'If you wish,' Adam said lazily. 'Although I daresay he'll find us in due course.'

As he said this there was another sound of gravel being crunched underfoot and Mr Tillyard suddenly appeared, with a lantern in one hand and waving a small gun in the other.

'Good God, Tillyard, what have you got there?' said Adam. As he spoke, two things occurred simultaneously to me: one, that Adam didn't care for Mr Tillyard very much: and two, that I was rather alarmed myself at the thought of one of our party carrying guns around. Mr Tillyard, however, seemed unperturbed by his tone.

'A derringer, Dr Ellis. I always carry one on my trips here, especially when I go upriver. One never knows when it might prove useful. Are you all right, ladies?'

'Of course, Mr Tillyard. It's very kind of you to be concerned for us, but I beg of you to keep *that* — I pointed to his gun — 'safely locked away. It really isn't necessary.'

'Certainly. I didn't wish to startle you, Miss Whitaker or Miss Wyndham-Brown, but I do like to be prepared.'

'Prepared for what?' asked Adam.

'For whatever comes along, Dr Ellis.' At

last Mr Tillyard seemed to notice his tone. 'Well, since the ladies are safe, I'll bid you goodnight. I apologize if I've intruded.'

He began to walk back the way he had come and I felt suddenly guilty. Both Adam and I had been a little censorious of his gun, when really it wasn't that ridiculous a precaution. News of Papa's find had indeed spread and there was evidence that plunderers had already made preliminary forays at our original digs. It wasn't completely beyond the realms of possibility that we might find ourselves in need of protection.

'Not at all, Mr Tillyard,' I said, getting up quickly. 'You weren't intruding at all and Bella and I were about to retire to bed anyway, weren't we, Bella?'

'Oh. Of course.' Bella seemed surprised but she stood up too. 'Yes. How kind of you to think of us. Goodnight, Mr Tillyard. Dr Ellis.' And she followed me down the hill, delicately stepping over the rocks and doing her best to avoid squashing the little lizards that lived in the tombs and scuttled about underfoot at night, hunting.

'Do you think Mr Tillyard admires me?' I asked when we were back in our own tent.

'I don't know. Perhaps. Why?'

'Oh, no particular reason,' I said, lighting the lantern by the side of my bed. 'Did Adam seem a little put out when he appeared, did you think?'

'Well, not that I noticed — although now I come to think of it, he . . . ' Suddenly she grinned at me. 'Kate Whitaker, don't tell me you were trying to make him jealous?'

'I don't see why he shouldn't have a taste of his own medicine,' I said, blowing out the match in my hand. 'Let's see how he likes it.'

Bella sat down on her bed and began to laugh.

'You know Kate, with a little effort I do believe we can have you behaving like a proper young lady after all.'

8

Ahmed was waiting for me as I left the tomb. '*Assalaamu aleikum*, Miss Katie.'

'*Wa aleikum assalaam*,' Ammi,' I replied, using the polite form of address towards an older man. 'I hope you are well.'

'*Inshallah*, Miss Katie.'

I had felt my heart sink at these words. In Egypt, as in most Muslim countries, this was the standard response. It means 'God willing' or 'if it pleases God' and the Egyptians used it as a reply to any number of questions ranging from 'is dinner ready?' to 'does your business prosper?' But my experience of the word tended to make me expect a pessimistic reply, so when Ahmed said '*inshallah*' to me, I had a feeling things were not good.

'Is there a problem, 'Ammi?'

'There could be, my heart.'

We had been digging for three days now. After we had cleared up the mess left by the plunderers at the original mummy-pit, and excavated further down the passageway, we had found a small chamber full of possessions. These were still relatively modest, but even so I was pleased with the finds. I had written to Papa last night, a second report in as many days, detailing all our treasures. I wanted him to miss out on as little as possible.

Ahmed crouched down beside a water barrel and took a drink, his white *galabiyya* stained with the red soil and dirt from the tunnels. I knelt beside him, knowing better than to rush him, and for a while we watched as the others worked around us. When, as a child, I had first met Ahmed he had been one of the few adults by whom I was genuinely intimidated. He was a tall, imposing man in his swirling robes, barking orders at his sons or his workmen. But he seemed to take a liking to me for some reason and he would often bring me *katif* — cakes made of honey and nuts, or *mahalabiyyah* — sweets made of rice and pistachios, when he visited the sites we worked on. I think it amused him that an infidel child could speak Arabic as well as I could. Papa had made him promise to come out to the site as often as possible to help me and he had spent the day with us, even going so far as to enter the tunnels, something he rarely did. Ahmed was very fond of Papa and greatly respected his ability to find precious artefacts, but he was not particularly interested in seeing where they had come from.

Now he pushed his rolled, turbanlike head-dress up a little on his forehead and dropped the tin cup back into the water.

'Last night one of your servants saw the Red Woman.'

'The Red Woman? You mean the ghost?'

He nodded, a serious look on his wrinkled face, and I felt my heart sink.

'How do you know? Who told you this?'

Ahmed spread out his hands. 'Alas, precious one, it is already common knowledge among the workers. Why else do you think they would be so keen to leave this early in the day?'

As he spoke he pointed to the diggers walking away from the site back to their village. Usually the local population were happy to stay chatting to the Egyptians we had brought with us and share a cup of tea or coffee. But today there was none of that. They strode purposefully out of the tomb area, the long lines of men looking like rats running away from a sinking ship.

I looked round at the servants by the cooking-tent. Although everything seemed to be normal, with the cook preparing the evening meal and his minions running round to do his bidding, suddenly I couldn't help feeling that there was a sense of anxiety in the way they kept giving darting looks at every sudden sound.

'Do you know what happened?' I asked and he nodded.

'The child who serves your young friend mentioned it to one of your grooms and he in his turn told the workers. It appears that last night, just as she was returning from attending her mistress, she happened to see a strange, red figure by the mouth of one of the old tombs. Apparently the figure disappeared as mysteriously as it appeared. Naturally she was terrified, but her story was dismissed by older, wiser heads as the over-imaginative ramblings of a child. However, this morning . . . '

His voice tailed off and I didn't need him to tell me the rest. This morning when the little groom who tended the donkeys mentioned it to the daily workers they would have been more than happy to supply him with all the details of our resident ghost. It would have been all round the campsite by midday.

'I don't suppose there's any chance the servants laughed out loud at the diggers' stories?' I asked.

Ahmed shook his head. 'None at all, Miss Katie. We Egyptians love a good ghost story.

Especially when it involves love and riches and betrayal.'

I nodded. 'Do you think we'll have any servants left by tomorrow?'

'Not if she's spotted again tonight.' He stood up, brushing dirt from the *galabiyya*. 'I would stay, but I have urgent business to attend to in town.'

I got up from my crouching position too. 'Not at all, 'Ammi. I know you're very busy. Thank you for coming today. And thank you for telling me this.'

Ahmed bowed politely and began to walk towards the corral where two of his sons and the horses stood waiting for him.

''Ammi!' I called. He turned back. 'Do you believe in the Red Woman?'

He paused. After a moment he said: 'Allah has given us a world of mystery and beauty, my heart, and eyes with which to behold it. There are many things in this life that I cannot explain except as the will of God. But I also know this — where men are concerned and riches are involved, look to the earthly to explain any inconsistencies before bowing to the infinite.'

He stared at me long and hard before turning round and continuing his journey back home for the night.

I walked into the tent and made a vain

attempt to beat the dust from my white linen blouse and bloomers before giving up and pulling my scarf off, glad to feel cool air against my neck. Then I put on my reading-spectacles and looked through the documents on my little desk at the end of my bed. The tent which Bella and I shared was the most spacious I had ever seen. Lady Faversham had insisted on the best — after all, Bella was an honourable — and after initially feeling decadent and spoilt, I had come to enjoy the luxury. Lady Faversham was rapidly going up in my estimation.

Just as I sat down there was a rapping sound on the stout wooden pole that was the central support of the tent. It was the nearest we could make it to knocking on someone's door.

'Come in,' I said.

Adam pulled across the canvas flap, letting in some welcome fresh air. Like me, he too was grubby and mud-stained: there were soil-smudges on his face and hands and clothes. White linen was the best defence against the heat, but it made any dirt stand out a mile.

'What did Ahmed want?'

'And a good afternoon to you too, Adam,' I said, rolling some paper into the typewriter. I began typing quickly, wanting this task done before dark. It was always more difficult to type with only the aid of a lantern. 'And how are you?'

'If you must know, I'm hot, tired, thirsty and in no mood to play games. What did Ahmed say?'

'Why don't you ask him?'

'Because he'll tell me only what he wants me to know and nothing I want to know. As far as he's concerned, Professor Whitaker is still in charge.'

'Yes, Ahmed's a dear, isn't he,' I said, silently blessing him for his loyalty to Papa. Adam sat down on Bella's luggage chest, resting his chin in his hands.

'Do you really need me to say *I* think this is still your father's dig, too?'

'That would be nice.'

Adam scowled at me. 'Kate, I did not tell the Board that I thought James's sponsorship should be curtailed.'

'So you say. But you also said — '

'If you mention that damned letter from Alice again, I swear — '

'Ah,' I said, before he could finish. 'So you admit there was a letter from her.'

He opened his mouth to speak, then suddenly changed his mind. Then he put a finger on my cheek, turning my face towards him. His eyes were narrowed with suspicion.

'You're trying to hide something from me.'

I mistyped a word and muttered under my breath.

'Yes, that's what you're doing. Nice try, Katie. It almost worked. Now, out with it. What did he say?'

It was my turn to scowl at him.

'If you're so clever find out yourself.'

He leaned back against the table, elbows resting on my completed work.

'Isn't this just like old times, Kate? You and I wrestling for the upper hand. But didn't I always win?'

'No,' I said, bashing down savagely on a key. He smiled lazily.

'Funny, I always thought I — Good grief, Kate, this is terrible.'

I looked up from my typing again.

'What? What's the matter?'

'This.' He held up a report that I had completed earlier. 'I thought you said you were good at this. Henry was devilishly generous in giving you the allowance he did if this is the best you can come up with.'

The disdain in his voice surprised me. I stopped typing, took the sheet from his hand and examined it for a moment. Then I turned back to my work once more.

'Sometimes you're a complete ass, Adam Ellis,' I said.

'But there are mistakes all over the place. And smudges. It's practically illegible.'

I looked at him briefly over my spectacles.

'That's not my typing, it's Bella's. She's getting bored because there's little to interest her at the moment and she refuses to go into the tunnels because the only time she did a bat flew past her and nearly got tangled into her hair. She noticed my typewriter and asked if she could help me, so I gave her some notes to type up. Here. This is my work,' I said, passing him the file I was intending to send to Papa. 'If you can't tell the difference, then you deserve to go back to London empty-handed.'

I could tell from the way his eyebrows suddenly went up that he *could* see the difference. I began typing again.

'I'm sorry,' he said after a moment. 'Can I take these back to my tent? I'd like to read them if that's all right with you.'

I quite liked the humble tone; it was definitely something new. But that didn't mean he was going to get me to do his work for him. He'd caught me out once, long ago, like that. It wasn't going to happen again.

'No, you can't. Get the museum secretaries to do your report-writing. That's what they're paid for, isn't it?'

'Kate, I wasn't going to . . . ' he started to

say in exasperation, then stopped and frowned. 'Listen, if I promise to be polite from now on and say nothing to annoy you, can we call a truce? I really didn't come here to make you angry.'

'No doubt. And yet you have. I wonder why that is, Adam,' I said, my eyes still focused on my typing. 'What is it that whips me up into a fury whenever I get into a discussion with you?'

'I don't know,' he said innocently.

I stopped typing. 'Perhaps it's the fact that I don't feel I can trust you, Adam. Do you think that might be it?'

We looked at one another. We were sitting very close by now and the sounds of the camp seemed far away. There was a smudge of red soil on his cheek and without thinking I reached out and wiped it away, feeling the rough grittiness as something completely new against my fingers.

'Kate, I wish I could — '

'Kate! Are you in here — Oh!'

Adam and I sprang back as Bella threw open the canvas flap, letting in bright sunlight.

'Oh, I beg your pardon. I didn't realize — '

'No, it's all right,' I said, turning back to my typewriter. 'Adam was just leaving. Weren't you.'

'Was I?' He leaned back again too. 'I suppose so. If you're not going to tell me what Ahmed had to say.'

'Ahmed? You mean that frightening old man who's always shouting at the workers?' said Bella. 'Never mind about him now. Have you heard the latest news?'

'No, what is it?' asked Adam with interest looking at her whilst behind him I shook my head frantically but to no avail.

'All the workers are getting hysterical about Kate's Red Woman. Isn't it ridiculous? Karima thinks she saw a ghost last night all wrapped up in red and now those silly Egyptians think the place is haunted. Honestly, you'd think grown men would know better.'

Adam turned to me, an eyebrow raised.

'Hmm, haunted eh? Would that have been what Ahmed was talking to you about, Kate?'

I had been hoping to keep the story secret at least for a little while until I had had some time to think about it. Now, however, there was no alternative but to admit the truth. I shrugged my shoulders, trying to keep my voice as casual as possible.

'He did mention it among other things. If we're not careful, there won't be any servants left out here after nightfall soon.'

Adam stared at me for a few moments

before rubbing his eyes, his fingers going white at the knuckles.

'Well, I suppose it was inevitable really, given the site and its history. I wonder what she did see.'

'Probably just a shadow or a flicker from someone's lantern. Candlelight can play tricks on one's eyes very easily and Karima is still a child. Would you like my advice?'

He looked up, surprise in his eyes.

'Of course. Always.'

'Keep a watch posted for the next few nights and make it clear to the servant that that's what we're going to do.'

He thought for a moment before nodding.

'That's a good idea.' He got up from his seat and walked towards the entrance. 'I'll see you at dinner, ladies. May I, please, Kate?' he added, picking up some of my old notes. 'I promise I won't crib from you. I just need to check something.'

I nodded as he ducked down through the tent opening.

'Oh, I forgot to tell you,' he said, just before he left. 'That inspector fellow, Bennett, will be arriving tomorrow. He wants to see what progress has been made.'

'Oh, how nice,' said Bella. 'I do so enjoy Mr Bennett's little visits.'

I groaned at this, but Adam just laughed.

As soon as we were alone, she sat down next to me, unable to contain her curiosity.

'Please tell me I didn't spoil anything important,' she begged.

I kept my eyes on my typing.

'Certainly not. In fact your arrival was very opportune.'

'Hmm. That's not what I thought.'

She sounded disappointed and I could see she wanted to continue this conversation, so I decided to head her off.

'Bella, you realize that if the servants think there's a ghost here, there's a good chance they'll all leave, don't you?'

'Not all of them, surely?'

'Probably.'

She thought about this.

'How ghastly. I suppose that means we'd have to leave as well.'

'Unless you want to do your own cooking and washing.'

'Good Lord, no. Although I daresay Uncle George would. I think he's rather in love with living in such a primitive fashion.'

I laughed briefly as I thought of our elaborate surroundings. This was hardly my idea of primitive.

'What about you, darling? You can't stay here on your own. What will you do?'

I stopped typing for a moment. I hadn't

thought of that before. Papa and I were quite used to living without servants in the desert, but he was ill at home and clearly I couldn't remain here alone with a group of single men, none of whom was a relative. And yet poor Papa had been adamant that I should not leave the dig.

'Perhaps Alice will want to stay,' I said, but although Bella nodded enthusiastically I could see that even she didn't believe it. Alice would be no more keen to live without servants than Bella was.

'Well, let's not worry about it now,' I said. 'Perhaps it might not come to that. So, what have you done today, Bella? Did Sir George eventually get you to venture into one of the tombs?'

Bella began to recount her day to me, but as I listened to her I couldn't help wondering what other problems the next few days would bring.

★   ★   ★

Dinner that night was a difficult affair. First of all Adam and Mr Tillyard were late, arriving some ten minutes after the rest of us. It quickly became clear they had had the devil of all rows. Then the news that we might soon be without servants was broken. When Sir

207

George heard about the Red Woman he was quite jovial at first, seeing it as no more than the simple superstition of the natives. But when it was pointed out that they might not remain at the site, he became distinctly less amused.

'No servants? Then what do we do for meals? And washing? And cleaning and all the rest of it?'

It was on the tip of my tongue to tell him that most adults managed to do all that for themselves, that Papa and I certainly had no problems when we came out here, but before I could say anything Adam spoke up.

'Well none of them has actually left yet. It may well be that the servants from the city are more sophisticated than we're giving them credit for and they won't believe in the stories any more than we do.'

'Yes, that's true,' said Alice. 'There's no reason to assume the servants are going to leave just because a little girl got somewhat over imaginative.'

'Right. And if we make it clear to them that we're going to have guards out for the next few nights we shouldn't have any trouble convincing them them that this is just a silly superstition.'

'Dr Ellis, I really don't see how taking it in turn to lose sleep for the next few nights is going to do any good.'

We all turned and looked at Mr Tillyard. His tone was sharp and it was obvious that this was the reason he and Adam had been arguing earlier.

'Yes, you've already made that clear, Tillyard. If you don't want to lose any sleep, fine. I'll do it myself.'

'Is there a problem, Adam darling?' Alice was beginning to get agitated now. She hated conflict.

'Tillyard doesn't think it's a good idea to post guards to keep a look-out for this Red Woman,' said Adam brusquely.

'Dr Ellis,' Mr Tillyard began irritably then paused, obviously trying to keep his temper. 'I just don't think it's a good idea to give credence to this ridiculous story. If you really want the natives to have faith in our ability to keep order, then I think we'd be far better off in carrying on as normal. It's the best way to show them how idiotic and childish this fairy tale is.'

'Good point, Tillyard,' said Sir George, taking a large gulp of wine. 'It's never a good thing to pander to the servants' whims. Makes 'em feel safer if we stand up to them.'

Adam glared at Sir George, but I don't think he noticed. He was too busy peeling an apple.

'Yes, Sir George, but what if Karima's ghost wasn't a ghost at all? There's already been evidence of plundering round here. What's to stop any thieves from taking advantage of nightfall to look for any treasures? And take advantage of the legend as well to achieve that end. I was trying to explain that to Tillyard before dinner.'

A howl from the desert hyenas distracted us all momentarily. It still seemed surreal to me to be sitting at this dinner table surrounded by uniformed servants and elaborate cutlery and shining candelabras while lizards scuttled under our feet and above us stars sparkled in the inky-black Egyptian sky. Then Adam pushed back his chair.

'Well, I'm going to explain to the servants what I intend to do and then start organizing shifts. If you'll excuse me,' he said as he got up. Sir George put down his knife.

'Wait a minute, my boy. Hold on there. I'm not so old I can't take a share of guard duty. Can't have the natives thinking we're not together on this.'

We all looked up, rather surprised that he was prepared to do something so arduous, although I could tell that Adam was less than ecstatic at the thought of the old man taking a turn at guard duty.

'Thank you, Sir George, but I'm not sure — '

'Don't worry about me, Ellis. I can still keep awake if need be. In fact, I'm probably better at it than you. You young folks would be surprised at how little . . . '

As they walked away from the dinner table, Adam still trying to dissuade him, Richard sighed and got up too.

'If you'll excuse me, Lady Faulkner, ladies. Wait a moment, Dr Ellis. I'm quite prepared to take my turn with you . . . '

For once it was the gentlemen who left the table first, not the ladies, although I didn't hold out much hope that we would be served port and cigars. As the three men disappeared Alice watched them go with an expression of relief on her face that they were all at last in accord about something.

Shortly afterwards we all retired to bed. I was exhausted as usual. For the last three days we had been working to a punishing schedule and I was always ready to fall into bed as soon as we had eaten. I was finding it hard to have to make polite conversation as well and was relieved that for once, dinner had been curtailed.

When we got to our tent, we found that Karima had already turned down our blankets and laid out our night-wear. Outside the crickets chirruped and the scarab beetles clicked their antennae ceaselessly. We undressed and I handed the lantern over to Bella so that she could check her bed for any insects or other creatures that might have crawled in. Bella had read somewhere that snakes regularly curled up in Western camp-beds and no matter how many times I told her that in all my years on digs it had never once happened to me, she still insisted on making a thorough, rather morbid, search for them. I had wondered more than once what she would actually do if she ever found one.

As we eventually climbed into our insect-free beds we heard voices murmuring and the sound of footsteps walking past the tent. I recognized Adam in quiet conversation with Sir George, obviously about to start their guard duty. Bella heard them too.

'I'm glad I'm not them,' she said as she lowered the lamp. 'I really wouldn't want to have to sit up now for another four or five hours.'

I pulled my blankets up to my chin.

'Neither would I.'

Bella squinted at me through the dim lighting.

'But it was your idea,' she said.

I grinned. 'So it was, my dear. That doesn't mean I'd actually want to do it. It's just fortunate that no one expects a fragile creature like myself to have to take on such an onerous task.'

Bella stared at me for a moment longer, before bursting out laughing.

'Kate, you're a wicked woman.'

I snorted as I turned out the lantern. I still hadn't forgotten Adam's remarks about me jumping off a cliff to prove him wrong. Somehow knowing he was losing sleep made me feel much better. To the sounds of the crickets and the occasional howl of a hyena I gently drifted off.

9

There was no sign of a ghost that night and when we woke up next morning none of the servants appeared to show any signs of wanting to leave. Either they had been reassured by the watch posted or they were more sophisticated than the desert-dwellers.

We worked hard that day and the next, digging carefully for any signs of entrances to rooms. The passageway had become a proper tunnel now and we were uncovering a marvellous pictorial recording of a funeral procession escorting an elaborate coffin into the tomb. There were fantastic images of life in the afterworld, the dog-headed figure of Anubis, Hathor, the mother-goddess in the form of a cow and last of all Osiris, weighing the hearts of the dead. The workers moved constantly in a stream from the tunnels, clearing the corridors of soil, their woven baskets always full to the brim. But although we kept finding enough to keep us encouraged, there was still tantalizingly little to suggest that this was the tomb of a royal.

On the third day after Karima had reported the ghost Adam caught up with me just as I was about to enter the tunnel. I was surprised to see him in a formal morning-coat and waistcoat.

'Hello,' I said. 'Is this a new fashion in tunnel digging?'

He smiled wearily. He and several servants had been staging watches every night, taking it in turns to sit the small hours out. I knew Sir George and Mr Tillyard had been helping, but although nothing was said, I got the distinct impression that the bulk of the guard duty had gone to Adam. Neither Sir George nor Mr Tillyard looked as strained as he did. He pulled irritably at the tie knotted around his high, starched collar. Adam hated wearing high collars.

'I've got to go back to Luxor for a few days, Kate. I've been trying to put this off but there's a number of matters that can only be resolved if I contact the museum in London.'

'What matters?' I asked, concerned by his pale face. 'Is there anything I can do?'

'No.' He smiled again, more easily this time. 'I wouldn't go if it weren't absolutely necessary, but I must get in touch with the museum and if I don't go to the telegraph office myself I can't be sure that the message will get to them as soon as possible.'

'Do you expect to be long?'

'No more than a day, two at the most.' He

grinned. 'Will you be able to manage without me?'

'We'll do our best,' I said drily. 'Actually you can do me a favour if you have the time.'

'Of course.'

'Take my latest report back to Papa for him to read. If you think it's legible, that is.'

I said this light-heartedly, meaning it as a joke, but Adam scowled.

'Of course I think it's legible,' he snapped. 'Do you have to harp back constantly to every comment I make?'

'I beg your pardon,' I said, feeling my face flush with embarrassment. 'I didn't mean to — '

'No, I'm sorry.' The anger left his face as quickly as it had come and he was left looking very tired. 'I had no reason to yell at you like that. Forgive me.'

'There's nothing to forgive,' I said, touching his cheek briefly. 'You're exhausted, Adam. You should get a good night's sleep.'

'Well, I will tonight. Now, where are these papers?'

I ran back to the tent where I quickly gathered the reports together, then went back out again to find Adam. I looked around for his horse, but to my surprise he was sitting in a carriage. Then I noticed Alice next to him. Bella was talking to her, holding

216

up a piece of paper.

'Here's my list, Lady Faulkner. Now you won't forget the coldcream, will you? I'm amazed at how quickly I've got through my jars out here. And if you could find that eau de Cologne I'd be indebted to you.'

'I'll do my best, Bella dear. Kate, is there anything I can get for you?'

'Just these messages to Papa, thank you, Alice,' I said. 'I didn't realize you were going too.'

'Yes, I need a few more provisions, my dear, and when Adam told me he had to return to Luxor I decided to accompany him. After all, there's no point in asking a man to remember all these things. I'm leaving Ruby here, since we'll only be gone for the night. Make sure she takes her quinine, won't you, darling? She makes such a fuss but I still maintain that that was why Rose was so ill.'

'Of course,' I said stiffly, holding my hand up as a shield against the glare of the sun. Alice was wearing a huge sun-hat in pale lemon, her gown was of the same matching chiffon and she looked cool and sophisticated, whilst I felt hot and bothered in my already grubby work-clothes. I tried to catch Adam's eye, but his head was buried in a pile of paperwork. As we watched the carriage drive off I began to feel the old jealousies rear up again, despite all my efforts to ignore them.

For the rest of the day I threw myself into work, scared to let my attention wander for more than a moment. Every time I did, I'd start thinking about Adam and Alice and how nothing seemed to have changed between them, no matter what either of them said. Their departure together nagged at me, although these days it was none of my business whom Adam took back to Luxor with him.

But I couldn't help wondering what was really going on. Apart from anything else we had never properly discussed last summer. Either someone else would suddenly appear and start up their own conversation about soil blockages or there would be a sudden scare as a nest of cobras was found. We never seemed to be alone long enough before there would some new problem to be solved. In a way I was glad, knowing that there was a good chance I wouldn't like the answers I got.

The day passed in a blur of work and worry. Then, at five o'clock, Mr Tillyard found me.

'How are you doing, Miss Whitaker?' he said, his voice echoey as he crawled into the space beside me at the end of the tunnel. I was trying to scrape away a stubborn block of

218

clay on a side wall without ruining the text just visible underneath.

'I'm fine.'

Actually my neck and back were aching abominably, my face was bathed in sweat and I had broken several nails trying to be as delicate as I could with the crumbling hieroglyphs. It didn't help that every so often one of the workmen would accidentally jostle me as they walked past with their heavy baskets of soil. But for the last half-hour or so I had started to get excited and I hadn't thought about Adam or Alice at all. The texts I was slowly and painfully revealing seemed to suggest for the first time that a royal person was the occupant of this tomb.

'Here,' he said, handing me a bottle of water. 'Drink this.'

As I drank, Mr Tillyard held his lantern up to the wall I was working on, his eyes screwed up in concentration. It was hot in the tunnels and his spectacles steamed up quickly in the humid atmosphere.

'These images really are interesting,' he said. 'I'd forgotten how exciting digs can be. My understanding of these texts is very limited, my dear. Tell me, is that the symbol for a royal personage?'

'I really think it is,' I said eagerly. 'Although I need to get to the rest of the text to verify it.

Oh, I wish Papa were here now. He'd be so excited!'

Mr Tillyard lifted the lantern away from the hieroglyphs and into my face. Long shadows flickered against the walls and the dim orange glow gave the whole place an eerie quality that I hadn't noticed until now. He smiled at me, his face shadowed.

'As you obviously are, Miss Whitaker. It makes me wish sometimes that I had remained on the practical side rather than turning my attention to administration.'

I wiped a trickle of sweat away from my eyes and smiled at him.

'I hope your career direction had nothing to do with my abominable behaviour.'

'Not at all, my dear. I'm enjoying myself immensely at the moment, but I think my talents lie more in the financial side of the field than in practical experience. Although I do enjoy my trips out here to check up on museum business. What does this image mean?'

I looked briefly at the pictogram to which he was pointing.

'It represents Nut, the sky-goddess. Do you travel to Egypt often, then?' I asked. I wiped a patch of dirt from an ibis-headed figure before scraping at it as delicately as I could with a thin scalpel.

'Occasionally. I was very pleased when Lady Faulkner asked me to join her and Dr Ellis in Luxor. I didn't realize she and your father were such good friends. Nor, especially, did I know how she felt about Khaemwaset,' said Mr Tillyard. His tone was so odd that I stopped what I was doing.

'What do you mean?' I asked curiously. His expression became suddenly guarded.

'Oh . . . well . . . I thought . . . I was just under the impression that you knew she didn't approve of Professor Whitaker's absorption with this particular project.'

'Alice?' I stared at him, shocked. 'Alice? Was it Alice who stopped the board sending us funds?'

'I don't think so, my dear. I merely got the impression that she felt Professor Whitaker was not in a position to know what the best use of his money might be at that time. I do beg your pardon, Miss Whitaker. I didn't realize that you didn't know that. Oh dear, I wish I hadn't said anything now. Are you all right? You look rather pale.'

'I'm fine,' I said again, but I was far from fine.

Mr Tillyard looked at his fob-watch.

'It's getting late. You've been here all day and you must be exhausted. Leave this now and come back to camp with me.'

'Yes, I think I will.'

We crawled slowly out to the passageway where we could stand upright. I felt a little dizzy as we reached the entrance and I fell against Mr Tillyard as the heat and glare of the sun hit me. He steadied me, his arms a comforting support around my waist.

'Thank you.'

'You're quite welcome. I apologize again if I've said anything to upset you. That certainly wasn't my intention.'

'No, of course not. You haven't upset me at all, Mr Tillyard. I'm just going to lie down in my tent for a while. I can feel a headache coming on and I think I need a little rest . . . '

We had reached the camp by this time. I stumbled inside my tent and collapsed on my luxurious bed. Bella was lying curled up on hers, reading a book, but she looked up as I came in.

'Hello. Gosh, what's the matter? You look as white as a sheet.'

'I'm just a bit tired. It was hotter in the tunnels than I realized,' I said, fanning myself with a sheaf of papers.

'Yes, I'm not surprised you're tired. You've been in there all day. Uncle George and I went up the Valley a little way this afternoon. There was a group of French people visiting . . . '

She chattered on about her afternoon and all I had to do was say 'yes' and 'no' occasionally. I still couldn't believe what Mr Tillyard had told me. It seemed inconceivable that Alice had been the one who had been behind the museum's distrust of our work. I knew I was jealous of her relationship with Adam but even I found it hard to believe that she was capable of this. And besides, if it was true that she had thought Papa was misusing the funds, why was she here now, helping us to find the tomb? My head really did start throbbing at this point.

'Kate darling, are you sure you're all right?' said Bella, realizing that I wasn't listening to a word she was saying. 'You really do look white, you know.'

'I'm fine. Really. We made quite an exciting discovery in the tunnel today and I expect that's taken more out of me than I realized.'

Well, it was half-true. Bella sat up, her face beaming with pleasure.

'Really? Oh how lovely, Kate. I am glad. After all this time . . . '

She began asking me all sorts of questions about the tunnel. As I answered I began to focus more on the reason for our being here in the first place and less on the confusion of ideas that had been whirling around in my mind. By the time the dinner gong had sounded I was already much more composed.

★ ★ ★

Dinner that night was a strange affair. Because we were two down there was much more space at the table and at first it seemed odd without Alice and Adam. But it was hardly quieter. Sir George was chattier than usual, laughing and joking with Mr Tillyard and almost giddy, although I realize that that seems an odd word to use to describe a fifty-six-year-old retired businessman. Mr Tillyard, too, seemed less restrained, as though the absence of Adam and Alice released him in some way from always watching his words. It had never occurred to me before, but of course they were both his seniors on the Board. Naturally, now that they were no longer present he would be feeling more at ease.

At about ten o'clock Mr Tillyard and Sir George got up from the table, Sir George swaying ever so slightly. We had all drunk more than usual and as the two men left, amidst much laughter, I got the impression they were having their own private little joke.

'Goodnight, m'dears,' said Sir George, as he and Mr Tillyard disappeared towards the

224

hill near the entrance to the tomb where the guard duty had come to be based.

'They both seem very jolly this evening,' I remarked, as we got up and walked back to our tent. The cook had given us little cakes called *basbousa* and *Uum Ali* still warm from the oven and fragrant with cinnamon and honey. We nibbled at these as we strolled through the camp, stepping round the flickering fires and stopping to listen occasionally to the music from the many lutes and tambourines the Egyptians had brought with them. The night air was balmy with the smell of incense and saffron, and the wine we had drunk at dinner had made both of us drowsy.

'I know. We all were a bit, don't you think?' said Bella. 'As though we were children who've been given permission to play away from the grown-ups.'

'I thought that too. Poor Alice and Adam. How they'd hate to think they were spoiling anyone's fun.'

'Well, this is their job. For me and Uncle George it's just a jaunt and a way of escaping from Aunt Augusta for a few weeks.' She looked at me and grinned. 'Kate, you didn't think Uncle George was really that interested in old mummies and tombs, did you?'

'Yes, I did as a matter of fact. Sir George and I had a very interesting talk about cartouches the other day.'

'Hmm. Uncle George is a bit intimidated by you as well as by Adam.'

'By me!'

'Yes, but don't say anything, will you? He's a bit embarrassed at being surrounded by young whippersnappers who know more about all this stuff than he does, poor love. That's why he keeps going out with Adam and Mr Tillyard on those wretched night-watches, because he doesn't want to feel that he's a complete old duffer. I wish he wouldn't.'

'Oh,' I said. I couldn't really think of anything else to say. The thought that Sir George was intimidated by me was a new idea to say the least. We were silent for several minutes as we undressed.

'We do love Aunt Augusta, you know,' added Bella after a while. 'She means well and she'd never ask anyone to do anything she wouldn't do herself. It's just that . . . you need a break from her sometimes.'

She sounded so earnest that I couldn't stop myself from smiling, but I nodded gravely so as not to upset her. We got into bed and talked some more, but our conversation was muted. Soon we were both fast asleep.

★ ★ ★

When I woke up next morning my mouth felt dry and sticky and as soon as I stuck my head out of the tent I knew it was much later than when I usually woke up. I found the water jug by my bed and took a few mouthfuls. I felt as though I'd had the deepest sleep imaginable. Usually I'm a very light sleeper and the sound of the first servant moving around in the morning is enough to rouse me. But not today. I dressed and was just picking up my notebook and tools and preparing to leave when Bella began stirring.

'What time is it?' she asked blearily. I looked at the watch pinned to my blouse.

'Just gone nine o'clock.'

'What? Really?'

'Yes. I think we both must have drunk more than we realized last night. And I was very tired after all the work I did in the tunnels yesterday. Anyway, I'd better go. I want to get started again on that wall text. Why don't you come and see it today? I promise you, no bats, rats or snakes.'

She yawned. 'Let me have some breakfast and see how Uncle George is and then I'll come up.'

I left her in the tent and after a brief conversation with Ruby, who made me breakfast, I climbed up the short, dusty slope to the entrance to the tunnel. I lit a lamp and began the long walk down the passageway, nodding and murmuring 'Good morning' to the workers as I passed them. I could just see Mr Tillyard in the gloom.

'Hello!' I called. 'How's it going?'

He looked up and smiled as he saw me but said nothing until I was right up close to him. His face and spectacles were smudged with dirt and the long white coat he wore to protect his clothes was also smeared with the red soil of the desert.

'Hello. Did you sleep well?'

I pursed my lips in mock indignation.

'All right, Mr Tillyard. I know I've overslept and you've been hard at work. I do beg your pardon.'

'Oh . . . I didn't . . . I mean . . . '

He seemed so anxious at the idea that he had caused offence that I couldn't help laughing as I knelt down beside him to examine his work.

'I'm sorry, Mr Tillyard. I was teasing you.'

'Oh.'

He stopped what he was doing and took his spectacles off to polish them. I had noticed that he did this a lot when he was agitated. It was rather charming somehow.

'You'll have to forgive me, Miss Whitaker. I'm not used to young ladies teasing me.'

'Duly granted,' I said. 'So. How are we doing?'

'Well, I've tried to continue the work you were doing last night on this wall, but the text seems to be less and less clear the more I uncover it. Or perhaps I simply don't have your light touch, Look.'

I settled down beside him, placed the lantern in the best spot to give myself the maximum amount of light and began chipping away at the clay. He was right. The figures, which last night had seemed so fresh and intact, were breaking down fast as more of the wall was uncovered. I pared and cleaned the dirt away as lightly as I could. Ahead of us, the workers were still moving forward, pushing further into the tunnel. After watching me for a few minutes, Mr Tillyard said:

'Miss Whitaker, may I ask you something?'

'Of course.' I blew a drop of sweat from my nose.

'Do you still believe you'll find the Scarlet Queen.'

I chipped away slowly, trying to ignore the flickering lights and the humidity which was making my blouse stick to my rib-cage.

'To be honest, Mr Tillyard, no. And I don't think Papa does any more. There was absolutely nothing about either her or the

Beloved on the last piece of text we found. I think she's just a lovely story, myself, although Papa still sometimes insists she was real. But even he's come round to thinking that if she or the Beloved ever did exist, then the Beloved was disgraced in some way and the Scarlet Queen was dismantled at the same time.'

'Do you still think the Beloved was a woman?' Mr Tillyard said.

'Why not? Doesn't it seem the most likely explanation? Khaemwaset sets his sights on a beautiful woman, she betrays him and in a fit of jealousy he has all mention of her removed.'

'Alas, she wouldn't be the first faithless woman.'

I sat back on my heels, looking at him curiously.

'I beg your pardon. Have I said something inappropriate?' he asked as he continued chipping away.

I began working again. 'No,' I said slowly. 'But it just occurred to me that men and women probably have completely different views on this, though. You immediately side with the man, assuming that the Beloved is some faithless minx who doesn't deserve to have an eternal resting-place alongside her lord.'

He smiled. 'Well, I wouldn't quite say that. But how do you see her, then?'

'Well, being a woman myself, I naturally take her side. It seems to me more likely that Khaemwaset saw her, decided he liked her and made a deal with her father. The poor girl probably had no say in the matter. Why shouldn't she fall in love with someone of her own choosing?'

'Because if she was a royal wife, she didn't have that luxury.'

'Exactly. That still doesn't make her faithless, though. Just trapped in a one-sided love affair and denied the right to live as she chose.'

'So you think she was executed, then?'

Again I stopped scraping the wall.

'Actually I'd never really thought about it so deeply before. But probably, yes.'

'Hmm.' He wiped a layer of dust from his cheek. 'Makes you wonder what we'll eventually find then, doesn't it.'

I grimaced. 'Ugh. You're right. Grisly hacked-up bones — '

'A smashed skull — '

'Knives still bloodstained after all this time — '

'Want to stop?'

'Absolutely not. Do you?'

'Of course not.'

We both laughed and continued in our work in companionable silence for a while, until we heard the sound of people coming down the passageway.

'Yoo-hoo, Kate, here we are!'

I immediately recognized Bella's voice and looked up to see a white-robed Egyptian slowly leading three other Europeans forward, his face in the lamplight clearly displaying the weary patience of a person unused to dealing with such decadent creatures. Behind Bella, I caught sight of Sir George, then grinned as I recognized the third figure.

'Hello, darling,' said Bella with a mischievous grin on her face. 'Look who turned up this morning.'

'Good day to you, Miss Whitaker,' said Peter Bennett.

'Peter, how are you?' I said, warmly. 'You've come at a very exciting moment.'

'Yes, that's what Miss Wyndham-Brown was telling me,' said Peter, tripping slightly on the muddy track.

'Oh, and I thought you weren't listening to me, Mr Bennett. You seemed so distracted on the way in here.'

Poor Peter almost whimpered at the thought that his goddess believed he was ignoring her, but luckily nobody else

232

was paying him any attention.

'By Jove, some of these pictures are quite gruesome, aren't they, Bella dear,' Sir George said, holding up his lantern and gazing intently at the walls. 'What's this fellow up to?'

'That's the ceremony called the Opening of the Mouth. Could I prevail upon you not to hold your lantern quite so close to the images, Sir George?' I asked. 'After so many years in the dark, bright light affects them adversely.'

'What? Oh, of course. Sorry.' He hastily pulled the lantern away.

'I don't know how you can bear to be cramped up in here all day, Kate,' said Bella with a shudder. 'It's so dark and — and — well, just horrible. I feel quite nauseated.'

I shrugged, looking round the tiny space with its slimy walls. I was so used to working in an environment like this that I never gave it any thought, but I knew many people were claustrophobic. It was just lucky that I wasn't.

'Well, why don't you come further down the tunnel and see what we've uncovered so far,' said Mr Tillyard. 'That might persuade you to see it in a different light, Miss Wyndham-Brown. Miss Whitaker, perhaps you and Mr Bennett could come last with the

233

lanterns. That's the way, Miss Wyndham-Brown, take no notice of the beetles, they won't harm you.'

Bella didn't look too happy as she stepped over the insects, but she followed him nevertheless. Mr Tillyard was a very skilful guide, describing the dig so far and pointing out any pictures of interest. He was also very adept at ending the tour rapidly without seeming to want to get rid of our guests. At last we returned to the place where they had met us.

'And is this the latest discovery, Miss Whitaker?' Peter asked. He stared intently at the text, making sure he held the lantern away from it. Whenever he forgot that Bella was around he was amazingly competent. I just wished Bella saw him like this more often.

'Yes, and I'm really quite hopeful that it will eventually show that we are in a royal tomb.'

'Hm.' He stared closely at it. 'It's not in very good condition. What did you do, Kate? Scrub with a wire brush?'

He was smiling as he said this, but his words unfortunately could well have been justified. While Mr Tillyard was pointing out different inscriptions on the walls to Bella and Sir George, I moved closer to Peter and we both examined the sadly fading texts.

'I hadn't noticed it before, but now that you mention it, Peter, it *does* look scratched, doesn't it?'

'Well, I suppose it's been in here, covered in mud and dirt, for thousands of years. You'd probably not be at your best under those conditions either.' He squinted at the images for a few more minutes, trying to get his lantern as close to them as possible without damaging them. Then he turned back to me.

'Well, I think I'd better be getting back to work, Miss Whitaker. I don't want to take up any more of your time.'

'Oh, are you leaving, Mr Bennett? We were looking forward to your staying for lunch, weren't we, Kate?'

Even in the gloom I could see Peter's face light up at the thought of Bella inviting him to lunch. But only for a second. Then duty must have reared its ugly head, because he looked suddenly miserable.

'That's very kind of you, Miss Wyndham-Brown, but I'm afraid I really must go.'

'Oh well, another time, perhaps,' said Bella carelessly. Sometimes I just wanted to kick her.

'Do you really have to go?' I said. 'Surely another hour won't matter?'

'Thanks, Kate,' said Peter, his eyes

235

following Bella hungrily as she and Sir George began walking back the way they'd come. 'But I really must get back.'

'If you insist,' I said, but already they were disappearing up ahead into the harsh sunlight.

I decided to stay a little while longer, in the vain hope that I might be able to uncover the rest of the images, but by the time Mr Tillyard returned from seeing Peter off, I knew I was wasting my time. The text had seemed so promising, but no matter how gentle I was the characters seemed to be almost vanishing before my eyes. In the end I sighed and sat back, leaning against the wall.

'This is no good, Mr Tillyard. We aren't getting anywhere. Whatever was under here is lost for good.'

Mr Tillyard wiped his forehead and sank down beside me. 'I think you're right. What a pity.' He handed me the water bottle and I took a few sips despondently. 'And it seemed so encouraging yesterday.'

I shrugged. 'Unfortunately our work is like that sometimes. Just when you think you've uncovered a treasure trove, it peters out to nothing. Papa and I are quite used to it,' I added but I must have sounded forlorn because he smiled and patted my hand.

'Now, now, my dear, you're just tired.

We've had a busy morning and, as you say, I don't think there's anything more we can do here today. Why don't we have some lunch and spend the rest of the day examining what texts we have got? I don't know about you, but I can't help thinking there must be more to those earlier scripts on the walls than we first thought.'

The artist Mr Tillyard had brought with him had already copied most of the texts from the tomb entrance and we spent the afternoon in the shade of some fig trees, trying to figure out exactly how important the person in the pictures was. He seemed to be a significant personage, but that still didn't make him a king and, more specifically, it didn't make him Khaemwaset. At last I sat back in my chair with a sigh.

'I need a break, Mr Tillyard. Dinner will be announced soon and I really must go and change.'

Mr Tillyard sat back too, rubbing his eyes from the strain of examining the tiniest detail in the pictures the artist had done. He nodded wearily.

'Yes, of course. I need a rest too. It's a pity Dr Ellis isn't here. Did he tell you how long he would be away for?'

'He said two days at the most, so I'm expecting them both back tomorrow.' I stood up and pressed my fingers into the small of my back, trying to smoothe out the aches. 'I'm afraid you'll have to excuse me, Mr Tillyard.'

'Of course, my dear.'

I left him under the trees and went in search of Ruby. She was hard at work beating clean the bedouin rugs from Alice's tent and was more than happy to stop. I prevailed on her to bring as much hot water as she could to my tent and I frittered away an hour pampering myself and wishing I was in a *hamman* (bathhouse) being scrubbed and cleaned by the expert masseuses.

For once, I was on time for dinner. The meal was less hysterically jolly than it had been last night; we all seemed to have private thoughts on our minds, but the evening passed pleasantly enough. Mr Tillyard and Sir George left before we did again, and soon after that Bella and I went to bed.

I felt bone-weary after another hard day's physical work, as well as the emotional whirlpool I had experienced, but there was something nagging at the corner of my mind. Although I just couldn't work out what it was, it niggled away at me, refusing to give me any peace. It was a long time before I fell asleep.

★ ★ ★

I woke up with a start. Something had jerked me into consciousness, but with the fogginess of sleep I couldn't be sure what it was. As I listened in the darkness, I suddenly heard it again, a low, shrill wailing that sent shivers down my spine. Beside me, Bella sat up suddenly.

'What was that?'

'I don't know. It sounds dreadful.' I got out of bed and pulled a coat on over my nightdress.

'Surely you're not going out there?'

'I certainly am,' I said, struggling to pull my boots on. Then I realized that I would waste precious minutes having to lace the wretched things up, so I just pulled them off and threw them to the side of my bed.

'But it's so dark!'

'Then I'll take a lamp,' I said firmly. 'It sounds like someone's in trouble and I want know what's going on.'

'Wait for me then.' She leapt out of bed herself and pulled on a frilly pink négligé. Even in the excitement of the moment I couldn't help being amazed at the incredible number of frivolous clothes Bella owned.

I pulled aside the tent-flap and we crept out into the night, Bella holding tightly on to my arm as we moved slowly away from the campsite towards the entrance of the tomb, from where the noise seemed to have come. The moon was full and bright, spreading a milky-blue glow around the rocks, making them look eerie and surreal. I held the lantern up higher.

'Hello?' I said, hoping I was the only one who noticed how shaky my voice was. 'Is anybody there?'

Silence. We waited, the chill night wind blowing our nightdresses around our ankles.

'Come on,' said Bella finally. 'There's no one . . .'

Suddenly, out of the corner of my eye, I saw a bright flash of red shoot past.

'Who's there?' I shouted, more forcefully this time. Without waiting for an answer, I let go of Bella, picked up the skirts of my nightdress and ran full pelt after the figure.

'Come back,' I shouted, sprinting past the tomb entrances and out towards the desert. But the only reply I got was from my own echoes and eventually I had to stop. I held the lantern up again, trying to see into the inky-black crevices of the desert, but nothing moved.

'What happened? Did you find anything? What did you see?'

Bella had appeared behind me, panting. As she struggled to regain her breath I scanned the area around us.

'I thought I saw someone. I was certain I did. They came this way.' I lowered the lantern, my arm starting to ache. 'I don't know, I must have been mistaken. It was probably just — '

Bella screamed. It was highest, loudest, most piercing scream I have ever heard and for a second I was so mesmerized by it that I almost missed what she was pointing at. Then I saw it too.

In the distance, about twenty yards away, stood a tall, redswathed figure. There was an unearthly red glow emanating from its middle. I dropped my lantern, my hands flying to my mouth in horror. Bella just kept screaming and screaming. Then the figure seemed to move slightly to its left and just vanish.

'The ghost! The ghost!' Bella wailed, managing to find her voice. 'It's the Red Woman!'

I wanted to contradict her, to tell her not to be so silly. But I couldn't ignore the evidence of my own eyes. I found myself starting to feel dizzy and light-headed and I clenched my fists as hard as I could.

'Listen Bella, that's rubbish and you know it. There's no such thing as ghosts and we — '

'Are you mad? You saw it. Are you trying to tell me you didn't see that — that — thing glowing in the distance? Are you . . . ?'

She was angry now, but at least she wasn't screaming any more. I caught her wrists and forced her to stop talking and listen to me.

'Bella, whatever it was, I guarantee we'll find — '

I got no further. Suddenly there was another loud piercing scream, resonant with agony this time. It was coming from the campsite and people were appearing out of their tents, woken up by all the commotion.

Bella and I took one look at each other and raced back to the campsite. There appeared to be a large crowd around our tent, which struck me as ridiculous because nobody was in there. Everybody was talking at once and because they were all Egyptians they were speaking in Arabic and Bella couldn't understand what they were saying.

But I could. I pushed and shoved my way past the crowd around our tent-opening, praying that they were mistaken or that I had misunderstood them. But there was no mistake. Lying there on the floor at the foot of my bed was Sir George, his face a deathly white, his breathing laboured and rasping. I gasped and knelt down beside him.

That was when I saw it. Just under his foot, now crushed and harmless was the desert scorpion that had stung him.

10

At first I thought Sir George was dead, but then I saw his chest move very slightly. Two of the servants picked him up off the ground and laid him down on my bed. Although it was still dark, the campsite had suddenly come to life, people shouting at each other and running around in panic. As I held on to Bella, trying to keep her calm, Mr Tillyard appeared at my elbow.

'What on earth's going on?' he said. 'I'd just taken over from Sir George when I heard the most dreadful noise by the tunnels. But there was nothing there.' He stopped suddenly, seeing Sir George. 'What happened?'

'Sir George was stung by a scorpion. Bella and I heard the same noise as you and we went out to look as well. When we came back we found him here.'

'Good Lord, is he all right? He looks very pale . . . ' he tailed off as I shook my head and glanced towards Bella.

'I'm sure he'll be fine,' I said with more conviction than I actually felt. But before I could say any more, a couple of servants returned to our tent with a steaming poultice of leaves, smelling strongly of coriander, which the Egyptians believed would cure scorpion-stings.

With Ruby to help us, Bella and I did our best to make her uncle as comfortable as possible. In concentrating on trying to cool his fever to keep him safe during the two terrifying convulsions he had, the time went very quickly. At six o'clock, as the sun began to rise, I knew there was no more we could do for him here and his best chance of survival was to return as quickly as possible to Luxor. So, leaving Ruby and Bella, I went outside to speak to Mr Tillyard. I had been so busy I hadn't noticed the activity outside our tent and had barely listened to Karima's nervous chatter whenever she appeared with another poultice, but now I realized that something was very wrong.

'What's going on, Mr Tillyard?' I asked, having spotted him over by the cooking-tent, where he seemed to be having a one-sided conversation in pidgin English with the cook, who ignored him except to glance at him with contempt every now and again. No one was doing any cooking. They were too busy bringing the tent down.

'I don't know, Miss Whitaker. I've been trying to get this chap to tell me what he's doing but no one's talking to me. They just keep packing things up.

I snapped a few questions at the cook. Although he looked a little more sheepish he remained resolute and I felt my heart sink.

'They know about the Red Woman. We couldn't have been the only ones who saw her.'

'What? Who? What are you talking about?'

'The Red Woman. Remember what I said earlier? Bella and I heard the same noise as you and when we went to investigate we saw the Red Woman.'

'You saw a ghost?' Mr Tillyard stared at me as though I'd gone mad.

'No, of course not,' I said. I had no intention of surrendering to foolish fancies. 'We saw someone dressed up and pretending to be her. Whoever did it the first night must have been scared off by the night-patrols at first, but they've obviously become bolder over the last few days.'

He nodded. 'Of course.'

'Anyway, the servants have heard about it and of course that's it as far as they're concerned. Sir George's accident hasn't helped, either. Apparently some of them are now convinced that we've angered the spirits and that they're responsible for the scorpion attack. Anyway, I've got to get Sir George

245

back to Luxor. I came to ask you to remain here until I return.'

'Of course. Whatever I can do to help.'

Just then I saw Ahmed arriving. I explained everything to him as quickly as I could and he agreed to come with me down to the river to find a boat, for which I was profoundly grateful. The Nile fishermen might not have paid any attention to a lone *khawaga* woman, but I knew that with Ahmed next to me we would have no trouble in finding a felucca for hire.

'By the way,' he said as we reached the river, 'the men have heard about the ghost from your servants and some of them have refused to work here any more. The ones who stay will want more money.'

I nodded. I didn't care how much we had to pay the workmen now. Somehow I knew we were coming to the end of this long journey to find Khaemwaset and I would not allow anything to set us back.

★   ★   ★

Bella sat shivering in the early morning light. Her face had lost its youthful, rosy plumpness and she looked pale and drawn. Her hands kept patting fitfully at Sir George's covers as though by pushing the blankets up further around his face she could make him better. We sat and waited for the sun to creep higher above the horizon. Sir George looked terrible. His face seemed to have collapsed in on itself somehow and several times I thought he was actually dead.

At last the fisherman whose boat we had hired gave the signal to embark.

'Everything will be all right, Bella,' I said as cheerfully as I could as she prepared to climb on to the boat. 'If the scorpion that stung Sir George had been one of the really venomous ones he'd be dead by now.'

'Do you think so?' she asked, desperation in her voice.

'I know so. Believe me, scorpions that kill don't let their victims linger for this long.'

I patted her hand reassuringly as she got on board and tried not to think about how old Sir George was. He just looked so ill.

'Hurry up, Ruby,' I said. She was lingering on the riverbank and I wanted Sir George and Bella away back to Luxor as quickly as possible. But Ruby just shook her head mutinously.

'I'm staying 'ere, Miss Katie. Lady Faulkner would be 'orrified if I left you alone.'

'Don't be silly, Ruby,' I said. 'Miss Bella needs help with Sir George and — '

'It's all right, Kate,' said Bella from the boat. 'Ruby and I have already decided you need her more than I do. Lord knows, *I* wouldn't leave you if it weren't for poor Uncle George . . . ' she trailed off as she looked at him again.

'Ruby,' I said sternly. 'This really isn't a good idea. You must get — '

'Miss Kate,' Ruby interrupted. ''Ow's it going ter look, a young lady all on 'er own back at that there camp full of men? If you're stayin', I'm stayin',' she ended firmly, a stubborn look on her face and I knew I was beaten. To be honest, I wasn't that sorry.

'Very well.' I nodded. Then, having made sure that all the other servants knew what to do with the equipment, Ruby and I climbed back on the donkeys that had carried us down to the riverbank and returned to the Tomb of the Nobles with only one servant left to escort us. It was a silent, cheerless ride back to the camp.

★   ★   ★

By the time we returned it was late afternoon and we were both hungry and thirsty, as well as exhausted by the events of the previous night. So, after a hasty meal scavenged from the now vastly reduced cooking area, we went

248

to lie down in the tent Bella and I had so recently shared. Ruby was a little unsure about this at first, but I was too tired to brook much argument from her. After I had pointed out that, since the whole purpose of her being there was to protect my reputation, the best place for her to be was with me, she soon gave in. I think, like Goldilocks, she rather wanted to try out Bella's bed anyway. We slept solidly for the rest of the afternoon.

It was getting dark when I eventually stumbled out of the tent. I could hear voices and knew that Mr Tillyard and the workmen had finished for the day. Our little campsite was now much depleted but it was still a lot bigger than anything Papa and I were used to. I made my way to the fire where a rough meal was being cooked.

'Miss Whitaker! What in God's name are you doing here?'

Mr Tillyard looked horrified to see me. His face went white and for a moment I thought he was going to faint.

'I want some dinner,' I said briskly. 'Just because we're not going to be dining off silverware any longer doesn't mean I'm not hungry.'

'But — but I thought you were going back with Miss Wyndham-Brown.'

'Only as far as the river. I got Ahmed to take her across.'

'But you can't possibly stay here.'

'Why not?'

I stirred the brown sludgy stuff at the bottom of the cooking-pot Mr Tillyard and his few remaining English employees, the artist and the secretaries, might be experts at their jobs, but they obviously knew nothing about cooking.

'Because . . . ' he glanced across at the three young men who were watching me with interest and then pulled me to one side. 'Miss Whitaker, don't you realize you're the only woman here now? Think of your reputation.'

I snorted. 'If I ever thought of my reputation, I'd be a poor, downtrodden governess living a wretched existence in somewhere dull like — like Eastbourne.' I'd never been to Eastbourne and for all I know it might be an extremely pleasant place, but it was the only English town I could think of on the spur of the moment.

'Quite, quite,' he said distractedly. 'But the point is — '

'The point is, Mr Tillyard, I have absolutely no intention of leaving here until we have completed our task. I've no doubt Adam and Alice will be back tomorrow anyway. Luxor is a small town as far as the English are concerned and I'm sure they will have heard about poor Sir George already.'

'But — '

'Besides, I'm not the only woman here. Ruby came back with me,' I pointed out as she came across and stood next to me, the stubborn expression back on her face. Not for the first time I was glad of her presence.

Mr Tillyard studied Ruby briefly, before turning back to me.

'Miss Whitaker, I hardly think a child — '

I could see Ruby's expression turning into a scowl and I struggled to keep a straight face.

'Ruby is seventeen, Mr Tillyard. Besides, there's nothing to be done tonight. It's too late to go back now.'

'I'm most disturbed by this, Miss Whitaker,' he said, frowning. 'But as you say there's nothing to be done tonight. But I really must insist that unless Lady Faulkner and Dr Ellis arrive tomorrow, you return to Luxor. I cannot allow you to remain here otherwise. Don't you realize how dangerous it's become here? Apart from any other considerations, I don't feel I can protect you.'

'I'll be fine, Mr Tillyard. And as for tomorrow . . . ' I stopped. Suddenly there was a sound of thundering hoofs coming from the direction of the Nile and we all turned and looked.

A group of horses was thundering up the primitive track, dust swirling around them, the long white robes of the riders flying out behind them like huge wings. As they reached us the leader of the group pulled back the cloth protecting his face from the desert dust.

''Ammi,' I said, bowing respectfully. Ahmed jumped down from his horse and the others followed, one of them taking his reins.

'Miss Katie. The old man is still alive or at least he was when I left him at the port. I've brought my sons back with me' — he gestured at the crowd behind him and there was a wave of bowing and murmurs of *assalamu aleikum* from six equally tall men — 'and two of my sisters.'

Behind the men were two women wearing *niqabs*, the full-length robe that covered the entire head and left only a slit for the eyes to see through.

'Thank you, 'Ammi,' I said.

Mr Tillyard, meanwhile, was looking at the group in amazement. 'What's he doing here?' he asked, staring at the crowd of white-robed figures. 'And who are all these people?'

'These are Ahmed's sons. I asked him to come back,' I replied, unable to stifle a smile at the baffled look on his face. 'I'm not

252

completely stupid or blind to my position, Mr Tillyard, despite what people might think. I'm aware that the situation has changed considerably in the last few hours and I certainly don't intend to stay here without protection.'

'Quite.' Mr Tillyard had taken his spectacles off by now and was polishing them in great agitation. 'Of course. Well done. But aren't they frightened of the ghost?'

I smiled. Nothing on God's earth frightened Ahmed or his sons, but before I could say anything, Ahmed roared with laughter. He spoke English perfectly well, being a refined and educated man. But, like Papa, he was contemptuous of foreigners who were so ill-mannered that they did not bother to learn the language of their hosts. Unless business was involved, he rarely engaged in conversation with them.

'Hah!' he snorted, walking back to the horses and helping his two sisters down. 'Tell this unbeliever we're not children! There are no ghosts here. There are only men who lust after riches. I'll give you two nights. If your menfolk have not returned by then, I'll take you back to Luxor myself.'

'Thank you, 'Ammi,' I said. 'And thank you for bringing your sisters. I hope we're not inconveniencing you too much.'

He grunted at this, as he began to unsaddle his horse.

'Two nights I can spare. And my sisters are both widowed and their children full-grown. They agreed that even an infidel woman should not be shamed by being left alone in the desert with no one to protect her reputation except a servant.' He walked off to settle the horse and I pulled my shawl about my shoulders, feeling a lot less nervous now that he and his sons were with us. Also, I was grateful that Ruby couldn't speak Arabic. Being spoken of so dismissively twice in one evening would have been hard for anyone, even an East End lady's maid.

★ ★ ★

Later, after we had eaten, I sat with Mr Tillyard for a while.

'How did the work go today?'

'Not so good.' He took his spectacles off and began polishing them. His face looked tired. 'We only had about half the number of workmen we usually have. I think they must have heard about the ghost.'

'That's right.' I told him what Ahmed had said earlier in this morning. He tutted several times and said 'Oh dear' twice. Then he leaned over and took my hand.

'Miss Whitaker, may I just say how much I admire you?'

I smiled faintly. 'You may certainly say it, Mr Tillyard. One can never have too many compliments. But I don't know what I've done to deserve it.'

'Really? One so young as you and yet even in the midst of such chaos you've organized the situation so deftly. I don't think I know half a dozen men who would have been so level-headed as you in this crisis.'

I flinched at the word 'crisis'. Certainly everything seemed to be going wrong. Papa's illness, that wretched ghost story, poor Sir George — but even so, even amidst all this gloom and misfortune I couldn't help feeling that some good was going to come of it in the end. I remembered Papa's words on the day we'd heard that the museum was sending Adam out here. He had refused to give in to depression. *I know the tomb is there, Kate. I know it!* And despite all our present woes, I understood at last why he had felt like that. Because I felt like that too. I stood up.

'You're very kind to say so, Mr Tillyard, but I'm simply doing what Papa would have done under the same circumstances. He trained me very well, you see. And now you'll have to excuse me. I'm exhausted. Goodnight, Mr Tillyard.'

'Of course. Goodnight, Kate.'

He stood up too, and as I left he took my hand and kissed it gently, reminding me of that first day we met. I gave him one last smile and walked over to my tent. Then I saw Ahmed and his sons sitting by their own fire, a *sheesha* passing between them. I walked across to them, and bowed to Ahmed, enjoying the familiar, distinctive smell of the tobacco mixed with molasses.

'*Assalaamu aleikum,* 'Ammi.'

'Miss Katie.' He wasn't looking directly at me, but over to where Mr Tillyard and I had been sitting. I got the impression he had seen Mr Tillyard's rather quaint gesture and hadn't approved of it.

'I really am grateful for you being here, 'Ammi. Thank you again.'

He grunted. 'I've sent my sisters to sleep in your tent. You should go too, Miss Katie. Your servant is annoying them.'

I grinned. I could just imagine how Ruby was taking to the idea of sharing a tent with a couple of exotic Egyptian women.

'Of course. Good night, 'Ammi.'

When I got to the tent Ahmed's two sisters had unrolled their sleeping-mats on the floor and were chattering away in Arabic, teasing poor Ruby who, of course, couldn't understand a word they were saying. They had also lighted an incense-stick and the heavy, sweet, pungent resin hung in the air.

'Miss Kate,' she gasped in relief as I slipped through the canvas and laced up the flaps. 'These two — creatures came in before I could stop them and they won't leave. An' the smell! An' they've taken their robe-fings orf too. Look at 'em!'

I suppressed a smile. Like all strict Muslim women Nawal and Huda wore the niqabs in public, but they had both married into wealthy families and in private they indulged their taste for expensive clothes. It didn't surprise me that Ruby was scandalized by their attire. Although they were respectably, and even modestly dressed, Egyptian fashions for women were definitely more exotic than the average lady's maid would be used to and I could see that Ruby was mesmerized by the lavishly beaded blouses and sequinned skirts in the sheerest silks. The gorgeous colours were breathtaking too: purple and aquamarine and turquoise; and since jewellery was a sign of wealth, Nawal and Huda were positively weighed down with heavy gold necklaces, rings and charms, their arms and wrists jingling with silver bracelets inlaid with dark-green emeralds and delicate pearls.

'It's all right, Ruby,' I said soothingly.

'*Es-sitt* Nawal and her sister Huda are staying with us tonight. It's an Egyptian custom,' I added. 'You didn't like the idea of my being alone here and neither do they. Now do get into bed, there's a good girl.'

Ruby muttered and grumbled under her breath but I don't think she was really sorry to see the two older women with us. She climbed slowly into Bella's bed.

'Why is this rude girl waving her hands at us so contemptuously, my heart?' asked Nawal. 'She is your servant, is she not? Does she have no manners?'

'Erm, Ruby was just a bit confused,' I lied. 'She thought you should be sleeping in the beds, as you are our elders.'

'Ah!' Both women nodded their heads, accepting the explanation instantly. I knew neither of them would have wanted to take the camp-beds, seeing them as hopelessly uncomfortable European contraptions, but the protocol would have been easily under-stood.

I undressed quickly and got into my bed, grateful for all these distractions. But as I drifted off I had that same feeling that I'd had the night before, as though there was something I should have done but hadn't. I still couldn't shake it off or remember what it was. Eventually sleep overtook me.

The next morning we started work early. I was determined not to let all the setbacks of the last few days delay us any longer. Mr Tillyard was right: only about half the number of workmen we usually had came to work that day, but we made the best of it and by lunchtime we found a section of wall which had more wonderful pictures of the funeral procession. This time they didn't crumble into dust at the slightest touch and once again I began to hope that our burial chamber might be the tomb of a king, after all.

After a hasty and rather meagre lunch which consisted mainly of figs and tinned corned beef, Mr Tillyard went back to work, but I had decided to write up a report for Papa while the details were still fresh in my head. I had just finished and was about to go back to the tunnel when I saw another dust storm of horses on the horizon. This time there was no mistaking who it was. Even from a distance I could see Adam in his white clothes. I looked for Alice, but she didn't appear to be with him.

As the group approached it was clear that Adam had brought reinforcements with him. I wondered where he had managed to get so many servants at such short notice and how he had avoided their hearing the lurid tales of ghosts and malicious scorpion spirits. But as they got nearer I realized that these were not servants, at least not the domestic kind. Adam had hired bodyguards, strong, tough mercenaries, not all of them Egyptian. As he reached the campsite, he jumped off his horse and raced up to me.

'Are you all right?' he said, taking me in his arms and pulling me up close.

'Yes, of course I am,' I said. 'Sir George was the one who was stung, not me. How is he?'

'He's fine.' Adam still had a tight hold on me and he seemed to be examining me, checking me over as though I were some kind of valuable horse which might be injured. 'At least, he was when I left this morning. The doctor seemed to think the sting was from a fairly harmless type of scorpion, and he was mainly suffering from side effects. What happened here?'

'Nothing. Sir George just stepped on it by accident, that's all. What side effects?'

Adam let me go. We were near the kitchen tent and he picked up a bottle of water, poured some into a glass, and swallowed it down in huge gulps. His face was smudged with the dust from the desert ride.

'He's an old man,' he said irritably, as though this were somehow my fault. 'The doctor said he was also suffering from mild heatstroke and exhaustion, which didn't help. And don't tell me nothing happened out here, Kate. All the servants have gone and none of them will return no matter how much money I offer them.'

'Adam, I have no intention of pretending nothing happened out here. Bella and I heard a noise and went out to investigate and — '

'Yes, so I hear. Didn't it occur to you how dangerous it was, going out on your own in the dark?'

'What would you expect me to do? Lie shivering in my bed like a child frightened by tales of ghosts?'

'I would have expected you to behave sensibly and go and get help. And as for that rubbish about ghosts, you knew perfectly well there was a good chance tomb-robbers had heard about the burial chamber. For God's sake, Kate, you were the one who said there should be a guard posted every night. Which reminds me, how the devil did this wretched ghost manage to get away without being captured?'

'How on earth should I know, Adam?' I asked irritably. 'Mr Tillyard went to look, but then he heard Sir George — '

'Yes, where is Mr Tillyard?' Adam interrupted.

'He's in the tunnels,' I said. 'We've made some really wonderful progress since you left. The walls on the south side — '

'Stay here. I haven't finished talking to you yet.' He began to walk towards the tomb. Not liking the look on his face and knowing how intimidating he could be when he was angry, I followed him.

'Adam, I don't know what you think happened here,' I said. 'But if you think blaming Mr Tillyard for Sir George's accident is — '

Adam turned round. His face was like thunder. 'Kate, if you really like Tillyard, stay out here. I can guarantee he won't want an audience for this.'

'Adam, will you just stop and listen to me . . . ' I began, but he ignored me and disappeared into the tomb.

I gave up and went back to my tent where my notes lay in a pile on my desk. Adam was right, poor Mr Tillyard wasn't going to want an audience for the scene that was about to take place and although I felt sorry for him, if I was going to be honest there was a part of me that felt he was at least slightly to blame for this mess. He had been against the guard watches from the start, clearly feeling that we were being over-sensitive about the possibility of tomb-robbers. I didn't blame him for that; after all, if you've spent most of your working life in a nice, safe museum in London, you aren't going to be particularly alive to the very real dangers that can occur in the field. But he had obviously let Adam take the lion's share of that duty, which I did feel was a little bit remiss of him, and when Adam had left I don't think either he or Sir George had given the watches the priority that Adam had.

It had occurred to me to wonder why the ghost had managed to appear and disappear so easily. But then I wasn't exactly blameless either. I suppose, in the end, I'd thought we'd been worrying needlessly, too. Adam's attention to detail had kept us safe and when he'd left we'd thoughtlessly put ourselves in danger because we hadn't bothered to take the same precautions as he had.

I ignored the sound of the workmen coming out of the tunnels. They were very happy to be given an extra break and the eccentric behaviour of the *khawagas* was always good for entertainment. I put on my spectacles and tried to work for a bit on my report to Papa, but in the end I gave up and went outside for some fresh air.

It was eerily quiet around the campsite and the reason why wasn't hard to understand.

263

The tunnel went down a long way underground now, but it was still possible to hear muffled shouts coming from inside. Adam obviously had a lot to say and although English people might have felt it good manners to try and ignore the storm that was taking place inside the passageway, the Egyptians suffered no such inhibitions. They were all sitting near to the entrance, tiny cups of coffee in their hands, their faces aglow with interest as they listened to the shouts from within. The fact that they couldn't understand any English wasn't detracting from their enjoyment of the argument in the least. Ruby was outside Alice's tent, folding some sheets, and as I went over to her she looked at me nervously.

'What's the matter wiv Mr Adam, Miss'?' she asked. ''E looked really angry.'

'Don't worry about it, Ruby,' I soothed. 'I think he's just worried because the workmen won't come here any more. You finish your work here.'

I patted her hand and then walked back over to the tunnel entrance. Just as I was wondering whether I should go in and try to pour oil on the waters, Adam came out, looking slightly less angry now. He ignored me and walked over to where Ahmed was sitting. They talked for a while, then Ahmed

264

shouted for the men to go back into the tomb and continue working. As they slowly got up and began filing back in, I thought about going over to see Adam and Ahmed, but they were still deep in conversation, so I decided to leave them to it and go back to my notes. I thought it prudent to leave Mr Tillyard alone for a while. Arguing with Adam has a tendency to take quite a lot out of one, as I knew from personal experience.

I had been working for some time when the flap of my tent opened and Adam came in.

'I've spoken to Ahmed and he's agreed to spend another two nights here,' he said.

'Oh good. Will Alice be coming back tomorrow? Because if not I must ask Huda and Nawal to stay until she does return.'

Adam scowled. 'That won't be necessary,' he snapped.

I stared at him. 'Oh really? Why not?'

'Because you're going back to Luxor with them tomorrow.'

We glared at each other.

'Don't think you can come in here and bully me, Adam Ellis,' I said icily. 'Save that for museum employees who don't have any choice but to bow their heads to you. I am not leaving here and nothing you say is going to make me.'

'Yes you are.'

'No I'm not.'

'Kate,' he said ominously calm. 'If I have to truss you up like a Christmas turkey and throw you bodily on to the ferry, then that's what I'll do. I can't believe you were so reckless as to come back yesterday after Bella and the servants left. And to let Ruby stay too. That was about the only thing Tillyard and I agreed on just now — '

'Well, I'm so glad you found something in common at least. But I am not leaving this place until Papa's theories have — '

'Your father is beside himself with worry. Do you know how quickly the news of Sir George's accident spread? Everyone back in Luxor is talking about it. It was as much as Alice and I could do to stop him from coming out here today. She's stayed behind to reassure him and I promised you would be back tomorrow as well.'

'Well then, you shouldn't make promises you can't keep. I'll write Papa a note explaining why I can't leave just now and he'll understand . . . '

'Pack your bags tonight, Kate, if you don't want someone else doing it for you. Because I promise you, you're leaving tomorrow whether you like it or not.'

'Adam . . . '

'You're not staying and that's final. This is

not your private little playground; the concession was granted to your father by the museum and both your father and I say you're going! Now, you can either accept that with a little grace and acknowledge that we're actually doing this for your benefit, or you can sulk like a child. It's up to you, but tomorrow morning you're going back to Luxor.'

I glared at him, my mind whirling with the few options left available to me. Unfortunately, he was right. The concession to dig here was granted to Papa, not me, and in fact the entire expedition was at the moment under the authority of the Cavendish Museum, which meant, in effect, Adam. My hands were tied.

'Very well!' I spat eventually. 'I can see I've got no choice. But believe me, I'll make sure every archaeologist in this hemisphere knows that you deliberately forced me out and made sure that neither I nor Papa was present when Khaemwaset's treasure was discovered.' I began to walk away.

'Would you really be that vicious, Kate?'

I turned back again. He no longer sounded angry; in fact, he looked as though he couldn't quite believe what I had just said.

'Without a moment's thought, Adam. That's what happens when you keep slaves.

You force them to choose between truth and justice.'

'I'm not . . .'

I turned away again, holding up my hand.

'Enough! You've got your own way. Now leave me alone.'

I ran back to my tent, so angry that I could hardly contain myself. I looked at the notes on my desk and then suddenly, without even realizing what I was doing, I swept my arm across and all my papers and inkpots and pens fell to the ground with a resounding, utterly satisfying crash. It was so satisfying, in fact, that I picked up the washing-jug and bowl and threw them towards the tent-pole, where they smashed and slivers of pottery arced in all directions. Some of the pieces came perilously close to me and my brief, destructive urge gave out as quickly as it had begun. I might be hot-tempered, but I'm not stupid. I sat down on my bed, arms folded angrily, looking at the ink from the pot seeping into the groundsheet, turning the khaki colour a dull black. After what seemed like hours, I heard a timid knock on the tent-pole.

'If that's you, Adam Ellis, you can just go away. I've said everything I ever want to say to you.'

'No, it's me.'

'Mr Tillyard!'

I jumped up and pulled the canvas flaps open. Truth to tell I needed a bit of company now. I really wanted to tell someone how much I hated Adam. Who better to understand that than Mr Tillyard?

He came in, stepping carefully over the shards of ceramic and the ink-soaked papers, tactfully saying nothing about them. He was still wearing his white, dirt-stained coat and his hair had spots of powder where he been cleaning the pictures on the wall. In his hands he held a cup of Darjeeling tea. It was expensive out here and we only treated ourselves to it occasionally. I could smell the delicate fragrance as the steam wafted gently from the cup.

'I thought you might like some tea,' said Mr Tillyard, offering it to me warily, as though he expected it to be thrown back in his face. I could see him looking round at the bits of broken bowl and jug on the floor.

'Thank you,' I said, taking the cup from him. 'How are things going in the tunnel?'

'Very well, actually.' He watched me nervously for a few minutes, then must have decided that I was no longer dangerous. 'That's what I've come to tell you. We've reached some very interesting pictograms which seem to suggest a doorway and I wondered if you'd like to come and see them.'

'Is he there?'

Mr Tillyard cleared his throat and pushed hair away from his spectacles.

'Um . . . well, Dr Ellis was the first to . . . '

I leaned against the tent-pole and took a sip from the cup.

'Then I'd rather cut my throat than be in the same room as him,' I said pleasantly.

'Ah.' He perched on the edge of Bella's bed, then realized he'd sat in an ink splodge and got up very quickly. 'You know, much as I hate to see you this angry, I'd feel a terrible hypocrite if I didn't tell you I am as concerned about your safety as Dr Ellis is. I don't think — '

'Dr Ellis isn't concerned about my safety. He's just a thug and a bully who enjoys making other people dance to his tune.'

I pulled aside the tent-flaps as I spoke and I shouted the words 'thug' and 'bully' as loudly as I could, which was quite pointless really because Adam wasn't going to hear me from inside the tomb. But the mercenaries he'd brought with him were all lounging around under the shade of a makeshift shelter, talking and drinking, so I repeated my words, shouting them in Arabic this time as I shook my fist towards the entrance, which

270

made them all sit up and laugh. With any luck they'd tell Adam what I'd said at the first opportunity.

'Really, Miss Whitaker, whatever you feel about this situation, I'm sure Dr Ellis only has your best interests at heart — '

'Really, Mr Tillyard,' I interrupted rudely. 'How can you stand up for that odious man after the way he treated you this afternoon? The whole campsite heard him, you know. He comes thundering in here, blaming everyone but himself for the problems we've had. I still don't know what was so important that he had to leave when he did.'

I might have said more but at that moment Nawal and Huda glided silently into the tent, only their eyes visible through the slits in their *niqabs*. Mr Tillyard looked at them nervously. Like most Englishmen he was a little bit disconcerted by women who looked like walking tents and never made eye-contact with him.

'Yes, well, just as you say, Miss Whitaker. Are you sure you won't come with me? You know,' he added gently, 'Dr Ellis did specifically ask me to tell you about the text.'

I gave Mr Tillyard a filthy look, not at all won over by this tender message.

'Tell Dr Ellis that I would rather drown — '

'Fair enough,' he said hurriedly and began

to move towards the entrance, then looked back. 'Oh, by the way, would you think me terribly tactless if I asked you to take some accounts back to Lady Faulkner to sign and return to London when you go back to Luxor tomorrow? I forgot to ask her before she left and it should be done before the end of the month. I believe the books are still in her tent.'

I sighed. Even Mr Tillyard had taken it for granted that I would be leaving tomorrow just as Adam decreed.

'All right Mr Tillyard. I might as well be useful to someone.'

He gave me one last sympathetic smile, then went back outside.

'You should be careful of that one, Miss Katie,' Nawal said as she and her sister removed their *niqabs*. I snorted.

'The only one I have to be careful of is that — that snake in the grass out there!' I said, with as much venom as possible.

'Do you mean the one who arrived just now? The tall one with the hair the colour of honey?'

Nawal and Huda began a lazy conversation about what they would like to do with Adam if he ever converted, which shocked me a lot less than it probably should have done. I had spent a lot of my formative years in the *haramliks*, and women-only *hammans* and, amongst themselves, Muslim women are very uninhibited. However, I wasn't interested in hearing about Adam's charms just then and I was about to make an excuse and leave when Huda suddenly clicked her fingers.

'Ah! He's the one who's a thug and a bully, isn't he?' she said brightly.

'Yes. Did the men by the shelter hear that?' I asked. Both Nawal and Huda laughed.

'Everyone in the entire camp heard it, precious one. You can be sure the infidel knows about it too, now.'

'Good,' I said, then realized that they were looking at the mess I'd made when I'd thrown my inkpots and water-bowl around in my childish temper tantrum.

'Sorry,' I mumbled, stooping to help them pick up the smashed pottery. Nawal patted my cheek as she knelt on the floor, the many thin silver bracelets she wore on her wrists clinking against my fob-watch.

'That's all right, my heart. Sometimes the foolishness of men can drive a woman to distraction.'

'It never hurts to let them know one can be pushed beyond endurance. Even the infidel looked a little worried when he heard the sound of your anger,' said Huda. Before I could get too smug about that, she added:

'And you also impressed our nephews with your passion. Just as we were leaving they were discussing how they would beat you into obedience before they embraced you.'

'Oh really? Did they?' I felt my temper rising again, but Nawal just stroked my hair.

'Don't worry, sweetheart. We boxed their ears soundly on your behalf. Young men should not talk like that in front of their esteemed aunts.'

'Whether they know we're listening or not!' cackled Huda and they both dissolved into laughter and began telling jokes, all of which had men as the butt.

All in all I was in a much better temper by the time Ruby appeared with some food and told me what she could about the new discovery in the tunnel. Adam and Mr Tillyard were apparently very excited about the hieroglyphs and practically had to be dragged away as the light faded and the workers wanted to go home.

It sounded as though they had completely forgotten their quarrel and I couldn't help feeling aggrieved once more. This was the great discovery that Papa and I should be making. It really wasn't fair. We had worked so hard and gone without so much to arrive at this moment and now neither of us would be present when the burial chamber of

Khaemwaset was at last uncovered. Once more I found myself becoming angry at the cavalier way we had been treated by the museum. I resolved to make sure that every eminent archaeologist in London and Egypt knew about it.

Sleep was hard to come by that night and I did nothing but doze fitfully until the sun slowly crept over the horizon and the heat of the day began to bake the camp. I gave up. Getting dressed quietly so as not to waken Ruby, Nawal and Huda, I walked out to see if I could find some breakfast.

There wasn't much in the way of food. Since none of the servants had come back with Adam, it was clear that the men who remained here were going to be eating out of tins for the next few weeks, which I had time to feel glad about. I hoped they would be thoroughly miserable with their lot, although I doubted it. Adam never really cared about food or the trappings of luxury.

I found a few hard crackers and some slightly dry figs and I ate them, intending to go over to the tunnel and see the hieroglyphs for myself before I was bundled off home like a parcel. But then I noticed Alice's tent, still with the flaps tied over. Obviously no one had dismantled it because they expected her to return. She was Lady Faulkner after all, I remembered bitterly. Widow of the chairman of the board and herself temporary chair and major stockholder. No one was going to tell her she had to leave the campsite if she didn't want to. She knew next to nothing about archaeology or Egyptology; she much preferred to be dressed in pretty clothes and to spend her afternoons and evenings socializing and yet she managed to come back here whenever she wanted. I sighed and swallowed the last of my figs.

Just as I was about to go up to the tomb, I remembered my promise to Mr Tillyard to take the accounts books back. I decided I might as well get them first so I walked across to her tent and unlaced the knots.

Alice's tent was slightly smaller than the one Bella and I had shared, but not too much smaller and she was alone in here. Her tent was much simpler than I expected it to be, with her bed in one corner and the large luggage-chest serving as a table to one side. There was a pile of books on it and I went over to find the accounts. But as I searched through the pile, I noticed one of her reading-books was opened to a page in the middle and was marked with her distinctive mauve ink. I put my spectacles on and glanced through it. It was a book on poisons.

I had been expecting genteel books on

etiquette or flower-arranging or perhaps some educational tomes or travel guides. Books describing the use and dosage on arsenic and cyanide, with graphic descriptions of symptoms and side effects were absolutely not what I had in mind. But as I leafed through the pages worse was to come. There were two chapters that had evidently interested Alice a great deal because she had marked them by folding the corners and had then underlined several passages. One was a passage on arsenic which described how small enough doses could often be misdiagnosed as an attack of malaria if the patient suffered from it. The other discussed the signs of chloroform overdose and how it could kill a patient by stopping the heart.

I let the book slip from my fingers, not believing what I was seeing and what my brain was telling me. Alice had a book on poisons. She had brought with her to Egypt a book on poisons and had underlined certain passages that were of significant interest to her. Sir Henry had died of a heart attack. And Papa had suffered another attack of malaria despite recovering well from the first one.

I was just about to leave the tent when Ruby appeared.

'Oh, 'ere you are, Miss Katie. I wondered where you'd got to. Mr Adam told me to come in 'ere and pack up as much of 'er ladyship's stuff as I could before we leave . . . ' Suddenly she paused. ''Ere, are you all right, miss?'

'I'm fine,' I said faintly.

'You don't look fine, miss, if you don't mind me sayin' so. You look like you've seen a ghost, which I suppose I shouldn't really say, wot wiv all the malarkey we've 'ad going' on 'ere . . . '

She chattered on, but I barely heard her, I was so busy trying to get my mind clear so that I could think about what I had read. Then she stooped down and picked up the book I had dropped.

'I'll put this in wiv 'er fings,' she said, looking at the title briefly. 'Blimey! 'Er ladyship don't 'alf like reading some queer books, miss.'

'How true,' I said drily.

'Mind you, it's no surprise really,' she went on chattily, picking up a few stray clothes. 'Not when you consider all them medicines she carries around with her.'

'What?' I snapped. Ruby looked up at me in surprise and I forced myself to remain calm. 'I mean, what medicines?'

'Well, you know, miss, all them ones,' Ruby said, pointing to a large brown sturdy box next to the bed.

I went over and pulled at the catch but it was firmly locked.

'What sort of things does she keep with her, Ruby?' I asked as guilelessly as I could.

'Oh well, miss, you know, sedatives an' fings. Stuff that Sir 'Enery 'ad to take an' what not. 'Er ladyship was always givin 'im medicines, but in the end nuffin' seemed to work. Cook used to say — '

'Yes, I see,' I said, picking up the book again. 'Ruby, I'm just going to go for a little stroll before we leave. Could you pack up my clothes?'

'Of course, miss.'

'Thank you.' I pulled the flaps of the tent aside. 'Oh, and if Dr Ellis asks where I am, say I've just gone into the tunnels one last time.'

'Yes Miss Katie.'

I left the tent and walked as casually as I could over to the corral where the horses were kept. Then I saddled a mare and led her quietly away from the campsite before jumping up and urging her away on to the plains.

I wanted time to think about this new revelation.

11

I sat under an acacia tree all morning. I had made the little mare gallop as fast she could down to one of the tributaries leading off from the Nile, and there I let her drink and graze whilst I sat and stared at the books I had slung across the saddle. I thought long and hard about everything that had happened ever since we had heard that Alice and Adam were coming to Egypt, and even before then. By the time Adam found me I understood some, if not all, of what had been going on.

But explaining it wasn't going to be so easy. When he arrived his face was dark with anger and his white jacket and collarless shirt were filthy from the ride.

'What the blazes do you think you're playing at?' he yelled, as he jumped off the horse, which dived gratefully at the stream next to my mare. 'Do you have any idea how many people have been looking for you? We thought you'd been abducted.'

At any other time, I would have treated this statement with contempt, but in the light of what I had been considering, it no longer seemed so absurd.

'Yes, I'm sorry — '

'You're sorry? Do you think that makes up for the utterly stupid, totally irresponsible way you've behaved?'

'Listen, Adam,' I said. 'I understand you're angry, but — '

'Oh really? That's very gracious of you. And there was me thinking you were going to give me all kinds of insane reasons why your actions are perfectly normal and shouldn't involve my having you sent back to England on the first available boat. Now get back on your horse. I've got the entire camp out looking for you, instead of working on the dig — '

'No!'

He had just put one foot in a stirrup, but he turned back and looked at me. 'Katie, I swear to God — '

'No! just listen to me for a moment, Adam. Just listen!'

'Look, you stupid woman,' he said, walking back across to me. 'Don't you understand it's dangerous out here for you? I'm not doing this to throw my weight around, I'm not trying to make you miserable. Your life is in danger if you stay here, and I — '

'I know.'

He stopped. 'What?'

'I know. It's been nagging at me for ages

why the museum was so obstructive to our progress and why no one would believe us when we said we were on the trail of the tomb, but I've finally worked it out. Someone has been deliberately misleading them about our work here in order to uncover the tomb themselves.'

He stared at me, but he didn't tell me I was being foolish. I felt vindicated but at the same time suddenly frightened. Because if Adam agreed with me then all the other awful things I had been considering down here by the riverside were probably true as well. The herons in the river were making a lot of noise; they must have just found a shoal of fish. A sudden breeze wafted across the water, bringing with it a welcome coolness and the sweet smell of the hyacinths.

'Yes. Which is all the more reason for you to leave here instead of — '

'Listen, Adam, I think I know who it is.'

Now he looked surprised. 'Who?'

I took a deep breath. 'You're going to find this hard to believe, Adam, so you've got to promise me you'll listen to everything I have to say before making a judgement.' I took his hands in mine and stared intently at him. 'I think it's Alice.'

'Alice?' He stared at me. 'You really have had too much sun, haven't you, Kate? What

282

did she ever do to you that makes you so unreasonable where she's concerned? What-ever I did — '

'No. Listen to me, Adam, really listen.' I took another deep breath. 'I'm not saying this because I hate her. A part of me can't believe it myself, but look — here, look at what I found in her tent.'

I picked up the books, but he did not seem very interested.

'So?'

'What do you mean, 'So'? Don't they seem odd books for Alice to have in her tent?'

'I'm not her librarian. I don't keep track of what she reads. What's this got to do with the problems you've had here?'

'Look, you idiot. Look at the chapters she's marked. Here! A whole passage on arsenic and how it can be mistaken for malaria if taken in small enough doses and here: chloroform. A passage highlighted about how it can cause heart attacks. Doesn't that strike you as coincidental?'

'Are you saying you think she was responsible for Henry's death?'

'I don't know.'

Hearing someone say it out loud like that sounded much worse than when I had only thought it in my head. Perhaps Adam was right. Perhaps I had had too much sun.

'I don't know,' I said again. 'All I know is that for over a year we've had hardly any money or support from the museum, despite the mounting evidence of Khaemwaset's burial chamber and now we're making real progress, yet somehow disasters keep happening to slow us down. Papa's illness, Sir George's accident, that stupid ghost. And the disasters all started happening when you arrived.'

'That's ridiculous, Kate and you know it. And anyway, if you're going to use that as a reason to start accusing people, why stop at Alice? Why not me? Or Tillyard? We got here at the same time too.'

'Because you and Mr Tillyard don't have books in your possession detailing ways of poisoning people and making it look like natural causes.'

He said nothing to that and I knew he was conceding the point, in his head at least, if not out loud.

'All right,' he said perching on the rock I had been sitting on. 'Suppose I agree with you. At least, some of it. Obviously not the ridiculous part about Alice . . . '

'Obviously,' I murmured, but he ignored that.

'But the part about someone sabotaging your links with the museum at least is certainly true. I know that. That's why I went back to Luxor.'

'What?' Now I was the one who was surprised. I sat down next to him. Behind us the two horses continued to graze peacefully, oblivious to our concerns.

'I went back to Luxor to get in touch with the museum because I realized that something was wrong when I saw your reports.'

'My reports? What's that got to do with anything?'

'When I saw those reports you'd written for your father a couple of days ago I knew something was wrong. They were nothing like the reports we'd been getting from you over the last twelve months. I saw one just before I left and it was completely different from the one you wrote to the professor. It was poorly done and with hardly any information of any relevance at all.'

'My reports?' I said again, stupidly. I remembered that on the ferry coming across Adam had made a suggestion that perhaps I'd like the museum's secretaries to write up reports for Papa, and his derision when he had seen Bella's attempt and had immediately assumed it was my work. But I still couldn't quite understand what he was getting at.

'I tried to check with the reports here, but

they've gone missing. The secretary who came with us swears he put them in with all his other documents but they're nowhere to be found and when I telegraphed back to London, no one can find them at all. I suspect we never will now.'

'You mean someone's stolen my reports.'

'They've been doing more than that, Kate. They've been replacing them. For the last year. Obviously they knew that the discoveries you were making here were very important and they couldn't take the chance on the museum finding out, so they've been intercepting your reports and replacing them with fake ones. The thing is, who? There are plenty of people who have access to the mail — not just Alice . . . ' he paused and gave me a hard stare before continuing ' . . . and it would have been the work of a moment to slip your reports into a bag and then be able to replace them at leisure with the fake ones. But who would do that?'

He put the books down on the ground and leaned over, flicking the pages idly as he kept finding more of Alice's mauve pen-marks. I knew he wasn't going to like what I said next, but I really felt I had no choice.

'Well, why not Alice?'

'Because Alice would have no reason to,' he said in a voice of deadly calm.

I stood up again, becoming angry myself now. Why was he constantly refusing to accept that Alice might be involved? Why did he constantly feel he had to protect her?

'How do you know?' I said heatedly. 'You don't know everything about her. There could be a hundred reasons why she'd do it.'

'Really?' He laughed harshly. 'Name one.'

'Because she was jealous!' I got up and walked nearer the stream, where it was slightly cooler. 'You're always accusing me of jealousy, but has it ever occurred to you that she might be the one who couldn't stand to see us together? Lord knows she did everything she could to separate us. Fifteen months ago — '

'Fifteen months ago my father was ill!' Now he stood up too. 'Why won't you believe me!'

'Because you're lying!'

Our shouts echoed around the river and even the two horses looked up, momentarily distracted from their peaceful grazing. We stared at each other, dimly aware of reaching some crossroads now, knowing that all the things we hadn't said to each other, all the secrets and lies were about to come out and neither of us was sure we were ready. But there was no way we could stop now.

'I know you're lying,' I said quietly,

frightened of what I might hear, but determined to face the truth this time. 'How many times do I have to say it? I saw the letter from Alice at your hotel. I kept waiting for you to tell me about it. I've been waiting all this time. Why do you keep pretending it was from your mother? Why do you keep . . . '

Suddenly I stopped. I could feel a great wave of misery threatening to envelop me and I turned away and stared out at the river, not daring to look at him for fear of bursting into tears. Adam didn't seem to notice this, however. He was looking down at the books again, nudging the pages with one foot.

Then I sat down on the rocky outcrop next to him again.

'Tell me about that wretched letter, Adam. We've been circling round it ever since you came back and you won't tell what really happened. I have to know why you left that summer, even if it's because Alice has a hold on you that I'm never going to break. If you have any regard for me at all, tell me why you really left Egypt.'

He looked at me for a few moments, then sighed.

'Very well,' he said slowly. 'But you have to promise me you'll never mention it to another soul, especially not Alice. I'm not proud of what I did, but she feels even worse.'

Despite the heat of the day, I suddenly felt a cold chill inside me.

'I *did* leave that summer because of Alice,' Adam said. 'My mother had written and told me my father had recently had an attack of influenza, but it certainly wasn't life-threatening and he was well even when she wrote. But it was Alice's letter that worried me. She'd only just got over the last miscarriage — '

'Miscarriage!' I looked at him, confused. 'What miscarriage?'

He rubbed a hand wearily across his face. 'Alice has had five miscarriages over the last eight years. The last one was the worst because the pregnancy lasted longer than the others, almost five months and she was beginning to hope it might come to term. But it didn't and she was beside herself with misery over it.'

My hands flew to my mouth. I *had* wondered, idly, a couple of times, why she and Sir Henry had never had a baby, and I'm ashamed to say I'd decided in the end that they probably couldn't bear the thought of an infant ruining their grand social lifestyle. It had never occurred to me that poor Alice had been trying and failing for years.

'Why didn't you tell me?'

'She didn't want anyone to know. Not outside the immediate family anyway. The last miscarriage seemed to affect her worse than the others, possibly because the doctors had warned her and Henry that she might not survive another pregnancy and no matter what Henry said or did, she seemed to feel she had let him down — '

'Wait a minute,' I said, interrupting him. 'Are you telling me that that summer when I was in England she had just had a miscarriage?'

He nodded and I thought back to the numerous times I'd seen Alice that summer. I remember all the afternoon teas and dinner parties that she had presided over, always with the same calm, pleasant demeanour, making sure everyone was happy and made welcome. For the life of me, I couldn't point to one occasion when she had seemed less than the usual perfect hostess. Of course, I know I had been wrapped up in my own romance with Adam but even so . . .

'Oh, Adam,' I said. 'The fifth one?'

He nodded again. 'I knew she was feeling miserable and I had offered to stay behind, but she wouldn't hear of it and in the end I just couldn't see how my staying would make her feel any better — '

'Oh! That was why you were so attentive to her!'

Now I felt even worse than before, remembering all the times I had accused Adam of jumping every time she whistled. He gave a faint smile.

'I'm sorry if I made you feel second best. I can see now it wasn't the most considerate behaviour, but — '

'Please, Adam, I feel small enough as it is, without you apologizing. If only I'd known.'

'She didn't want anyone to know, so I didn't tell you, but on reflection it wasn't really fair on you at all. I see that now, but at the time . . .'

He trailed off and we sat in silence for a while, both of us, no doubt, thinking about how different things would have been if only I had known.

'I did try to tell you,' he said, eventually. 'I wrote so many damn letters telling you that I regretted all that had happened and that if you would only give me the chance I would explain, but when you never wrote back I thought you didn't care any more and I was so miserable and sick of everything that in the end I just decided to hell with it and threw myself into work.'

'I never got any of your letters,' I said miserably. 'I wrote too, you know, but there are only so many times one can say sorry and when you never replied — '

'I know. Believe me, I know.'

We looked at each other, almost unable to believe the string of bad luck which had decreed that none of our letters would reach the other. I took his hand in mine and squeezed it tightly, then suddenly felt his lips on mine and we were kissing each other fiercely, holding on to one another, desperately making up for lost time. I forgot the heat of the day, forgot where we were and all the problems back at the burial site and all the other people out looking for me. All I could think was that he wanted me after all. Even poor Alice and her problems seemed to vanish.

Eventually I pushed him away from me, gasping for breath.

'Adam . . . we shouldn't . . . '

He nodded without speaking and we got up. I picked up the books by the rock and he walked across to the horses.

'What happened with Alice?' I asked, more for distraction than anything else. 'When you got back? Was she ill again?'

'No.' He sighed again. 'Actually, she'd called me back to London because she thought Henry was having an affair.'

'What?' I'd started to tie the books back on

my saddle, but at his words, I stopped and just stared at him. His face was grim as he began tightening the girth on his horse.

'She thought he was having an affair. Her letter was bad enough, full of wild accusations of women she was convinced he was seeing, but I kept finding cables at every port we stopped at with her suspicions all written in bad French so the telegraphists wouldn't understand. I kept trying to make her understand that they usually only spoke French, but she didn't seem to be reading any of mine. She just kept sending these appallingly long telegrams telling me about all the music-halls she thought Henry was frequenting.'

I looked down at the sandy riverbed for a few moments, trying to control myself, but in the end I just couldn't stop myself giggling. I didn't mean to and I couldn't help it, but the idea of Sir Henry, of all people, sneaking around London, and carrying on with music-hall actresses and loose women was the most ludicrous thing I'd ever heard. I tried to imagine the state poor Alice herself must have been in to think that, but then a picture of Sir Henry in some squalid back-street hotel in his underdrawers would leap unbidden into my mind and I was off again.

Adam watched me for few moments, a

cross expression on his face as he finished attending to his horse. When I didn't stop laughing as he came across to my mare, he gave me a sharp smack on the bottom.

'Well may you laugh about it, my dear,' he said irritably as I squeaked and tried to look grave. 'But it was not funny in the least. I spent the entire voyage thinking she was going mad and by the time I got to London, I think she was more than halfway there.'

I took a deep breath, cleared my throat and made my expression serious.

'So what happened?'

'We had a terrible row and she burst into tears and begged me to follow Henry the next time he went out. He was hardly leaving the house at all at that point, because he was so concerned about her, but he'd left that afternoon soon after I'd arrived. He was so pleased to see me and so desperate to get away, a part of me couldn't help wondering if her suspicions were correct.'

'Well,' I said, trying to put myself in Sir Henry's place, as I climbed on top of the mare. 'If she was as bad as you say and he didn't feel he could leave her, perhaps he just needed a break. So what did you do?'

Adam mounted his own horse and we began the journey back to the campsite.

'I followed him, of course. The next

afternoon.' He paused and looked at me. 'I'm not proud of what I did.'

'Well, you were only trying to help her. So where did he go?'

'To Harley Street.'

'Harley Street?' I had heard of the famous medical quarter of London, of course, although I had never been there. 'For help for Alice?'

'No. Although I thought that too, when I got out of the cab. But I managed to find out, by means of the most inept detective work possible, I might add, that the doctor he was seeing was a heart specialist.'

'A heart specialist?' I was aware I was begining to sound like an echo, but then I realized what this meant. 'Oh. It was for him, wasn't it?' I gasped as Adam nodded, feeling every bit as small as he had said I would. 'Oh no! Poor Sir Henry!'

'He'd been having problems for the last six months or so, but since Alice was so ill, he was trying to keep it from her which was why he had been leaving the house and not telling her where he was going, or giving her such flimsy excuses that she saw through them at once and of course thought the worst.'

'So what did you do?'

He smiled briefly, his sense of mischief coming to the rescue.

'I spent the next two hours sitting on a park bench opposite the surgery waiting for him to come out so that when he did I could pretend to be there as if by accident. Anyway, when he appeared, I went across to him and gave him some ridiculous story and suggested we have a drink.'

'Did he believe you, do you think?'

Adam snorted. 'Not for a minute. And anyway, in the end, when he'd told me the prognosis — which wasn't good: the specialist told him if he didn't slow down, he'd be lucky to last another six months — I was so sick of the whole thing that I confessed to him why I was there and begged him to talk to Alice.'

'Oh.' I thought about Sir Henry. He wasn't the sort of man who would take lightly to others interfering in his business. 'Was he angry?'

'No. He knew how miserable Alice was, of course, but didn't realize she'd become so low that she was thinking such things about him. When I told him about the music-hall business he even laughed.'

'Poor Adam,' I said. 'It must have been awful for you. And I said those dreadful things to you too.'

We rode in silence for a few minutes. The sun was now almost at its zenith and the heat was becoming unbearable. The horses were almost dragging their hoofs and the smell from the river was no longer fragrant hyacinth but a boggy, almost putrid stench. By mutual consent we got off them and began walking slowly towards the campsite again. It would take longer that way, but we were in no hurry. Adam took out a water bottle he had brought and we both drank from it.

'So what happened then?' I asked when we had both quenched our thirst.

'We caught a cab back together to their house, but I left Henry to talk to Alice alone. I don't know exactly what went on between them, but the next time I saw Alice she was much calmer. I think that, in a way, knowing Henry was so ill gave her something else to think about. Anyway, we only spoke briefly. I'd only gone there to tell her about my plans to leave immediately. Henry had offered me the job in Persia the day after I'd followed him in fact, although to be frank it was less of an offer than an order.'

'Oh! I thought you said . . . '

Adam shrugged, his smile ironic. 'Henry was a first-class chap in many ways, but no man is going to feel particularly fond of the young idiot who's so besotted with his wife that he's prepared to sneak around after him looking for evidence of infidelity. Under the circumstances I think I got off lightly.

Actually that was the worst thing about it all, you know.'

'What, my dear?'

'Knowing you were right after all. I had plenty of time to think about it in Persia in between arguing with bureaucrats and filling in forms in triplicate which I knew were going to end up in the bin two minutes after I'd left the room.'

'Right about what?'

'Right about me and Alice. I *did* jump when she called. All the time.'

'Oh Adam, that's not true,' I said, feeling guilty myself now. 'She was ill and you knew she needed — '

'Oh I don't mean that summer particularly, although that was when I excelled myself if I'm going to be truthful. I always did what she wanted, right from when I was a child. The trip to Harley Street was just the culmination of that relationship. She was desperate and I was so hopelessly infatuated I never even stopped to think about what I was doing.'

'Adam, I think you're being too hard on yourself,' I said gently, but he shook his head.

'No. She had the excuse that she wasn't thinking properly. How could she with the terrible misfortune that had just happened to her? But I should have known better. She should have been able to rely on me to think straight for her, but all I did was follow her commands, exactly as I had always done. You know, seeing her in the house when I arrived back — she was distraught, her hair was untidy, her clothes just thrown on . . . '

'Alice? Untidy?' I tried to picture this, but failed. To me, Alice was never going to be anything but a perfectly made-up lady of fashion. But Adam just nodded.

'I should have known then. But I didn't, you see. And even when I confronted poor Henry and he told me what the problem was, even then it didn't occur to me how stupid I'd been. It was only later, when I had hours and hours alone with nothing but my thoughts and you never replied to my letters and I kept writing new ones, hoping that you'd finally forgive me, that I realized how stupid I'd been. You've no idea how pleased I was when Alice proposed that we should come out here. It was the perfect excuse to see you again and hope you might have forgiven me for being such a fool.'

We walked on silently for a while. Then Adam spoke again.

'We really made a mess of things, didn't we?'

I nodded. 'A spectacular mess,' I said, then started to smile. 'You know, it almost has a funny side really . . . '

He scowled. 'One day, Kate, your sense of humour is going to be the death of you.'

'You used to like my sense of humour.'

'I still do . . . '

Suddenly he let go of the horse's reins and, pulling me up close, began kissing me again. We might never have stopped, but suddenly we both became aware of the sound of a horse's hoofs on the sand. We pulled apart and watched in astonishment as a single horse came into view from the direction of the river. The figure on top of the horse seemed unaware of the effect his frenzied ride was having on his mount in the scorching midday heat.

'That horse is going to collapse if he's not careful,' said Adam shading his eyes with his hand to get a better focus on the two figures. I did the same.

'Yes, but — wait a minute.' I screwed my eyes up against the glare of the sun. 'That's not a man on that horse, it's a woman. It's Bella!'

12

I helped Bella over to the shade of a palm tree and sat her down, while Adam saw to the horses. She had almost run us both down at first. After a few minutes she began to regain her composure. Adam crouched down so he was on a level with her eyes.

'What on earth are you doing here, Bella?'

'I managed to slip out this morning, before anyone noticed. Aunt Augusta is still beside herself with worry over Uncle George, although he's getting better. I knew if I could get out early enough, no one would notice until it was too late.'

She paused and took a sip from the water bottle I had given her. She was wearing her desert clothes and at long last they looked dirty and used.

'But what . . . '

She shook her hand at me again and took several deep breaths. Adam and I exchanged glances.

'I had to come,' she said at last. 'I had to warn you, Kate. As soon as Uncle George told us. I begged Aunt Augusta to send someone, but the doctor insisted he was just delirious and poor Aunt Augusta isn't thinking straight at the moment and just kept saying: 'Don't bother me now, Bella.' Although he *did* seem a bit mad, poor thing, even I could see that. But I knew he wasn't. I knew he was telling the truth.'

'Calm down, Bella, you're not making any sense. What did Sir George tell you?'

'The scorpion, Kate. It was in your boot.'

'The scorpion?' Adam frowned. 'The one that stung Sir George? How could it have stung him if it was in her boot?'

'It wasn't in her boot when it stung him. He had come to our tent to check that we were all right after he'd heard that noise and he knocked Kate's boots over as he walked in. When the horrid thing scuttled out, he just reacted without thinking, forgetting he wasn't wearing any shoes. That was when it stung him. The doctor said he was lucky it wasn't a lethal one, although it gave us all a scare.'

I sat down next to her, putting my arms around her.

'I know. I'm so glad he's all right, Bella. But I don't see what it's got to do with me. I know you're a bit squeamish about creepy-crawlies, but it's really not that unusual for scorpions to get into boots and things.'

'Yes, but you'd put your boots on just five minutes before Uncle George got there, don't

302

you remember? Then you couldn't be bothered to lace them up. I didn't realize it straight away, when Uncle George was telling us, but when I was thinking about it afterwards, it occurred to me that your boots were upright the whole time. Somebody put that scorpion in your boot deliberately. While we were outside. To make it sting *you*. How else could that horrid little thing have got in there so quickly otherwise?'

'Well you know, Bella, it's more likely that they fell sideways when I threw them down. Scorpions like dark — '

'No! I picked them and put them straight,' she said firmly. 'You're so untidy, Kate. It was driving me mad.'

'Well, I still can't see why you'd automatically assume someone would put a scorpion in my boot, hoping I'd pull it on without checking first. I always shake my boots out before I pull them on. I know how dangerous it can — '

'No, you don't,' Bella interrupted, looking rather cross. 'In fact, whenever I did it, you used to tease me.'

I frowned. 'Well maybe not *all* the time,' I said. 'And just because I — '

'You know, I think Bella's got a good point,' said Adam.

'You would.'

Adam and I had spent so long discussing Alice and her problems this morning, we'd never got round to resolving the original dispute we'd been having, namely my remaining at the dig until the burial chamber was unearthed. Now I could see he was going to use this as an excuse to make me leave. Much as I appreciated Bella's concern for me, I couldn't help wishing she hadn't come.

'You've got to agree it's yet another coincidence, Kate,' said Adam. 'If you'd gone back to your tent with all that commotion going on, there's a good chance you would have pulled your boots on without bothering to check first.'

'Why should anyone bother to get rid of me? You were due back any day, Mr Tillyard was still there with all the work crew, what possible reason could anyone have for wanting me to leave? As you've already pointed out so tactfully, Adam, I don't exactly have executive powers here, do I.'

'I don't know,' he admitted. 'Maybe you know something no one else does, you just don't know yet you know it. The point is, the more I hear about this dig, the less happy I am about it. To be honest, I'm tempted to order everyone to pack up now and leave and let the Antiquities Service sort it out. I know the hieroglyphs look promising but — '

'No!' I shouted, so loudly that Bella and Adam flinched and all three horses, who were enjoying their rest immensely, looked up in surprise.

'No, Adam, don't do that. You know what will happen if the Service takes over. They'll get all the credit and everything that Papa had worked for over the last three years will have been a waste. It won't be fair!' I wailed.

I was near to tears at this point. I just couldn't let Adam ruin this last chance Papa had of proving he wasn't some mad old fool who'd spent too long under the Egyptian sun.

'Listen, stay one more night here. Just one! If nothing's turned up by tomorrow, I swear I'll go back to Luxor quietly and you can do what you want; stay here and dig yourself or hand it all over to the Antiquities Service; I won't say anything. But just give me one more night, Adam. Please! I know we're close. Look, you're here now with all those guards and I know I can persuade Ahmed to stay. One more night, Adam. That's all I'm asking.'

He hesitated and I knew he didn't really want to go to the Antiquities Service and hand over what could potentially be a magnificent find.

'Very well. One more night, Kate. But if we don't find anything . . . '

'We will,' I said confidently.

We led the horses slowly back to the campsite.

* * *

We arrived back at the campsite shortly after one. It was quiet in the heat of the afternoon and the place was deserted, except for Ruby who rushed up to us, relieved to see me and surprised to see Bella. Just as we were giving her a greatly edited version of Bella's story, Mr Tillyard appeared at the mouth of the tunnel, his spectacles skew-whiff on his face which was covered in soil and dirt. His white coat was filthy and his hands were caked in mud. He looked at us all in surprise.

'Oh hello! And Miss Wyndham-Brown! You're here too.'

'Yes, hello, Mr Tillyard,' said Bella. 'Uncle George is much better and I thought I might come back and see how you were getting on.'

'Alone?' said Mr Tillyard.

'Why are you here, Tillyard?' said Adam. 'I told everyone to go looking for Kate.'

'What? Oh. Yes. I did. I took a group of men and searched all over the lower plain, but found nothing, obviously, because here you are,' he said, smiling at me. 'Are you all right?'

'Fine thank you, Mr Tillyard. Have you been working some more in the tunnel?'

'Yes. I thought I might as well, since I was doing no good in the desert, but unfortunately it isn't going as well as I had hoped. The hieroglyphs have started to — '

Suddenly he was interrupted by a workman who came running out of the tunnel, shouting with excitement. When he saw me and Adam he rushed up to us and began yelling about a shining doorway. He seemed so animated that we all followed him into the tomb without protest, even Bella and Ruby, neither of whom were very fond of the dark, cramped tunnel. The passageway was head height to begin with and not too unpleasant with the light of several lanterns illuminating the way, although it was soon close and humid in the enclosed space. At first there was nothing but dark, packed earth and mud and the lanterns made their weird, eerie shadows dance with a dull orange glow. But as we got further into the tunnel, the light started to show the pictures from the funeral procession painted so many thousands of years ago, so that in some way it was as though we were part of that original party, escorting the dead person on his final journey out of this world and into the next. After about five minutes we reached the end of the passage and as we stopped, I found myself gasping in wonder.

There at the end of the tunnel, partly exposed, was a yellow-coloured door, beautiful despite the dirt which clung to it. I scrambled up to it, desperate to touch the cool metal, to feel the lines of the engravings beneath my fingertips. I ran my hand over the exposed part gently at first, then greedily, brushing away specks of dirt that obscured some of the characters.

'It's fabulous,' I whispered to Adam who was beside me. 'Exactly what we were expecting. It *must* be the door to a king's burial chamber. Papa was right!' I turned to the grinning workmen beside me who had first discovered it. 'Well done!'

'Here, get that brush. Let's uncover it all,' said Adam and we all grabbed tools and set to work, chipping and brushing the mud and dirt of centuries away.

It seemed to take no time at all before we were standing in front of a gold-worked, exquisitely crafted door, the hieroglyphs as sharp and detailed as if they had just been engraved yesterday, the lamplight sending shafts of golden colour on to the faces of everyone who beheld them. There were thousands of birds and animals, ibises and dogs and cats and humans with fantastic heads representing the gods, crossed sceptres and counsellors with their own cartouches. And last of all we found what we were looking for: the burial seal of the King. I fumbled in my pocket to find my spectacles and stared in wonder at the characters. Now at last I knew that all Papa's hard work has been worth it.

'Blimey!' said Ruby.

'It's amazing.' Beside me, Bella's eyes were wide with astonishment. 'I can hardly believe we're standing in a horrid little hole in the ground looking at something as grand as this. How do we open it?'

Adam laughed shortly, as he held up his own lantern beside her to inspect the hieroglyphs more closely, but it was Mr Tillyard who answered her.

'I'm afraid that's impossible, my dear. At least today.'

'Why?'

'Because, my dear Bella,' said Adam, 'the Antiquities Service insists on an inspector being present whenever a new tomb is discovered. It's part of their policy to try and stop all Egypt's ancient wealth leaving the country.'

'Oh, what a shame,' she said, then looked at him and grinned. 'Couldn't we take just a tiny peek?'

'No. We couldn't,' said Adam curtly and I knew he wanted to as desperately as I did.

'And shame on you for suggesting it, Miss Wyndham-Brown. That's how so much of value is lost for ever to this wonderful country,' Mr Tillyard added, but Bella just shrugged.

'Well I've heard that lots of stuff gets pinched by black marketeers anyway,' she said. 'Isn't this El Nummy person supposed to be a marvel at sneaking things out under the very noses of the authorities?'

'Il Namus,' I said, absently, still gloating over the door. Bella shrugged again.

'Il Numus, then.' She paused. 'What odd names these people have.'

Mr Tillyard smiled. 'It's not really a name, Miss Wyndham-Brown. It's more in the nature of a description really. It means 'mosquito'.'

'Ugh,' said Bella. 'How horrid.'

'Actually I think it's meant to be a compliment, my dear. You know, it's an annoying little creature, but it can give you lots of nasty little bites and nine times out of ten there's no way you can fight back, because you never even see it.'

'I suppose so,' Bella replied doubtfully.

While they were discussing this I was still on my knees, touching and stroking, almost

310

caressing the smooth metal of the door. But as my fingers moved towards the edges at the bottom, I fell slightly and my thumb and index finger were driven briefly against the hardened wall. At first, I just pulled back, then from my vantage point on the floor, I realized something. As my fingers pulled away the mud, they showed a different colour underneath the top layer. I stared at the crumbling mud in amazement at first, then started scrabbling madly at the wall. Ruby saw me first.

'Miss Kate, what on earth are you doing?'

'The wall!' I gasped, still fumbling at the upper layer. 'The wall! It's a fake. It's a robber's hole!'

'What!' Suddenly both Adam and Mr Tillyard were on their knees beside me, Adam holding the lantern over the spot where I was still frantically scraping.

'What's a robber's hole?' asked Bella, but we all ignored her.

'My God, you're right.' Adam leaned forward and wiped away the top layer of dirt, the disguise which had kept the secret of the unauthorized entrance for millenia. We looked at one another and grinned.

'Well, they can hardly criticize us for taking a quick peek now,' I said, anticipation of what we might see in the tomb almost making my mouth water.

Adam rubbed his nose reflectively. 'True. Besides, we could always fill it up again if we wanted.' Again we looked at one another and grinned.

'Dr Ellis! Miss Whitaker! I hope you're not suggesting we open this hole?'

I turned round to see the look of horror on Mr Tillyard's face and I felt slightly guilty. But only for a second. After all, this project was mine and Papa's before it was anyone else's here. Why shouldn't I get just a quick preview? It wasn't as if I was suggesting stealing anything.

'Cheer up, Mr Tillyard. I promise it will only be the quickest of looks. Besides, aren't you even the slightest bit curious?'

Before he could answer that, Bella interrupted.

'Will someone please tell me what's going on here? What's a robber's hole? And why are we going to take a look now when you said just a few minutes ago we couldn't?'

'Robbers' holes are exactly what they sound like, Bella,' I said, still digging. 'After the people were buried in here robbers used to turn up and dig their way in to steal the treasures left with the corpses. Not all the ancient Egyptians were terrified of retribution in the after-life.'

'And there's an unwritten rule that if there's a robber's hole in a tomb, then the excavators are entitled to use it as a means of access,' Adam added.

'That is totally untrue, Dr Ellis, and well you know it,' Mr Tillyard said, sounding even more disapproving than ever. But Adam just smiled at him.

'Well, it may be and it may not be. But this robber's hole is here and I intend to open it just a tiny bit to have a look inside. Kate, if you don't mind?'

He held out his hand for the shovel which I had already picked up, and began hacking away at the discoloured stain around the door. I seem to remember Mr Tillyard making more protests about this sacrilegious assault on an ancient artefact, but his complaints fell on deaf ears. Bella and Ruby were almost beside themselves with excitement and as for me, I could hardly wait for Adam to finish. It seemed to take hours, but at last he managed to dig a big enough hole in the wall to allow his head and shoulders through. He took the candle out of the lantern for a moment and held it up in the hole to check that there were no foul gases from this ancient burial-place. He made as if to go into the hole, then he checked himself.

'Kate?' he said, holding the candle towards me. 'I think you should look first.'

I was touched by this. On impulse I took his hand in mine, smoothing out the palms, still muddy from the remains of the hole. Then I took the candle and gently pushed myself through the hole. Holding the flame high, I waited for my eyes to grow accustomed to the gloom.

For a moment I couldn't believe what I was seeing. The chamber was huge and every corner was filled with so much treasure it could only be the last resting place of a king. There were finely carved chairs and chests, beautiful gilt couches with the heads of fantastic animals on their sides, life-sized statues of servants to attend to the king on his journey, richly painted caskets with all his personal belongings, weapons, musical instruments and in one corner a magnificent chariot, sparkling with jewels, ready to take him wherever he wished to go. And everywhere the glint of gold, so rich and precious it almost blinded me. And then, in the corner I saw it; a shrine of gold and blue faience, almost hidden by the mass of wealth around it. Inside would be housed the huge stone sarcophagus that held the body of Khaemwaset.

'What can you see?' The muffled voice of

314

Adam behind me made me remember the others.

'It's amazing,' I answered. 'So much gold, so much . . . '

I trailed off, unable to say what I was thinking, just drinking in all the splendour of the treasures in here. I was loath to pull myself away, but common decency told me the others would want to look too, so reluctantly, I withdrew my head and shoulders from the hole and let Adam take my place. As he disappeared into the gloom, Bella hugged me.

'What was it like? Is it fantastic?'

I nodded. 'It's absolutely just what Papa and I always believed we'd find,' I said with joy. 'Oh, I wish he could be here now! It's so unfair. If it weren't for his persistence and determination we would never have come this far.'

'You shouldn't be so modest, Miss Whitaker,' said a voice behind me and I turned to see Mr Tillyard looking at us. He was cleaning his spectacles with such vigour I feared for the lenses. I smiled at him.

'What do you mean?' I said.

'You possess as much persistence and determination as Professor Whitaker, my dear. I doubt we'd be here now either if it weren't for your equal diligence in this task.'

'That's not true, but you're very sweet to

say so..' I began, but just then Adam withdrew his head from the hole.

'It's fantastic, truly amazing. Here, Tillyard, you may as well look.' He handed the candle to Mr Tillyard, who hesitated for a second then popped his head through as well. 'But I suppose we had better make some effort to block it up again. Tillyard's right,' he said in response to the protests I began to make. 'The Service will have a fit if they think we've been meddling with the evidence and there's really no point in annoying them needlessly. And it's probably better that no one else knows about this anyway. Cheer up Kate. At least you got to see it first.'

I sighed, but I knew he was right. There was no point in making trouble for ourselves when the inspectors would be here to tomorrow.

'Come on, Tillyard. Let's let Bella have a look — and you too, Ruby — and then we'll seal it up again and work on our spontaneous shouts of surprise for tomorrow.'

With renewed energy we set about blocking in the hole again.

★ ★ ★

Adam sent a messenger back to Luxor to inform the Antiquities Service of our find as

316

soon as we had finished blocking in the hole and we spent the rest of the afternoon deciphering the texts on the door.

Ahmed agreed to stay one more night. I think he would have stayed anyway now that the doorway had been found; he always had been curious about Papa's obsession and I felt safer knowing that he and his sons would still be with us.

We worked all afternoon and much of the evening, laboriously copying the images around the doorway on to paper, but eventually had to give in to fatigue at about eight o'clock that night. Reluctantly, we made our way back to the campsite, leaving two guards to remain on duty until we returned in the morning.

After dinner we sat round the fire for some time discussing the day's finds. Everyone was excited by the discovery, even Bella and Ruby, who I don't think really cared one way or the other normally. Soon Ruby began yawning so I sent her to bed, walking with her to fetch my coat as it was beginning to get cold. Nawal and Huda had agreed to sleep in Alice's tent for the night as ours was beginning to get somewhat cramped and I know Ruby felt happier about this. She chattered amiably with me as she rolled some blankets up on the ground to sleep on. I left her, promising to be back soon, and as I walked across to the fire I heard a noise beside me. Turning, I saw Mr Tillyard. He was wearing a dark coat and he seemed to be making for the tomb again.

'Hello,' I said. 'Can't you keep away?'

He smiled. 'I thought I might just take one last look at the tomb before I turn in. It's getting late and I need to be up early in the morning. I must return to Luxor tomorrow.'

'Must you?' I asked, surprised.

'Yes,' he said firmly. 'I must. If for no other reason than to remove myself from Dr Ellis's presence for a day or so. He makes it quite clear that he still hasn't forgiven me for allowing you to remain here.'

'Really, Mr Tillyard,' I said. 'You're being foolish.'

'No, my dear. I have to go. I should speak to Lady Faulkner personally anyway, about this magnificent find. After all, she is my employer.'

'Well — if I can't dissuade you. But you will be back soon, won't you?'

He was walking away from me as I said this, but he turned back, smiling.

'Oh, I will. Believe me, nothing would keep me away from here for too long.'

And with that he disappeared into the tomb entrance, swallowed up by it as though

318

he were entering the mouth of a voracious
animal.

★ ★ ★

I walked slowly back to the fire to find Adam
alone.

'Bella went to bed,' said Adam, stretching
and yawning himself. 'She was tired and you
were so long, she thought you'd already
gone.'

'I was talking to Mr Tillyard. Adam?'

'What?'

'Who do you think has been behind all our
problems? Who's been trying to sabotage this
dig?'

'Well I don't think it's Alice,' he said firmly
and I felt obliged to nod my head.

'No, neither do I. But even so . . .'

I couldn't help thinking about those
strange books and he must have read my
mind because he took my chin in his fingers
and turned my face towards him.

'I don't know why she had those passages
marked out or even why she had those books.
Perhaps it's a reaction to Henry's death. We
all thought she was coping remarkably well
with it. Maybe too well. I don't know. I'll talk
to her about it when I see her. But I do know
that Alice is no more capable of flying to the

moon than she is of murdering her own husband or plotting some long-drawn-out conspiracy to cheat you and your father of your rightful rewards.'

It was quiet in the camp now. Most people had withdrawn to their tents and only a few of the mercenaries remained, drinking and playing cards.

'Come on,' said Adam, standing up and pulling me up with him. 'Let's go for a walk. We haven't had a chance to talk since this morning.'

He put his arm around my waist as we walked slowly away from the fire. It reminded me of the time we had had in London and the few short weeks at sea before everything had started going wrong. We had enjoyed ourselves. I'm sure it's the same for every couple, before familiarity breeds contempt, but we were well suited. I remember thinking it then and thinking it now.

'I wonder who it was. It must be someone who has contacts here and in London too,' I said as we walked along listening to the busy chirrupings of the desert insects.

Adam shrugged. 'It's got to be someone connected to the Cavendish because they managed to get to your reports. But even so, that doesn't help much, either. There're several ex-employees that I know of working further up the Valley, not to mention just across the river at the Temples of Karnak. And by the time we got out here there were plenty of people who knew about your work. Especially after those articles in *The Times* were printed. It could be anyone.'

I thought about this. 'I suppose so, but Papa and I know all the archaeologists here. I know they thought Papa was a fool, but even so I can't believe they'd — oh!'

'What is it?'

'I've just had a thought. Supposing it's Peter.'

'Peter Bennett?' Adam stopped walking for moment to stare at me. 'What on earth makes you think it's Bennett? I thought you liked him.'

'I do, but just think for a second. He's only been over here for six months, so that would have given him enough time to find out about my reports back in England . . . '

'Who from?' Adam's tone was sceptical, but I wasn't going to be put off now.

'From his accomplice, of course, and also he was here the very day the ghost appeared for real in front of me and Bella — and then Sir George got bitten,' I said, rather wildly, I have to admit, but the germ of an idea was forming.

'What's that got to do with anything?'

'Because he saw the progress we were making in the tunnel and realized that he would have to do something to put us off the scent,' I said triumphantly.

After a moment or two of thought, Adam nodded.

'OK, but I thought you said you'd actually lost quite a bit of the mural when he arrived.'

'Yes, but — oh!' I gasped again and Adam looked at me, one eyebrow raised.

'Now what?'

'We've sent for an inspector. What's the likelihood he'll be the one to come out here to see us. We've delivered ourselves right into his hands!'

'Kate, if he really is the culprit — which frankly I doubt — what exactly is he going to be able to do? We've found the doorway now. The place will be crowded tomorrow with people watching as it's opened. Whoever is responsible for your problems has lost, despite their best efforts. Really,' he added as I hesitated, 'stop worrying about things you can't change and come over here.'

He pulled me off the track as he said this. I hesitated for a second, then followed him. He grabbed a small lantern hanging on a post and we moved quietly away from the main sites, off behind one of the many little hillocks and slopes. But as he took off his coat and spread it on the ground, I started giggling. He frowned.

'Now what?'

'I'm sorry,' I said, lying down beside him. The coat was thick, fortunately, but the ground was so dry it was impossible not to feel the sharp stones beneath the material. 'I just had a thought. This is a tryst.'

'A what?'

'A tryst. You know, a lover's tryst, a romantic assignation, a — '

'Kate, you talk too much, do you know that?'

He was beside me now; we were both lying on the ground, looking at one another gravely. Suddenly I found I no longer wanted to laugh. Around us the cicadas chirruped noisily and a slight breeze brought the smell of smoke from the fire. From somewhere I could hear a lone flute being played.

'Well then, what are you going to do about it?' I asked softly. In reply, he leaned over and began kissing me, gently at first, but with increasing urgency, his hands roving all over my body as his fingers searched for the buttons on my blouse. I kissed him back, only mildly surprised to find myself as eager for his touch as he was to touch me. I could feel the bristles on his cheeks as he kissed me with increasing passion, his hands moving further down my body. But as I moved closer towards him, a small noise to my left distracted me. I pulled away.

'Did you hear that?'

'Hear what?'

'That noise. It came from over there.' I pointed vaguely into the distance, but already I was beginning to forget exactly where the noise had come from.

'Forget it. It was probably just a hyena or a rat.'

'What a lovely thought, Adam. You know just how to create the right atmosphere.'

He grinned. 'Don't tell me you're frightened. You'll spoil all my illusions about you.'

I stroked his cheek, inviting him to touch me again.

'It's nice to know you still have some. I thought you knew everything there was to know about me.'

'Not everything . . . '

We didn't speak for a while, but the noise still nagged at the back of my mind. If it had been a hyena or some other animal, why hadn't it come closer to investigate? I couldn't help feeling distracted and after a few minutes of fidgeting, I sat up again.

'Adam, did you arrange for your men to guard the tomb?'

Giving an exasperated sigh, he rolled back

away from me. 'Yes, Katharine. I did. It was such a good idea of yours I thought I might carry on with it until we leave here, especially considering we might have just found the biggest haul so far this century. Or perhaps it's more important that the guards get a good night's sleep. What do you think?'

'All right. I know it was stupid that we weren't as diligent as you. I'm sorry. You were right and we were wrong,' I grumbled. 'What more do you want?'

He smiled then, before pinning my arms down.

'Katie,' he whispered. 'You have no idea.'

★ ★ ★

Much later we left the little rocky hideout and made our way back to our tents as quietly as we could. The camp was silent now; I don't know exactly what the time was but it seemed to be well past midnight and there was no sign of anyone about. I found it hard to behave as though nothing had happened. My entire body was tingling with the excitement of new sensations and I was wondering how I would ever be able to face anyone in the morning without their realizing what we had done. I was grateful that Nawal and Huda had withdrawn to another tent. They would certainly have been able to read me like a book.

Adam walked with me to the tent, but just before I leaned down to lift up the flaps, he pulled me back towards him and kissed me once more with passion. This time I made more than a token effort to push him off.

'Adam, enough. It's late. I need to go to bed and so do you.'

'Hmm.'

'No, I mean it, Adam,' I whispered fiercely. 'Go to bed now. Or you'll wake up the entire campsite.'

'All right.' He let go finally and began to turn away, then suddenly he looked back again. 'You *are* going to go to bed, aren't you? You're not going to go for another little midnight ramble the minute my back's turned?'

'Don't be ridiculous,' I whispered. 'I'm dead on my feet. I only got up the other night because I heard a noise.'

'Oh. Like the one you heard just now, you mean?'

'Oh shut up and go to bed,' I said, then pulled him towards me for one last kiss.

I undressed as quietly as I could and slipped into my narrow little camp-bed. It was more comfortable than Adam's coat on the pebble-strewn ground, but I felt myself wishing I was still back there, lying next to him.

I curled into a ball, thinking about all the events of the day, fighting sleep with ever more difficulty until at last I was in a strange surreal dream doze, neither properly awake or asleep. It was then that I had my epiphany.

I sat up in the bed suddenly. The thing that had been nagging away in my brain for the last few days had come free at last. It floated to the front of my mind, while I was dozing, relaxed and happy. In fact it was so sudden, I almost didn't know how to react. Then I got out of bed and bumped around the tent, looking for matches for the lamp and my boots and coat. Now, at last, I knew what I had to do.

I had to go back to Khaemwaset's tomb.

13

As I blundered around the tent Bella woke up.

'Kate! What's the matter?'

'I'm just going back into the tomb to check something.'

'What, now?' She squinted at the lamp that I'd just lit. 'It's still dark.'

'Well, it won't take long. Go back to sleep, Bella'

'How can I, with all the row you're making? What on earth is so important that it can't wait until morning?'

'Just go back to sleep, Bella. I'll take the lantern and you can go — '

'What's the matter? What's goin' on, miss?'

I sighed. 'There! Now you've woken Ruby up too.'

'I didn't wake her up. You were the one making all the noise.'

Ruby was sitting up now, rubbing her eyes. 'What — ?'

'Go back to sleep, Ruby. It's all right.'

'Wait a minute.' Bella pulled the blankets from her bed. 'I'm coming too.'

'Comin' where?' Ruby was fully awake now

and beginning to frown. 'What's goin' on, Miss Kate? Miss Bella?'

'Nothing.' I was beginning to get exasperated now, but before I could continue Bella stood up.

'Miss Kate is going back up to the tunnels, Ruby. For some insane reason she has to go at this ungodly hour, and I'm certainly not letting her go on her own, so I'm going with her.'

'Orright, miss, me too,' said Ruby, leaping up now and pulling her boots on.

'For heaven's sake, will you two stop this. Bella, get back into bed. Ruby, take your boots off . . . '

'Certainly not.' Bella found her black velvet coat and put it on. 'Why should you get all the excitement? We can come too if we want, can't we, Ruby?'

'I should say so, miss,' said Ruby, pulling her own navy-blue serge coat on with a grin. 'I don't know what Cook would say if I let two young ladies go out in the middle of the night on their own.' Cook was clearly a very important influence on Ruby. I gave up, shrugging.

'Very well. But keep quiet. I don't want everyone to know what we're doing.'

I waited until they were ready, then just as I was about to open the tent flaps, Bella fumbled with something at the bottom of her bed. She had arrived with much less luggage than the first time of course, although after the confusion of her departure there was still a lot of her stuff left. But she had brought a few things back with her and one of them was a bulky-looking object that she had been curiously reticent about.

'Very well,' she said. 'We can go now.'

'OK. Are you — ? Bella! What on earth . . . ?' I stared at her in amazement and even Ruby looked surprised.

'Blimey, miss, wot you got there?'

'A gun,' said Bella, looking obstinate. 'A little protection. After last time.'

'Protection!' I stared at her. 'What do you think is going to attack us, an elephant?'

She was holding possibly the oldest, largest gun I've ever seen. When people come to visit Egypt, the men particularly feel that their trip isn't complete without at least one day spent along the river, trying to kill as much of the wildlife as possible. I'd seen quite a few hunting rifles in my life and watched a lot of birds and other animals being wounded by the antics of these idiots, but I don't ever remember seeing a gun as antique as the one Bella was holding, at least not outside a museum.

'It was all I could get hold of at short

notice,' she said defensively. 'Uncle George is fanatical about keeping his guns under lock and key and of course I couldn't ask him to lend me a better one.'

'Well, thank heavens for small mercies. It's a blunderbuss, isn't it?'

'Yes. Uncle George is very proud of this one. Says it was last fired fifty years ago.'

'Does it still work?'

'Well Uncle George says not, which is why it was easy to take. But it looks as though it might, doesn't it.'

I opened my mouth to make some sarcastic remark about shooting at ghosts, but then changed my mind and shrugged. After all, if she was prepared to come out with me now in the middle of the night to sneak down the pitch-black passageway into the tomb of a long-dead corpse, who was I to challenge her on her choice of accoutrement?

We set off. The last time Bella and I had done this we had had the sound of ghostly wailings ringing in our ears, but I hadn't been that scared then and to be honest, I wasn't particularly worried now. If I had known what was about to happen, I would have never dared venture out of the tent; I would certainly never have taken Bella and Ruby with me.

'What are we doing here?' asked Bella,

holding tightly on to my arm as we got nearer to the entrance.

'I just want to check something out — oh. That's funny.'

'What? What's funny?'

I said nothing for a moment, waving my hand at her to keep her quiet. I moved slowly into the tunnel entrance, holding the lantern up high to catch even the slightest movement, but no one stirred. The place was empty.

'That's odd,' I said.

'What's the matter, miss?' Ruby asked nervously.

'There are no guards. Adam was very insistent that he had left guards outside the entrance. I wonder where they are.'

We looked at one another.

'You know, Kate,' said Bella, 'perhaps we ought to get Dr Ellis out here. And Mr Tillyard. And perhaps . . . '

'All right,' I said slightly anxious myself now. It seemed very quiet. 'We'll go back for Adam.'

We crept back down the hillside, keeping much closer to each other this time. It only took a couple of minutes before we were standing in front of Adam's tent. Like Alice, being the top dog of the expedition meant he was entitled to private accommodation. I rapped sharply on the wooden pole.

There was the sound of someone slowly getting up. It seemed to take ages and we were all beginning to get less nervous and a little impatient by the time Adam eventually pulled the tent-flaps aside. He looked sleepy and dishevelled and I noticed he was still dressed in his shirt and trousers. This confirmed the suspicion I had that men were less fastidious than women.

'Kate,' he murmured, smiling sleepily. 'What's the matter?'

'Well, Bella and Ruby and I have just been up to the tunnels and — '

'Bella?' He rubbed his eyes and peered over at them. 'Ruby? What on earth is going on?'

'Nothing. It's just — there's a bit of a problem with the guards at the tomb.'

'What problem?'

'They've disappeared,' I said. 'Get your coat and come with us.'

'Disappeared?' He frowned, but made no move to do as I said. 'What are you talking about? And what are you three doing up at this time of the night?'

'We got bored and decided to go for a stroll! What do you think?'

'I think,' he said, looking at me through narrowed eyes, 'that when you and your little friends wake me up at . . . ' he peered blearily at a watch in his hand and groaned, 'oh, God

— three in the morning, that you're up to no good, that's what I think.'

'For heaven's sake, this is no time for behaving like an idiot.'

'Yes, and for your information, Adam Ellis, I am *not* up to no good and you are no gentleman,' said Bella crossly. Adam grinned at her.

'Then you shouldn't let yourself get dragged into one of Kate's little schemes,' he said, turning around to go back to bed.

'Adam! We need your help.'

'Not at three in the morning, darling.'

'Yes *now*. The guards are gone! Doesn't that worry you in the slightest?'

'Oh, for goodness' sake, Kate!' Now he was beginning to sound irritable. 'They've probably gone into the tunnel to keep warm. Go back to bed.'

'No they didn't. I checked. I'm not completely stupid, you know. But fine,' I said, moving away from the tent. 'If you won't help we'll do this alone. Come along Bella, Ruby.'

I began to walk away, gratified at how eagerly Bella and Ruby followed me. He let us get about ten yards.

'Kate! Wait a minute.'

Gesturing for Bella and Ruby to wait, I turned and went back to his tent.

'What the he — ? What made you decide to

go strolling up to the tomb at this time of the morning anyway?' he asked, pulling viciously at the laces on his boots.

'What difference does it make? Hurry up!'

He looked up at me briefly. 'I must be going mad,' he muttered, as he put on his coat. 'Come on.'

We walked back up the slope towards the tomb entrance, Adam in front, holding a lantern and leading the way with great ill-grace. But as we reached the dark opening to the tunnel and it became clear there was no one around, his bad temper began to give way to surprise.

'That's odd,' he said. 'I don't know why they — good God, Bella, what's that?'

Bella had lifted her gun up from under her coat by now and was holding it out firmly out in front of her as though she expected to be assaulted at any second.

'It's a gun, silly,' she said, peering ahead of her into the gloomy distance.

Adam frowned. 'I can see that. What are you doing with it?'

'I'm using it as protection of course. In case we're attacked.'

'Here, give it to me a minute.' He held out a hand and after a brief pause Bella gave it to him to examine.

'Forget the gun, Adam,' I said. 'I told you

the guards were gone and I want to get on and search the tomb.'

'Yeah and anyway, it don't work, Mr Adam. Does it, miss?'

'Be quiet, Ruby,' Bella hissed. 'There! Now anyone listening will know we're unarmed and vulnerable.'

'We're not vulnerable, Bella and there's no one here to listen anyway,' I said, testily. 'That's the whole point. The guards have gone and — '

'It's loaded,' said Adam.

'What!' I shrieked. Beside me, Ruby gave a small scream.

'It can't be!' Bella was horrified. 'Uncle George would never have left it out if it was.'

Adam gave her a sardonic look, but refrained from comment. Much as he liked her, I knew he regarded Sir George as a bit of an old fool. Which apparently he was.

'You'll have to take it back.'

'Certainly not. I'm not going in that awful gloomy tunnel without any form of protection. We don't know who's in there.'

'Good point. Which is why you'd all better go back to the campsite and get Ahmed and his — '

'Don't be ridiculous,' I interrupted. 'I'm not going back now. Although he's got a point about that gun, Bella. Best not take it in here.'

'Why not?' Bella asked.

'Because it could go off at any time,' said Adam. 'Those things were never very reliable at the best of times. And I really mean it about you all going to fetch the others.'

I ignored him and began to walk quickly into the tunnel. Behind me I could hear Adam arguing with Bella. Even Ruby was being difficult. I smiled to myself.

'Kate! Wait! Wait!'

I turned and waited until he caught up with me.

'Bella fetching the others, is she, darling?' I asked.

He scowled at me. 'You know this is a really stupid thing to do, don't you? Probably the stupidest thing you've ever done and that's quite a feat.'

'Why?' I asked, resuming my slow tramp down the passageway. It was muddy the further underground we went. The flood plains of the Nile weren't so named for nothing.

'Because . . . ' He began by speaking in a normal voice, then changed his mind and started whispering. 'Because we have absolutely no idea what's up here. Those guards should be here but they're not and . . . '

We were almost at the end of the tunnel now and the doorway gleamed gold even in the pitiful glow of the lantern I had in my hand. I put my finger to my mouth.

'Listen,' I said in a low voice and, pointing towards the door, I walked over and put my ear up to it.

Obviously still disbelieving, he followed me and stood with his own ear against the ancient doorway. For a few seconds we heard nothing. Then, as our hearing grew accustomed to the acoustics of the place, we gradually heard thumping sounds and the low hum of unhurried, calm conversation. Adam gasped as he realized what he was listening to.

'Gr — '

I put my fingers to his lips, signalling him to keep quiet. He nodded.

'Grave-robbers? In there? How did you know?' he asked, his voice barely audible.

It was hard not to look smug. I pointed to the robber's hole.

'Didn't it occur to you that it was odd the air in there smelled so fresh this afternoon?' I said. 'The place was supposed to have been closed up for thousands of years and yet we hardly noticed any change in atmosphere at all.'

He thought about this for a few minutes, then nodded slowly.

'I suppose, now that you mention it, it was

odd that it didn't smell worse. But I was so excited . . . '

'Exactly. So was I. But then there were other things about this whole dig that have been nagging at the back of my mind for some time. And tonight, just as I was dozing off, it occurred to me — '

'What are you doing here, Miss Whitaker?'

We had been whispering this conversation, still on our knees at the foot of the door, but now the sound of a voice talking in normal tones made us jump. We looked up and saw Mr Tillyard standing just behind us, fully clothed and wearing a dark-coloured version of his white duster-coat. Adam looked up, briefly shocked, but his expression changed to one of no concern when he realized who it was. I, on the other hand, now experienced my first jolt of real fear.

'Oh, it's you, Tillyard,' Adam said quietly. 'Keep your voice down. There are grave robbers at work in there. We don't want them to know we're here.'

Mr Tillyard rubbed his forehead and sighed regretfully.

'Unfortunately they already do.'

'Already do what? What do you mean?' asked Adam stupidly. I felt my mouth go dry and I seemed to watch Mr Tillyard's hand go to his pocket almost in slow motion.

'They already know you're here, Dr Ellis,' he said, as he pointed a gun at us, the very one he had shown us only a short week ago. I had completely forgotten about it, but now at last I knew exactly why he always carried one. 'At least, *I* know and essentially it's the same thing.'

'What?' Now Adam looked at Mr Tillyard with totally new eyes. He stared in fascination at the gun. I put my hand on his arm.

'Adam, Mr Tillyard's the grave-robber. He's the one who's been sabotaging the dig. He's Il Namus.'

Mr Tillyard smiled, still in that quaint way of his, although now I wondered how I could ever have found it charming.

'Well done, Miss Whitaker. So you managed to work it out. What was it that gave me away?'

I gulped, trying to bring some moisture into my mouth.

'Well, for someone who was supposed to know no Arabic, you seemed to get by extremely well both here and in Luxor. The first day I met you outside our house I noticed that the cab-driver didn't make any attempt to cheat you, which struck me as strange at the time. And you knew what Il Namus meant.'

He thought about this. 'Someone might

have told me in passing whilst I was here. And don't make any sudden movements, please. Just get up slowly.' He gestured with the gun and we did as he said.

'Yes, but there were so many other strange things happening around you,' I said, trying to drag out this interview as long as possible, so that Bella and Ruby and the others would arrive before he got away. 'You didn't want us guarding the tunnels at night and as soon as Adam left you made sure the guards were cancelled. You told me you were impressed with my reports, and yet Adam said they were dreadful. And then when I thought about it, it was always you at the bottom of any rumours about people's obstructions to this dig. I bet Alice never did say anything disapproving about Papa, did she?'

He shook his head without speaking and I pursed my lips.

'And it was you who sent me into Alice's tent yesterday morning when I found that book on poison. I don't suppose that's hers either, is it?'

'Of course not. That was just insurance. I knew you wouldn't be able to resist sneaking around in her tent and it would cause even more friction between you and Ellis and keep you out of the way just for a bit longer.'

I found myself gulping with fear.

341

'You killed Sir Henry, didn't you?'

Again he nodded. 'He found out about the reports I'd been — shall we say — editing? He summoned me that morning to his house in order to give me a chance to explain myself before he called the police. Which was jolly sporting of him, I must say. I felt quite bad having to repay his kindness by killing him, but what could I do? If I'd let him get the police, it would have been a short step from there to everyone discovering my alias. He had to go. Besides, I console myself with the thought that he didn't have much longer anyway.'

He sounded so sincere I felt lost for words, but Adam was looking at him in amazement.

'You were the one reading and changing all the reports?'

'Of course,' said Mr Tillyard. 'I oversee all the correspondence from the archaeologists to the Cavendish. That's where I get my best finds from. And I've been keeping my eye on Professor Whitaker's project right from the start. I knew my old mentor wouldn't let me down. By the way, Miss Whitaker, thank you so much for using that cheap little typewriter. It made it so easy to replace your reports with bogus ones. However, we can't stand around here all night gossiping.' He waved the gun in front of him towards the entrance. 'If you would be so kind.'

'Where are we going?' asked Adam warily. I could tell he was having difficulty reconciling this new, ruthless Mr Tillyard with the mild, almost timid character he was used to. I felt the same myself. Mr Tillyard looked at him with slight scorn.

'To the tomb of course. Don't you want to see Khaemwaset's treasure? It *is* Khaemwaset, by the way Miss Whitaker, although of course you knew that anyway. It was his name on the section of wall I had to destroy a few nights ago.'

'It was you!' I spun round and glared at him. 'I knew I hadn't done anything to cause such rapid disintegration.'

I was beside myself with fury at the thought of what he had done and my anger must have surprised him because he stepped back slightly at the sight of me. Seeing this, Adam sprang forward and almost managed to grab the gun. But Mr Tillyard was just slightly faster. He moved back, caught me by the throat and pulled me close up to him, the barrel of the pistol rammed hard against my neck. Adam stopped.

'I had to do something to stop you getting too enthusiastic about your little project. After all, I've been sabotaging this dig for the last fifteen months. Very successfully too, even if I do say so myself. It was the work of a few moments to drug the wine that evening and make sure you all slept very soundly. Sir George certainly benefited from the rest and I like to think you and Miss Wyndham-Brown did too, Miss Whitaker. Please don't try anything like that again, Dr Ellis,' he continued, pushing the gun a little harder into the flesh of my neck. 'Otherwise Miss Whitaker will pay the price.'

'All right.' Adam nodded, trying to sound calm. 'What do you want to do now?'

Mr Tillyard pushed me back towards the entrance.

'We're going to walk out and along to the other tombs over the hill. I'm going to ask you both to be very quiet now and you understand that if either of you shouts, Miss Whitaker will be the first to die.'

'But what happens if we meet someone else on the way there?'

If Adam was hoping to stall him it didn't work. Out of the corner of my eye I saw Mr Tillyard's mouth quirk up into the slight grin that I had always found attractive, but now it chilled me to the bone.

'Pray that we don't, Dr Ellis,' he said quietly.

The walk to the main Tombs of the Nobles

344

on the far side of the hill was short and terrifying, besides being, for me at least, very uncomfortable. It is actually quite difficult trying to walk up hilly inclines and along rocky paths in total darkness with someone's arm clamped around your neck and a gun barrel pressed into your throat. But we arrived at the Tomb of the Nobles and it was then that Adam and I got our first glimpse of just how organized Mr Tillyard — Il Namus — really was. The tunnels, usually silent and dark at night-time, were dimly, but comprehensively lit throughout as a procession of men strode purposefully through them, carrying pile after pile of priceless artefacts. They took very little interest in us. Beside me I heard Adam gasp as he recognized some of the men. They were the mercenaries he had brought back with him from Luxor. Mr Tillyard heard him and nodded.

'Thank you for being so kind as to supply with a fresh batch of workmen, Dr Ellis. I knew a couple of nights ago that I was going to have to finish this project more quickly than I had hoped and I didn't think I'd have enough men to take everything I wanted. But your foresight in bringing these characters out here saved me a great deal of time.'

Adam frowned, but before he could say

anything, he tripped over something and nearly fell. We all looked down instinctively and it was then that I screamed.

Sprawled by our feet, completely still and covered in blood, were two dead bodies.

14

Mr Tillyard reacted instantly to my screams. Still with the gun at my neck, he clamped his other hand over my mouth.

'Please calm down, my dear. Besides, they're only natives. I thought I'd need a couple of decoys for later on and they weren't very keen on joining their colleagues in this venture,' he said, kicking a foot away from his path. 'Anyway, here we are. Would you like to take a look? I think it's only reasonable under the circumstances.'

He spoke like a considerate host taking pains to keep his guests happy and I wondered briefly what he meant by 'under the circumstances'. But whilst he had been talking we had been moving further down into the less well-known areas of the Tombs of the Nobles. We had been made to descend a steep incline until we reached a passageway. From a distance it seemed to be a dead end but then, as we drew nearer, I saw a robbers' hole not unlike the one we had found in our tunnel. This one, however, was much larger, head-high and wide enough to allow easy access. I didn't need it to be explained to me that it was so wide in order that all Khaemwaset's wealth could be removed. But as we were prodded forward into the chamber I forgot all about the trouble we were in and just stood, breathless, drinking in the wonders before me.

We were once again looking at all the priceless treasures in the burial chamber of Khaemwaset. But this time we were actually there, not just spying through a tiny, uncomfortable hole in a wall with barely room to move. I relaxed almost involuntarily and Mr Tillyard felt my compliance and let me go. I pulled my coat tighter over my nightdress and moved forward into the chamber, walking around, touching everything I saw with a kind of reverence. There was just so much to admire and wonder at. All the things I had glimpsed in the robbers' hole, the gold, the jewels, the marvellous furniture; now I was actually in the same room as them. It was impossible not to pick things up or touch them, revelling in their cool, smooth elegance and their beauty. The care with which they had been made was all for the use of a dead king, buried for thousands of years.

'This is fantastic,' said Adam at last, reluctantly setting a small statue of a female slave back in her place by the shrine. 'It's so perfect, as though they were placed here only yesterday . . . '

I looked at him and he checked himself. It wasn't perfect at all. Despite all the dazzling riches before us, it was impossible to miss the fact that much more was missing. There was so much empty space in this vast chamber. Clearly it had been constructed to house a lot more. And what was left was in a state of great confusion. Caskets had been left carelessly open with the contents spilling out, and some of the great gilt couches were left lying on their sides, with no regard for their value. We suddenly found ourselves returning to the real world with a bump.

'So much wealth I have to leave here,' said Mr Tillyard sadly, as he picked up an alabaster vase. He paused, then handed it to a mercenary who nodded and walked out with it. 'Still, it doesn't do to be too greedy and I have to leave something to keep the Antiquities people happy.'

Adam gave a brief, hollow laugh.

'You know, I can hardly believe it's you doing this, Tillyard. And to think I saw you only as an unimaginative bureaucrat. I really did make a mistake about you.'

'Yes, you did,' Mr Tillyard agreed. 'Your contempt was obvious and extremely insulting. Miss Whitaker, however, was much kinder.'

He slid a hand over my shoulders as he said this and I shuddered, horrified to think that I had ever considered this man pleasant and attractive. I even hated to think how I had let his lips linger on my hands and I pulled sharply away now. Adam took my arm, but before either of us could speak, Mr Tillyard lifted the gun up again.

'Never mind, Ellis, I wouldn't want her anyway. Not now she's soiled goods.'

'Soiled . . . ?' For a moment, I was confused. 'Oh! It was you back at the campsite, wasn't it? You were spying on us. Just before we . . . '

I could see in his eyes it was true and I couldn't finish my sentence, but I didn't have to. He smiled nastily.

'It was quite stimulating watching you two love-birds consummate your union with such passion. Almost made me wish — '

He got no further. Before any of the men around us had time to react, Adam leapt forward and struck him across the face. He fell to the ground, blood beginning to trickle slowly out of his nose. Two mercenaries, meanwhile, had grabbed hold of Adam and were holding him whilst a third was punching him in the stomach. Mr Tillyard watched them for a few moments before snapping out a sharp order. Reluctantly they stopped beating Adam.

'That's enough. It won't do to have them looking too damaged,' he said in perfect, almost accentless Arabic. Then he switched back to English. 'Well, I'm sorry it has to end like this, Miss Whitaker. Or may I call you Kate? I feel as though I know you so well now and I've become quite fond of you over the last few weeks, even though I expected to hate you. You were an odious little baggage, by the way, when you were a child.'

'I hope I made your life a misery while you were out here,' I hissed at him.

'Oh you certainly did that. You know, even now I can't decide whether it was the laxative in my morning tea which made me hate you more or the time you locked a pack of flea-ridden cats in my room. I was itching for weeks after that. And your doting father always took your side. It really was too bad. Did she behave so monstrously when you were out here, Ellis?' he asked chattily, but Adam was leaning against a gilt couch, barely conscious. 'No, probably not,' he continued, perching on a wooden chest. 'Puppy love can be very enduring, can't it? Lord, all those letters you two wrote to each other! It got quite an ordeal in the end, having to wade my way through so many nauseating outpourings of emotion in case either of you said anything important. I was very relieved when you both eventually gave up.'

'You read our letters too!' I cried.

Mr Tillyard looked at me in mild surprise. 'Well, of course I did. I couldn't take the chance your knight in shining armour might come charging back to help you and the professor.'

For a second I just looked at him with utter disbelief: then I did something that I have never done in my life before. I spat at him. I'd seen Egyptian men do it in the streets many times and my nannies and governesses had always turned their heads away in disgust, appalled at such behaviour. Mr Tillyard hardly batted an eyelid. He merely took a handkerchief from his pocket and calmly wiped his cheek. Then he stepped forward and slapped me hard across the face.

'You really are quite an uncivilized little creature, aren't you, Kate,' he said, before snapping some more orders to the men still standing guard by us. One of them picked Adam up and threw him across his shoulder. Tillyard grabbed my arm and steered me towards another doorway at the bottom of the chamber.

'Down that way, if you please Kate. That's right, keep going.'

He pulled at a huge door which led into yet

another tunnel. As I stared down into its gloomy depths, I began to feel a sudden dread clutch at my stomach. I had spent all my life wandering in and out of tunnels just like this one and never once felt any fear. But suddenly I understood what claustrophobia was.

'Lively now, Kate. It's quite a trek down to the next level and we don't have much time left before someone realizes you've gone. It's amazing how wealthy the ancients were, isn't it? Khaemwaset didn't just have one chamber full of treasure, he had several, although I won't be telling the Service that, of course. I've already taken most of what's down here, but I've got to leave a few things for future discovery.'

He kept up this awful chatter as we descended ever further into the ground, the heat becoming more stifling and the sense of oppression weighing me down. We seemed to walk for ages before reaching another doorway. This one was simpler, less ornately decorated, but still sturdy despite its aeons in the dark. The mercenaries prised it open and we were hustled in.

The chamber was smaller and although there were treasures inside, it was clearly meant for a less important purpose. The couches were not so fabulously carved, the statues seemed more utilitarian and there was a general air of common sense about the items chosen to acompany their owner into the next life. Mr Tillyard nodded to his men and they dropped Adam on to the floor near the back of the chamber.

'You won't get away with this, you know that,' I said.

'Really?' He looked up at me, with an interested smile on his face. 'How are you going to stop me? Oh wait a minute, there's Miss Wyndham-Brown, isn't there, and that vulgar little maid? You must be expecting them to arrive any second with a horde of rescuers. Of course.'

He walked across to one of the large wooden chests and knelt down by a tarpaulin. I had barely noticed it and now looked at it, expecting to see a new pile of treasures. But as he threw it back, I gasped.

Bella lay crumpled on the floor, Ruby beside her. They were both unconscious, but breathing. Bella had a huge, purple bruise on her forehead, but she seemed the less injured of the two. Even in the lamplight I could see blood on Ruby's face.

'I don't think Miss Wyndham-Brown will be doing any rescuing, do you Kate?' he enquired in a jolly tone and I resisted the urge to spit at him again. 'You know, you all gave Ali over there quite a shock when you turned up at the tomb. It just goes to show you how important it is to keep a guard posted at all times, doesn't it, Kate?'

'You are the most despicable excuse for a human being I have ever met in my life,' I said coldly. 'And I suppose you thought it was funny having people dressed up as ghosts and putting scorpions in my boot.'

'Good heavens, Kate, that wasn't me. Although I do rather wish it had been. You know, you've been out here too long, my dear. Ghosts indeed! And as for the scorpion — well that was just a stroke of luck.'

By now, half of what he was saying made no sense, but as he moved towards the chamber entrance to leave us alone in here, I said the first thing that came into my mind. Anything to give us a little more time and a little more hope of rescue.

'I don't care what you say, Richard, you won't get away with this. As soon as we're free, we'll tell everyone what you've done. You won't see a penny of all this treasure.'

He shrugged and looked slightly bored.

'Well, frankly, Kate, unless you can shout very loudly, I don't see how you're going to escape. This tomb is far below the original one found yesterday and once I leave there's going to be an unfortunate cave-in along the tunnel that you and your friends found when you came snooping in here. I doubt very much that you'll be able to shout loud enough to attract anyone's attention and the air won't last for ever down here. And the lantern will give out soon enough. And I certainly intend keeping the whole campsite busy looking for you in all the wrong places, until it's too late. But do try. It's important that when we eventually find your dead bodies it looks as though you've done your best to escape.'

He stood the lantern on the shrine next to us and walked briskly away.

'Goodbye, my dear. Give my regards to Dr Ellis and Miss Wyndham-Brown when they wake up.' And with that, he stepped through the chamber entrance. Almost immediately I heard the sound of rocks and boulders being pushed back into place. I knelt down beside Adam, still unconscious on the floor by my feet.

'Wake up, Adam,' I said, at first patting him gently with my hands. This brought no response at all and I soon gave up and began shaking him briskly. 'Adam, wake up!'

I was trying not to give in to hysteria, but as the seconds ticked by and the sounds of the men outside the entrance faded away to silence, it became almost impossible. But just as I despaired of getting any signs of life from Adam, his eyelids fluttered feebly.

'Adam! Wake up!' I shouted and slowly his eyes rolled open, closed, then opened again.

'Will you stop yelling in my ear?' he said irritably, pushing himself up, then groaning with pain as he remembered the battering he had taken. 'Oww! That hurt! Where's Tillyard?'

'Adam, get up. We're in terrible trouble.'

He had managed to lever himself into a sitting position, still rubbing gently at his stomach, but he looked up at my words.

'Really? Do you think so?'

I bent over him as he sat back against the wooden chest. 'There's no need to be sarcastic. How much of what he said did you hear?' I asked as I wiped a trickle of dried blood away from his mouth.

He grunted. 'Most of it up to the part where he said you'd put laxatives in his tea. Oww!'

'You would remember that,' I said crossly.

He took a few careful, deep breaths.

'Laxatives. Honestly, Kate, I don't know how you ever made it to adulthood.'

'I was twelve, Adam,' I said irritably. 'I wasn't very sophisticated. Besides, considering what he's done to us, I wish I'd put arsenic in his tea now. Oh my God!' Suddenly

I realized what I had just said. 'Papa! Adam, Papa is in danger!'

'Not as much as we're in. Besides, I doubt whether Tillyard will be bothering himself with the professor. Your father is safely out of the way back in Luxor. We were the ones causing him trouble.' He grimaced as he levered himself up with great care. 'Is that Bella and Ruby? How did they get here?'

I went across and checked on them. They were still out cold and it seemed kinder to leave them that way. As I explained to Adam what had happened, there was a short boom, followed by a dull thudding sound. Adam and I looked at each other.

'What are we going to do, Adam? The lantern is only good for another hour at the most and we don't know how long the air in here will last.'

There was a slight pause while we both realized that the atmosphere in the chamber suddenly did seem stickier. My skin seemed to become clammy, despite the uncomfortable heat that was developing and try as I might, I could not stop myself from saying:

'Does it seem to you that there's a funny stale smell in here, Adam?'

'No,' he said firmly, but I knew he was lying. When you lie a lot yourself you recognize it easily in others.

'We can't just stand here, hoping someone will find us,' he continued. 'Let's take a look around. There might be another way out of here. The tunnels in these tombs honeycomb all over the place. If one leads *in* to Khaemwaset's tomb, it's possible there might be another one that might take us away.'

I nodded and began helping him examine the mud walls of the chamber. We inched our way slowly round the room, our eyes straining to find the slightest sign of a robber's hole or a blocked-up doorway. We ignored the vast collection of treasure behind us, oblivious to its charms now. It was difficult working the smooth surface of the mud chamber, especially since we only had the one lantern between us and the wick kept guttering fitfully. We worked slowly, trying to conserve as much oxygen as we could, whilst at the same time give ourselves something positive to do, but it was hard going. Sweat had begun trickling down my forehead and along my rib-cage and I could feel myself becoming more tired with every step. Then, suddenly, I stopped. I gestured for Adam to hold the light up closer to the part of the wall I had been examining, my fingers scrabbling tensely as I detected a definite change in texture.

'Look Adam! There's the outline of a hole!'

'Here,' said Adam, holding out the lantern

for me to take. 'I'll go and see if I can find something to dig with.'

He stood up and walked back to the middle of the room, coughing with the exertion. Eventually, among all the pots and vases, he found a solid-looking sword. Panting with the effort, he hefted the weapon above his head, then swung it down. Mud and dust flew up around us, making us cough as it entered our nostrils and mouths and for a few seconds I felt as if I were choking. But at last the debris settled and we found ourselves peering once more into a small hole.

At first it was hard to make anything out. The lantern was definitely growing weaker now. I stared into the hole, taking shuddering breaths as I did and almost gagging on the stale, old smell from the tomb, proof that this was one chamber that hadn't been opened for centuries. As our eyes grew accustomed to the gloom we began to see better what we were looking at. It was a very small chamber, hardly bigger than the inside of a coal cellar and almost immediately we knew two things: one, that it was not a tunnel to another tomb; and two, that it was empty.

Adam wiped his dust-covered face on the sleeve of his shirt and sank down on to the ground beside me.

'I'm sorry Kate. It doesn't look as though we're going to get out of here by another route after all.'

I sighed as he put an arm around my shoulder.

'I should be the one apologizing to you,' I said. 'After all, it was my stupid idea to go into the tomb at the dead of night without telling anyone.'

He laughed. 'True. Remind me to break off our engagement if we ever get out of this.'

'I don't remember you ever proposing.'

'Didn't I?' He was starting to sound as weak as I felt.

'Trust me, Adam. It's the sort of memory we girls treasure.'

'Well, I'll take your word for it. I just thought . . .'

He stopped, interrupted by my gasp of surprise. I had looked away briefly and something in the far corner of the foul little chamber had glinted, catching the last feeble glow of the lantern. I sat up, my body tensed again.

'Adam, there *is* something in there. Hold the lamp up.'

I turned away from him and began to crawl slowly into the little hole. The floor was quite smooth and my nightdress was almost in shreds by now, the slick feel of the mud beneath my knees revolting. Then, as Adam followed closely behind me, the lamp held high above our heads, we saw it together, shoved up tightly at the back of the chamber. A tall, slim, sleek statue of a cat. It stood over five feet tall, covered in rubies, carved in the most exquisite pink gold. The Scarlet Queen.

We stared at it for a long time without speaking. At last I crawled up to it, slowly, reverently, like a heathen on her knees before a false god.

'It's the Queen, Adam,' I said at last. 'It really is. The Scarlet Queen. Papa was right. She did exist! She was made and put down here to be with . . .'

I stopped. Now that the first rush of excitement had abated, it occurred to me that this tiny, crude little hole was an odd place to put such a magnificent piece of workmanship. By rights, she should have pride of place in the centre of the chamber and not this chamber either, with its simple tools and plain bowls. She should have been in the main tomb, the royal tomb.

'Hmm, who *was* she put down here with?' wondered Adam, as he moved closer to the statue. We both looked curiously up at the Cat-Goddess, with her inscrutable smile.

'Oww.' I felt Adam flinch, then draw back slightly. 'Hello, what's this?'

I dragged my eyes away from the face of statue and looked down at her feet. There were a couple of objects on the floor by her sharp claws, dull and dusty from lying unused so long. Adam poked at them gently with his finger, careful not to push too hard for fear they might break. One object was a dagger, long and pointed; the other a small clay vial, broken in two.

'Odd,' said Adam as he rolled a piece of the vial away from the dagger. 'I wonder what the significance of this is. It seems to be some kind of — '

'Oh God, Adam! Look!'

'What?'

I was pointing to a pile of bones, lying near to the statue, when suddenly, just for a second, it seemed to me that they shimmered away and in their place was a person. It was surreal, but in the heat and haze I was staring into the face of a beautiful young woman, dressed in the clothes of an ancient Egyptian, living and breathing although logic dictated she had no right to do either. For a few seconds our eyes met and she smiled at me. Then, with horror, I saw the knife at her throat, red blood oozing beneath the blade.

I screamed. I was vaguely aware of Adam's hands on my face, trying to calm me, but the light had gone by now and the darkness was so absolute and so thick and stifling that I couldn't even begin to control myself. Then, just as it seemed our situation couldn't get any worse, there was a thundering noise above us. Something large and heavy fell on top of me, cracking against my skull and I was aware of nothing more.

15

I came to in dim candlelight, feeling light-headed. After a while I realized I was back in my bedroom in Luxor. It was dark outside and silent, except for the soothing sound of the crickets. I could see a jug of water and a glass on my bedside table and it suddenly occurred to me that I was parched, but the idea of having to move myself into a sitting position to reach them seemed exhausting. Still, I was very thirsty. Slowly I began to pull myself up. It was then that I sensed there was someone else in the room with me.

'You're awake,' said a voice in relief. 'Adam, she's awake!'

I looked up. Alice was sitting next to the bed, Adam was nearby, dozing in a chair.

'Darling, we were beginning to worry,' Alice whispered, as she leant over and kissed me. 'Don't try to get up. Are you thirsty? Adam, help me sit her up.'

They lifted me up into a sitting position and Alice held a glass of cool, lemon-scented water to my dry, cracked lips.

'You gave us all quite a scare for a while,

Kate,' Adam said, as I sipped feebly. 'We thought you were dead when Bennett and his men eventually managed to find you.'

'Peter?' I said. At least, that's what I tried to say. Actually what came out was a dreadful, rasping croak. Adam and Alice exchanged looks.

'Here, darling, keep swallowing,' said Alice. 'You've been unconscious for three days now and hardly drunk a thing.'

'Thank you,' I whispered after a few minutes. This time my voice sounded stronger. 'What happened? The last thing I remember is the lantern giving out and then something falling on top of me.'

'You got injured when Bennett and his men were trying to dig you out. They heard you screaming in the tomb but it was so faint they feared they wouldn't reach you in time and they were working so fast they didn't realize how close they were. The floor — our roof — caved in and one of the men accidentally hit you with a spade.'

I lay back on the pillows and Alice pressed a cool hand on my head.

'You still feel hot, my dear.' She stood up and looked at her watch. 'It's nearly five o'clock. I'm going to send Sayeed for Dr Murray. Adam will stay with you. He can tell you everything that happened.' She leaned over and kissed me again. 'It's so good to have you back.'

Still feeling dazed, I watched her leave the room, then I turned and looked blearily at Adam.

'Where's Papa? Is he . . . ?'

'He's fine. Still tired from the malaria, but finding the Scarlet Queen and Khaemwaset's tomb seems to have taken ten years off him. He's desperate to see them both, but wouldn't leave the house while you were unconscious. I'll go and wake him in a little bit.'

'No, leave him,' I said, thankful he was well. 'And Bella? And Ruby? Are they . . . ?'

'Bella's fine. Ruby we were a little bit worried about at first. She took a nastier crack to the head than Bella. But she's on the mend now and enjoying her fame immensely. We're all well except for you, Kate, which seems a bit unfair.'

Adam sat down in the chair beside the bed and I could see the cuts and bruises on his face from the beating he had received from the mercenaries.

'You don't look fine.'

He smiled. 'A few souvenirs from my ex-employees. I'll survive.'

'What happened, Adam? I remember finding the statue and the bones, then it all becomes a blur. What's Peter got to do with it? What men?'

'Peter Bennett, my love, is not the humble Service inspector we thought he was.' He paused. 'Obviously he wasn't Il Namus either.'

'No. Who is he then?'

'He's a private investigator.'

'A what?'

'A private investigator. A sort of private policeman. The Antiquities Service engaged his services six months ago after the last theft by Il Namus. They were so fed up with constantly losing all the best finds in the Valley and the temples and they knew they'd never catch Il Namus on their own, so they decided to send to London for the best private detective they could find.'

'A private detective? Like Sherlock Holmes? It sounds fascinating. And Peter's the best there is?'

My scepticism made Adam smile. 'You shouldn't sound so surprised, Kate. If it wasn't for him, we'd all be dead now.'

'I'm very fond of Peter, as you well know, but . . . ' I paused, lost for words. 'Really? Peter? The best private detective there is? Really?'

'Really.'

'But he's so young.'

'Actually, he's only two years younger than me. And now the game's up and he doesn't have to play the clumsy *ingénu* any more, Bella's nose has been put right out of joint. He's barely been paying any attention to her and it's driving her wild.'

I smiled at the thought of Bella suddenly realizing that her admirer was no longer so keen. It wouldn't hurt her at all to find out how it felt to be ignored.

'He was good enough to save us, anyway,' Adam continued. 'He was only three miles down the valley when all the fun started.'

'Some fun,' I muttered. 'Why was he there?'

'He was waiting for Il Namus, to show himself. Ahmed sent for him just in time.'

'Ahmed! Ahmed knows Peter?'

'Ahmed knows everyone, my love. He's been helping Bennett ever since he arrived here. He and his sons know most of the black marketeers in Luxor and quite a few in Cairo too. They don't object to a little healthy local enterprise, but they didn't like Il Namus's methods.'

'But why didn't Ahmed tell me all this?'

'Bennett insisted he didn't.' Adam's mouth quirked into a smile. 'Apparently he thought you were Il Namus.'

'Me!'

'Well you and your father.'

'Me and Papa! Well, really!' I huffed, moving restlessly about the bed. 'I've never heard such nonsense.'

'Well, you thought he was Il Namus for a while. Why shouldn't he think the same about you?'

'Hmph,' I snorted.

Outside the window faint streaks of light were appearing on the horizon and there were sounds of the day beginning. A donkey brayed half-heartedly in the distance and I heard the sound of the muezzin calling the faithful to prayer from the top of the mosque nearby, his song a mesmeric, oddly melodic chant. Adam got up and walked towards the window.

'It's almost daylight. You look tired, Kate.'

I smiled. 'I'm fine. But there's something I don't understand. If Ahmed and Peter were expecting trouble in our camp, why did it take so long for them to rescue us?'

'Because they didn't know Tillyard was Il Namus and therefore that he was already in the camp. But they knew that once the tomb was finally excavated Il Namus wouldn't be able to resist and it would only be a matter of time before he showed up. What was really worrying Bennett was the sight of so many people around which he thought might put Il

Namus off, so he sent the ghost in, hoping to persuade the Egyptians to leave.'

'You mean it was Peter who was responsible for that wretched ghost?' I said in astonishment. Adam laughed.

'He got one of Ahmed's sons to dress up. And he was very annoyed when we posted guards instead. Then, when he visited the tunnel and saw the murals on the wall, he had an inkling that something was about to happen. He knew he had to do something to get everybody out of there and he thought the best way to get most of you away from the tomb was by staging an accident, as well as another visit from the ghost. Bella was right by the way: that scorpion was meant for you.'

'Peter put that scorpion in my boot?' I scowled. 'I must remember to thank him next time I see him.'

'So you should,' Adam said cheerfully. 'I told you: we'd be dead without him. Anyway, after you came back from the ferry, he realized that there was nothing more to be done and he'd just have to let you stay. Ahmed told him about the doorway as soon as we found it and they had a pretty good idea then that something was about to happen, but of course they were expecting Il Namus and his men to arrive from the outside and go into the campsite. No one realized that Tillyard had already found the treasure by that time and was using the tunnels in the Tombs of the Nobles to get to our tomb. In fact, Ahmed and his sons were some way outside the main camp, waiting for the next development, when one of them heard either Bella or Ruby scream. That was when Ahmed decided it was time to fetch Bennett and whilst they were waiting they had a good scout round and eventually found that ridiculous gun of Bella's near the Tombs of the Nobles. When they saw all the footprints, they began to suspect what had happened. Then Bennett and his men arrived and they began searching the caves.'

'But surely Mr Tillyard was still there? With all those awful mercenaries?'

Adam nodded grimly. 'Oh yes. He must have known that his plan was falling apart, but he was determined to take as much of the treasure as he could and that was his downfall in the end. Bennett says they cornered him in one of the tunnels between the tombs. It was blocked up, probably as a result of the explosion they created to seal us in the Cat's tomb. Bennett tried to get him to surrender, but it did no good.' He sighed and rubbed his eyes. 'From what Ahmed told me, he was quite insane at the end. Shooting madly at anyone he could with that damned little pistol of his. Several of Bennett's men were injured and one was killed.'

'Oh no,' I gasped. 'And — and Mr Tillyard?'

Adam grimaced. 'Dead. He didn't stand a chance really, especially after he'd killed the serviceman. They got most of the mercenaries as well, although a couple managed to slip away in all the confusion. And all of Khaemwaset's treasure was recovered. The Antiquities Service is very pleased.'

I looked out of the window where I could just see the sun, making great strides on the horizon by now, the delicate pink streaks suffused with a deeper red at the edges. There is nowhere in the world more beautiful than Egypt at dawn, but just at that moment its beauty was lost on me as I thought about Richard Tillyard and all the evil he had committed.

'Those books — did he really use chloroform to kill Sir Henry?' I asked after a while.

Adam nodded. 'That's the general opinion. Alice says she's sure she remembers an odd smell in the room when she found Henry, but of course it was so long ago now, she can't be absolutely certain. And she was more concerned with Henry at the time. It seems that after he killed Henry, Tillyard decided that your expedition would have to be the last robbery, at least for a while. He's been doing this for years, by the way. Ever since he came out here in '97 and realized how much money could be made by stealing antiquities.'

I frowned. Poor Papa; he certainly didn't expect his assistants to learn that sort of thing while they were with us.

'Anyway,' Adam continued, 'he'd been keeping a careful watch on developments out here and knew you were very close to finding Khaemwaset's tomb. It wasn't that difficult for him to get himself invited on this trip — he'd made himself invaluable to Alice during the first few weeks of her widowhood and he didn't anticipate any problems getting the expedition to go his way. He put enough arsenic in your father's medicine to trigger a relapse, but not enough to kill him, assuming that you would naturally stay behind and nurse him. We think he also assumed he'd only have me to deal with once we were at the site. It must have been quite a shock to realize that you were still coming on the expedition. And not only that, but that Alice was intending to accompany us as well as old Faversham and Bella. Still, he made the best of a bad job.'

I sighed and rubbed my eyes. 'That odious man! I can't believe I actually liked him.'

'Don't upset yourself, Kate. Richard Tillyard was a master manipulator. He even had your father thinking Alice and I were on a mission from the museum to cheat you out of the treasure.'

I nodded, remembering the day Papa had made me promise to go on the expedition in his place. His strange, delirium-fuelled rantings about parvenus stealing his glory made sense at last.

I shook myself. 'Tell me about the Scarlet Queen, Adam. What was she doing in that awful little hole? And where were we? Not in Khaemwaset's tomb, I'm sure.'

Adam shook his head. 'Tillyard took us much further down to another level. Judging by the weapons we found there, I'd say we were in a high-ranking soldier's tomb, probably a general. And it was later than the Third Intermediate. Probably the twenty-seventh or twenty-eighth dynasty.'

'Oh.' I frowned. 'And the bones?'

Adam smiled at last. 'Your father and I are almost certain they belong to the Beloved. Actually they are the remains of two people, a woman and a man and there was a scroll in a pot, detailing why they were there. I brought it back here for your father to see the same day we got out and he's been working on it ever since, in-between sitting with you.'

Adam sat back in his chair. 'It turns out she was killed. Stabbed. By her companion in the tomb with her.' He paused and grimaced. 'Her lover.'

'Her lover stabbed her! Why?'

Adam rubbed his fingers across his eyes. 'Her name was Meresankh,' he said. 'She was one of Khaemwaset's secondary wives and she was caught having an affair with Nebnufer, a soldier in his army. Apparently, Khaemwaset was besotted with her; he worshipped her and caused her to be referred to constantly as the Beloved in his texts. And that's why he had the statue made.'

'To bribe her,' I said softly.

Adam nodded. 'To try and win her love. He knew she didn't care for him, but I suppose he hoped to win her with precious gifts and symbols of status. He was quite old by the standards of the day and she was young and beautiful. Anyway, it's easy to imagine his horror when he found out she was having an affair with one of his lieutenants, giving all her love to this young upstart instead of her sovereign lord. He had intended that she should share his tomb with him, but after they were found naked together along the banks of the river he had a tunnel built as far away from his tomb as possible in the week following their arrest and they were both thrown in, blocked up and left to die.'

'What was the Scarlet Queen doing in there?' I asked.

'Well, I suppose that after all the love and care that had gone into making it for her, he felt she'd thrown it all back in his face and he couldn't bear to look at it any more, so he had it put in there with them, as a reminder during the last few hours of her life of what she had thrown away. He certainly had all traces of her existence erased extremely comprehensively everywhere else.'

'Poor girl!' I murmured. 'What a terrible end. But why was she stabbed? And by her lover, too. Surely . . . ?'

'It seems Khaemwaset had a slight change of heart at the last minute. Even though he couldn't bear the thought of anyone else having what he had been denied, he must had had some small streak of compassion left for her at the end, because he ordered a small vial of poison and a knife to be placed in the tomb with them. They were given the chance to end their lives quickly if they wanted, without having to wait in increasing pain and fear for the end.'

'Oh. But what was the knife for? Surely poison would be a much more painless — '

'There was only enough poison for one

person, not two.' Adam shrugged as I looked at him, appalled.

'You mean he deliberately forced them to choose which one would take the poison, knowing the other would either have to commit suicide or murder? Lord, the poor girl.'

I closed my eyes, suddenly remembering the strange dream-woman who had flashed into life for a few short seconds in the tomb. It must have been Meresankh. I recalled the sweet smile on her face as she waited for Nebnufer to deliver that last final, fatal embrace, and hoped she was happy wherever she was.

'Poor both of them,' said Adam. 'At any rate, they elected Nebnufer to take the poison and before he did he wrote down everything that had happened. The scrolls are quite brief — he must have been granted papyrus and writing materials as a final request and it gets a bit patchy at the end as his light fades and I suppose the oxygen goes. But he gets the main gist of the story in. Some of it is quite poetic, actually. It ends with him calling her 'the most beloved, who rules my heart'.'

I looked out towards the window. It was now early morning and I could hear all the familiar sounds of Luxor: donkeys and camels braying raucously as they were driven along with their burdens, the clip-clopping of horses' hoofs on the road, vendors crying out to people to buy *aysh* and *ful* and figs and hot, sweet coffee. I could almost smell the acrid tang of roasting coffee beans and I suddenly realized how hungry I was. I looked back to Adam, to ask him to ring the bell for Sayeed and saw him picking up his jacket from the back of the chair and pulling it on.

'Are you going?'

'I have to. I've got a meeting at the Antiquities Service with Bennett at eight o'clock and I shall be late if I don't leave now.'

'When will you be back?'

'As soon as I can. I won't be long.' He bent over, stroking a stray lock of hair away from my eyes. 'Don't fret. Alice will be here soon.'

'I'm amazed she let you stay in here alone in the first place,' I said. 'That's not like her at all.'

Adam grinned as he went across to the window and blew out the last of the guttering candle.

'I've told her we're engaged. No doubt that removes any impropriety.'

'I thought you were going to break off our engagement if we ever got out of that tomb.'

He walked back across to the bed and sat down next to me, taking my hands in his and gently kissing each finger.

'I decided to forgive you.'

'Oh you did, did you?' I said, reaching up and stroking his chin. It was bristly where a beard was just starting to grow and I realized I had never seen Adam in the morning before he had shaved. The idea fascinated me for some reason; I had seen him half-dead, but never with a stubbly chin.

'Yes.' He leaned further over the bed and whispered in my ear. 'I've decided to take you with all your faults.'

I laughed as he kissed my ear then moved down to my neck. 'Adam, do you think Peter will be terribly upset if you're a bit late?'

He looked at me for a moment. 'I don't know,' he said at last. 'Let's find out.'

We do hope that you have enjoyed reading this large print book.

Did you know that all of our titles are available for purchase?

We publish a wide range of high quality large print books including:
Romances, Mysteries, Classics
General Fiction
Non Fiction and Westerns

Special interest titles available in large print are:
The Little Oxford Dictionary
Music Book
Song Book
Hymn Book
Service Book

Also available from us courtesy of Oxford University Press:
Young Readers' Dictionary
(large print edition)
Young Readers' Thesaurus
(large print edition)

For further information or a free brochure, please contact us at:
Ulverscroft Large Print Books Ltd.,
The Green, Bradgate Road, Anstey,
Leicester, LE7 7FU, England.
Tel: (00 44) **0116 236 4325**
Fax: (00 44) **0116 234 0205**

Other titles published by
The House of Ulverscroft:

THE SEA BREAK

Antony Trew

Lieutenant Commander Widmark had truly earned his nickname, 'The Butcher', in Mediterranean waters. He derided the Geneva Convention: in his view, war was a bloody business in which those who stopped at nothing would be victorious. And in November 1942 his greatest adventure begins: the organization and execution of a private cutting-out operation, designed — regardless of any consequences — to strike a telling blow for his own side. Widmark plans to seize and sail an 8,000-tonne German vessel, *Hagenfels*, from the neutral East African port of Lourenço Marques . . .

THE BONAPARTE PLOT

Hugh McLeave

In 1803 it seems nothing can stop Napoleon Bonaparte from invading and conquering England. So Prime Minister William Pitt plans to thwart his enemy. He recruits French royalist General Georges Cadoudal, with orders to kidnap or kill Bonaparte and restore the Bourbon monarchy . . . But Bonaparte, a master tactician, detects and unravels the murder plot. In order to rule as Emperor of France, he constructs a plan that will cost many lives . . . This fictional account is based on the testimony of Bonaparte himself and his contemporaries.

THE DAMNED

John D. MacDonald

A mixed group of American tourists never expected to be trapped together, unable to cross the river to continue their journey. They were all strangers and didn't really want to get to know each other, but the stalled river ferry takes away the luxury of choice. Under the brutal Mexican sun their personal relationships, their values and dreams are exposed in a way that leaves them no excuses. Their lives would never be the same again — and crossing that river was not even to be a journey they all would make . . .

THE SPANISH HAWK

James Pattinson

There were five dead men in the cabin of the boat, lying under ten fathoms of Caribbean water. They had been shot through the head at close range . . . John Fletcher had gone down to photograph a sunken ship, but he took photographs of the boat and its cargo of dead men instead. Soon he is having trouble with the island police, some men from President Clayton Rodgers' private army of thugs and two CIA agents. Now Fletcher wishes he had followed his first impulse and said nothing to anyone . . .

STEEL RAIN

Tom Neale

Special Agent Vincent Piper of the London FBI Field Office is a newcomer to this vibrant city. There is anger simmering beneath its surface. He's only here to patch up his marriage . . . But when his daughter Martha is murdered in a terrorist bomb attack in the city, Piper realises he's staying. He knows who planted the lethal device: all he has to do is find him . . . Sarah, his daughter's tutor, and the mysterious Celeste, help him piece together his shattered life. Piper invests his trust in them, but what exactly are their motives? Before he can find out, he has a man to kill.

IOOF
WP
ST.
MM.
Roblo.
RL
YP.

JS

MC.

BRH.